Turn Back the Clocks

Also by Bonnie Schroeder

Write My Name on the Sky

Mending Dreams

Turn Back the Clocks

Bonnie Schroeder

Published by Bonnie Schroeder, Boise, Idaho

Copyright © 2023 by Bonnie Schroeder

This is a book of fiction. Names, characters, places, and incidents are either the product of the author's imagination or are used fictitiously. Any resemblance to actual persons, living or dead, business establishments, government agencies, events, or locales is entirely coincidental.

International Standard Book Number 979-8-9857529-4-6

Library of Congress Control Number: 2023907619

CREDITS

Cover Photo: Mihaela Rosu/iStock

Cover Design: Paula L. Johnson

Page Design: Vellum

Author Photo: McCarthy Photo Studio

Proofreading: Dorothy Read

FIRST EDITION 2023

Printed in the United States of America

For Jayne
Best friend and teacher

Chapter One
"Old Girl"

My life changed forever on a bright May morning, the year I turned sixty-five.

Steven and I had just begun our usual Saturday hike, with him in the lead, when he called out, "Hurry up, Old Girl."

I gritted my teeth and straightened the straps on my backpack. "Right behind you," I muttered as I sprinted after him, careless of the bumps and holes in the parking lot asphalt.

My husband had started calling me "Old Girl" back when we were dating, after he learned I was born four years before him. I laughed about it then, but lately it annoyed me, and he knew it. Over thirty-eight years of marriage, a lot of things about him had annoyed me, but most of them weren't *personal*.

At the trailhead, he turned and smiled at me, and my irritation eased off. It was a glorious May morning, a perfect start for our hike to the top of Griffith Park. Much of Los Angeles was just waking up as we set out, early sunlight kissing the back of my neck.

I let my thoughts wander as I followed Steven, keeping part of my attention on the trail so I didn't stumble. One of our sometime hiking companions had broken her seventy-year-old hip in a fall the summer before. My own left hip had been complaining, and my doctor had hinted at a replacement. I hated the idea and put off deciding, but a fall would have decided for me.

We stopped at the water tower to rehydrate and catch our breath, and often I needed the break more than Steven. That morning, though —maybe it was the scent of spring in the air—I wasn't winded.

Then we tackled the aptly-named Cardiac Hill, the most challenging part of the climb where I knocked myself breathless every time.

Steven seemed to be going more slowly than usual, and where the trail made a sharp upward left, I overtook him. Before I realized it, I'd reached the level patch at the foot of the gentler grade up to the sixteen-hundred-foot Mt. Hollywood summit.

I heard Steven panting behind me, and my mean-spirited self couldn't help but relish the sound. *Who's the Old Girl now, Steven?*

I kept going, and when I couldn't hear him behind me anymore, I turned to see if he'd gotten his second wind. For an instant I couldn't make sense of what I saw: Steven, doubled over, hands on his knees, his faded jeans and red t-shirt the only color on the wide, dusty trail— except his face, which was an alarming shade of purple.

No! Nonononono! This can't be happening.

I blinked hard, but the scene didn't change. *What should I do?* I couldn't move, couldn't even think for a few agonizing seconds before I broke through the paralysis of shock and fumbled for my cell phone as I ran toward Steven. Who to call? *Do I dial 9-1-1? No—the park rangers! Where's their damned number? I know I put it in here!*

Steven snatched the phone away from me. "I'm okay," he gasped. "Just… let… me… breathe… for… a… minute."

Sweat dripped from his forehead, but his sides quit heaving. I throttled my panic as his color faded to its usual ruddy tone.

I yanked a water bottle from my backpack. "Good God, Steven. What the hell happened?" I handed it to him and grabbed my phone back while he gulped water.

"Go sit on that rock, Steven. I'm calling the rangers."

"No." He took another deep drink.

"Then we're going back."

"I'm fine," he panted. "Anyway, we're almost there."

Typical Steven. Now that my heartbeat had quit thundering in my ears, I could consider my options. Let him continue to the summit and risk another episode of whatever-it-had-been. Or start back down and pray he would follow.

"You are not *fine*. You scared me half to death. I thought you were having a heart attack."

"No," he said again, and then he glared at me. "Jesus, Diane. You were going so damned *fast*. What got into you?"

Oh, sure. Blame me. "Was I? It didn't feel like I was."

"You were. Believe me."

He was breathing normally by then, and I couldn't help a gentle jab to his arm. "Maybe you were going so damned *slow*."

He didn't reply but turned and trudged toward the summit, where a cluster of picnic tables waited. I hoped he'd sit down and rest, but he didn't. He walked to the outer edge of the clearing and stood, hands on hips, taking in the view. I followed him, spread my arms and let the breeze dry my sweat, grateful our Saturday morning hadn't turned tragic. Los Angeles fanned out below us, pristine and innocent in the morning light.

I took hold of his arm and leaned into him. "Mr. Resilient," I said. He chuckled and bumped his head gently against mine.

I broke out a bag of trail mix and offered it to him, but he waved it away. I took a few bites, then popped out a second water bottle, since he'd almost drained the first. He didn't look at me when I offered it to him but kept his gaze on the distance.

What was he thinking? I was pretty sure I knew. Steven had more than his share of manly pride, and in his mind at least, it must have been breached.

My husband was intensely competitive, in sports, business, and life in general. He liked to win—a good trait in a lawyer. But he never won by cheating, and he rarely gloated. He coached our son Jeff's Little League team to victory three years in a row, but not by intimidation. Playing cards with him could suck, though.

"Okay," he said after a few minutes contemplating the urban sprawl below. "Let's head back."

No lollygagging for us today, but I already knew that. Steven had brought home a thick folder of legal documents for review and commentary. As *the* Devlin in Jernigan, DeWitt, Royce and Devlin, he was lead counsel on a contentious copyright infringement case soon to go to trial, and the work had consumed him for weeks.

We went down Cardiac side by side, mindful of loose rocks coating the trail, and me mulling over my new take on that trail's name.

Steven nudged me. "Gonna share your new vitamins with me, Di?"

I let out a long exhale. "Same old stuff. I just felt extra peppy this morning. Maybe I took a double dose by mistake. You know us senior citizens can be forgetful."

He put his hand on the back of my neck and squeezed gently. "You do pretty good for an old broad."

Ouch. I pulled away from him. "Sure wish Elsa could still come with us."

Elsa, our twelve-year-old German shepherd, had accompanied us on our hikes until recently; arthritis was crippling her joints. My gallant girl never complained, but I *knew* she was suffering. We started her on Rimadyl, which eased the pain, but the vet discouraged strenuous walks. Instead, Steven and I took her on strolls around the neighborhood and gently tossed her favorite ball across the back yard to keep her exercised without injuring those worn-out legs.

"She did love her hikes," Steven said quietly, and maybe he was wondering the same thing I was. How did Elsa get so *old*, so *fast*?

Steven's breathing became audible despite our descent, so I deliberately slowed my pace, glancing at him occasionally. His color remained normal, but I was relieved when we reached the foot of the trail.

Only a few more yards to go. I hadn't realized how tense I was until I saw Steven's Lexus, sunlight bouncing off its silver hood.

The parking lot was filling up, and as we approached Steven's car, I noticed a young couple beside a dusty Chevy sedan, a few parking spaces away from us. She was crouched, lacing her hiking boots, and he was pulling a backpack from the trunk. *That was us a few decades ago.* An adorable Golden Retriever puppy sat with them, head cocked, watching the activity around it. The puppy made me think of Elsa, because she had that same gangly, curious look when she was a pup.

Steven pressed the remote to unlock the Lexus's doors, and the car chirped in response. That got the dog's attention, and it stood.

No leash, I thought. *Don't those kids know how dangerous that is?*

The puppy loped toward us on those big clumsy paws, tongue flopping, ears flapping. Suddenly I saw a Range Rover between us and the dog, backup lights blazing white—but not the red glow of brakes. The Range Rover jerked backward, the puppy right in its path.

Time froze. My legs worked before my brain, and I sprinted toward the puppy and snatched it out of danger. The dog felt weightless in my arms. My momentum shot me forward, and I felt the Range Rover's fender whack my backpack. Brakes squealed, doors slammed, and someone yelled, "Lady, are you okay?"

And I was. The puppy and I were just fine, thank you. The dog squirmed in my arms, and I realized I was probably squeezing so hard it couldn't breathe, so I shoved it into the arms of the woman who had been tying her boots and now stood, mouth open, eyes wide.

"Oh my God, oh my God!" She held the quivering dog close, and it nuzzled her, unaware of its brush with death.

Her companion stepped up to me and seized my shaking hands. "Thank you, thank you, thank you!"

Then Steven was there, his arms around me. "Good grief, Diane— you could have been killed. And you moved so fast—I've never seen you like that!"

"I don't know what came over me. I didn't think. I just moved!"

He stroked my hair. "Obviously."

"You *did* move fast," the woman said. "Are you a marathon runner or something?"

I shook my head. "Just an old woman who cares about dogs." I rubbed the puppy's ears. "And you should keep this one on a leash. Puppies can get into trouble in a flash."

The man crossed his heart. "We will!"

While they were still thanking us, I took Steven's arm and returned to the Lexus. I should have felt winded after all that, but I wasn't. I was ready to climb Cardiac Hill again, only I didn't want to. All I wanted was to get Steven safely home, and to hug Elsa.

* * *

I expected an interrogation from Steven about my newfound bursts of energy, but he mostly kept silent on the ride home. I did catch him glancing at me with a mixture of bewilderment and something else I couldn't identify. Fear?

"Steven, that was just an adrenaline rush—nothing extraordinary. I saw that puppy and I knew what would happen if I didn't act. Fast."

His fingers tapped the steering wheel. "You certainly did *that*."

I patted his knee. "Drive through Starbucks, and you can treat me to a latte for rescuing the puppy."

He did.

* * *

Back at the house, Steven took a quick shower and headed for the downstairs bedroom, which we had converted into an office, mostly for him. Until three months earlier, I'd used part of the room for my own work, but then Gardner Engineering had outsourced its employee relocation department. Since I was the department's manager, I became superfluous, almost overnight. I was eligible for a generous retirement package along with the severance, but I wasn't prepared to leave the workforce that soon. My age hadn't troubled me much until then, but I had never felt as old and unwanted as I did the night I turned off my office lights for the last time. If I'd been my younger, prettier self, they'd have found a way to keep me. But I wasn't, and they didn't.

* * *

The rest of the day passed in tranquil semi-silence, with Steven immersed in his trial preparations and me doing laundry and planning the week's meals.

When I took down Elsa's leash, her ears went up. She pranced to me, whining softly, and thrust her wet nose into my hand. She was a good dog, loyal and smart, intensely aware of her surroundings and the moods of her humans.

The afternoon air was heavy with spring. My roses bobbed in a breeze, the Double Delights scattering their sweet fragrance. I stopped to sniff them—isn't that a benefit of retirement, being able to stop and smell the roses, guilt-free? Elsa tugged at her leash, however, so we took off down the sidewalk at a good clip, until she began lagging and throwing out her right hind leg. I patted her head.

"You okay, baby? Want to keep going?"

She did, but my pleasure dimmed at this reminder that Elsa was probably the equivalent of my age—and feeling every minute of it.

By the time we got back, and we didn't go far, Elsa's tongue was hanging out and dripping drool, her sides heaving. Guilt dug into me for letting her get so worked up; I hadn't meant to and had consciously slowed down after I noticed her struggle.

Steven was taking a break, and we found him in the dining room with the *Los Angeles Times* spread out in front of him. Elsa went to him and sat, tail thrashing, as he ruffled her fur and stroked her big pointy ears. If he noticed her panting, he didn't comment.

"Looks like I'll be free for the play Friday night," he said, stretching and cracking his knuckles.

We had season tickets to the Pantages, but we never knew for sure if Steven could make the performance. If he got stuck at work, I'd usually go with my friend Maura, who always gushed about our aisle seats in the Orchestra section.

"Great!" I said. "It sounds like a good one—and funny. I could use a laugh."

I kissed the top of his head and inhaled a whiff of Old Spice as I savored his sturdy maleness. Steven was my rock, my protector. Those terrifying moments on Cardiac Hill had shaken me. *I don't know what I'd do if anything happened to you, Steven.*

I grabbed a glass of water and joined him at the table while we worked out plans for the coming week. Our son Jeff had a book signing Thursday afternoon, but Steven had back-to-back depositions and couldn't make it.

Jeff had become something of a celebrity as the author of a successful series of children's books featuring a character called "Defender Dog." His latest book had just been released, and he was on an author tour that included our local bookstore.

"I suppose you're taking Maddie?" asked Steven.

"I am. Nancy has a faculty meeting."

He peered at me over his reading glasses but didn't say anything.

Our daughter Nancy had resumed her teaching career after a five-year break that started when Maddie was born. Back in the workforce, Nancy had hired part-time childcare, but still she had to juggle schedules, and her husband Nick wasn't much help. Steven and I filled in when we could, but back then we both had demanding careers. When things went haywire, however, I was usually the one who stepped in. What mother could refuse her daughter's tearful call for help with a last-minute emergency when the caregiver took sick and couldn't fetch Maddie after school?

"If she'd married someone with a real job," Steven muttered as he turned back to his paper, "she wouldn't have to lean on you so much."

"Someone like a lawyer?"

Steven had been on partner track when Nancy was born, earning enough to support all of us without my needing to work, which gave me the luxury of being a full-time mom during the kids' early childhoods.

"Nick makes good money," I added, aware I was poking a beast.

Steven scowled. "When he's working."

After Gardner and I parted company, and with a lot of free time, I began picking Maddie up after school, chauffeuring her to ballet class, soccer practice, and piano lessons, and hanging out with her until one of her parents got home from work. She was a delightful child, and I loved her with all my heart. Being with her, I almost forgot my yearning for the fast-paced business world I'd left behind—or, more accurately, had left me behind.

Steven had not been enthusiastic when I told him I'd signed on as Maddie's part-time nanny, and at first I didn't understand why. I enjoyed Maddie's company, and I was glad to help Nancy. If it wasn't the life I had chosen for myself, at least I was doing something useful again.

"She takes you for granted," he said, not looking up from his paper.

"She always has. And who taught her to do that?" I had to chuckle. "Who treated her like his little princess who could do no wrong?"

That got his attention. It always did.

He snapped the paper shut. "I admit it—I spoiled her. But what can I do about it now? Forbid you to short-stop for her?"

"Like you could do that! Since when do you—"

He held up his hands. "I didn't mean it literally, and you know it. But I don't like the way she takes advantage of you."

"And what would you have me be doing instead? Taking a pottery class? Working the crossword puzzle half the day? Sitting in a rocking chair on the porch and spying on the neighbors?"

He tapped the paper on the table top. "I was thinking more of that astronomy course you talked about taking. Or the Italian class. Or the—"

My God, we're bickering just like my parents.

I stood. "Don't you ever get tired of being right?"

I didn't wait for an answer.

* * *

We managed not to quarrel any more for the rest of the day, and Steven praised the chicken and pasta I made for dinner, like it was something special—even though it wasn't, really. That was one of his endearing traits; if he felt responsible for causing friction between us, he didn't apologize but went out of his way to be complimentary for any little thing I did.

That night as I was brushing my teeth before bed, I thought back on those surges of energy I'd felt in the park. My legs had felt as light as bird wings—as if I'd been visited by my younger self. Wouldn't it be nice if she stuck around?

"Be grateful for what you've got, Diane. Don't go wishing for more," I told my toothpaste-spattered reflection.

But I couldn't help wishing for more. Elsa wasn't the only one showing her age. My body had begun to let me know I was sixty-five, and I hated every reminder.

I usually avoided the mirror; firm skin is one of the first casualties of age. Yes, I was—or had been—vain, but my looks had opened a lot of doors when I was younger. I even suspected Steven Devlin would never have asked me out if I hadn't been pretty. Not movie-star gorgeous, but better than average, and I knew it. Feeling pretty gave me confidence, and I used it. But those days were gone, and I missed them.

The changes in my body were even harder to accept. I fought back, joined the Y and took exercise classes, worked the elliptical and weight machines. Most of the time, though, I barely held my own, and I had never—even in my thirties—been able to keep up with Steven.

Until that morning. What *had* happened?

My mirror image had no answer, but she looked mighty pleased with herself, and, I imagined, a tiny bit less wrinkled and worn than she had the day before.

Chapter Two
Beautiful Child

When I awoke the next morning, I expected to feel the effects of my spurts of energy the day before. It usually took me several minutes to work out the kinks and sore spots when I first got up. My muscles had lost strength and flexibility—another cruel reminder that I wasn't thirty-something anymore. Not that morning, though. I felt perfectly fine—not a twinge anywhere. *This is nice*, I thought. *Maybe my reward for a good deed, rescuing that puppy?*

I usually worked out three mornings a week in the YMCA circuit room to try and combat time and gravity. One of the perks of retirement was being able to go the gym mid-morning, when a lot of people were at work. The few regulars I encountered on the circuit were mostly around my age, mostly semi-fit. Like me. None of us were shooting for the Olympics, merely keeping our bodies from falling apart.

The circuit consisted of ten machines designed to strengthen each major muscle group, and you controlled the resistance by adjusting weights and pulleys to make them easier or harder to move. The resistance levels started at one and ended at twelve. A buzzer sounded at forty-five-second intervals, and then you went on to the next machine.

Never a bodybuilder, I generally started out at level three for one circuit, did a second at level four or even five, and then fell back to three for the final round. I couldn't lift 100-lb. weights, but I *could* haul three or four bags of groceries in one trip from the car.

On Monday, I sat down at the first machine, adjusted the resistance, and started lifting and lowering my ankles, working my quads and the tendons and ligaments around my knees. That machine and the squat were my least favorites, but I noticed that it didn't feel nearly as hard as usual. *Maybe the machine needs a tune-up*, I thought as I upped the resistance. Still too easy. I went all the way to level seven before the buzzer sounded, but since there was no one right behind me on the circuit, I went for a second set of reps. I wasn't even straining.

Still thinking the machine wasn't calibrated right, I moved to the next station, set the resistance, and started raising and lowering a bar to work my shoulders. Same thing: level three felt like nothing, so I tried seven. A little harder, but not much.

The woman who followed me on the circuit seemed in pretty good shape. I'd seen her there before, enough to mouth a hello to. She got onto the machine I'd vacated and started to work. After a couple of seconds, she looked at the resistance setting, then I saw her ease off on the pressure. She glanced over at me, eyes wide, and called out "WOW!" with a thumbs-up.

The buzzer sounded. I returned her thumbs-up and went on to the next station.

Usually by the time I finished, I was sweating and breathing heavy from pushing my muscles beyond their comfort level. That morning I couldn't even tell I'd done a workout. In fact, I felt so peppy I went to the cardio room for a twenty-minute session on the elliptical, after tweaking the resistance level to a challenging five. I could feel the blood flowing through my body, my muscles flexing as I pumped the pedals.

Wednesday morning, I upped the resistance on the circuit machines but still had energy to spare when I finished. Back to the cardio room. This time I started the treadmill at a brisk walk. Easy. I bumped up the speed until my feet skimmed the belt, my arms pumping in time. It felt so good! Most other exercisers ignored me as they worked their own routines, but one fellow simply stopped and stared. I was barely aware of them as I finally felt sweat trickle down my neck.

I went thirty minutes before I began to feel like I'd *really* exercised.

Maybe, I told myself on the drive home, I'd been getting stronger all along and simply hadn't paid attention until that morning with Steven at the park. Maybe it was one of those things that crept up on you; months or even years of work finally paying off. Maybe.

Enjoy it while it lasts, I told myself, hoping my body would let me down gently when it remembered my true age.

* * *

Thursday afternoon, I took Maddie to Jeff's book signing in Glendale. The store had set up rows of folding chairs, most of which were already taken by children and their parents; the babble of excited young voices filled the store. *All this for my son,* I kept thinking.

Jeff's *Defender Dog* book series had become a huge hit. Defender Dog looked something like Snoopy from "Peanuts" except he was reddish-brown and possessed uncanny intelligence. Oh, and he could fly. Defender Dog cruised the planet, rescuing children, and often their parents, from danger, and his exploits usually ended with some type of light moral lesson: don't fib to Mom and Dad; don't be fooled by friendly strangers; be kind to other kids and defenseless animals. I loved the stories, but I found it hard to believe that my Jeffrey had created this phenomenon. As a boy, he'd always like to write, and he'd always loved animals, but Steven and I thought he'd follow his father into law. Instead he got an MFA in creative writing, and not long afterward, Defender Dog was born.

The irony of Jeff's achievement often struck me, because I'd always expected Nancy to be the successful one. She got better grades, excelled in everything she tried: the volleyball team, Honor Society, editing the school newspaper, starring in the Senior Play. Her SAT scores got her the choice of universities, and I saw a brilliant future for her. Then she met Nick Ross, and any ambitions she had went straight out the window. She did go on to college, but close to home, so she and Nick could date. The teaching credential was almost an afterthought, but thank goodness she had it because there were years when she was the sole breadwinner.

Meanwhile, Jeff—my daydreaming, take-it-easy, pot-smoking son—went on to literary fame. He'd even been approached by Hollywood about a TV series, maybe a movie. So far the talks hadn't led to anything, but stranger things had happened in the Devlin family.

Including a sixty-five-year-old woman whose body had seemingly forgotten the laws of time and gravity.

* * *

Maddie and I found Jeff in the front of the store, surrounded by his young fans. His smile broadened when he saw us.

"Uncle Jeff!" Maddie called out, easing her way toward him through the cluster of kids. Her blond hair fanned out around a perfect face, rosy cheeks and deep blue eyes.

Even allowing for motherly prejudice, I believed Nancy and Jeff were two of the most attractive people on the planet. Jeff had yet to marry and have children, but Nancy had produced the most adorable little girl the world has ever seen: a proud grandmother assessment, but everyone who met Maddie agreed. People stopped on the street for a long look, and more than once I heard someone murmur, "What a beautiful child."

Maddie wasn't just pretty—she was good-tempered and well-behaved. Nancy had seen to that.

"Maddie!" Jeff lifted her off the ground. "Aren't you gorgeous! And you smell like peppermint candy." He pretended to nibble on her neck, and Maddie giggled in delight. The other children around him regarded Maddie with obvious envy, and I didn't blame them.

When Jeff turned to me, his face registered surprise. How long had it been since we'd seen each other? A month at least.

"Hey, Moms," he said, releasing Maddie and planting a kiss on my cheek, "don't you look spiffy today. New haircut?"

I hugged him. "I love you too, Son."

* * *

Jeff held his standing-room-only audience spellbound, and afterward the line of people who bought his book and wanted an autograph backed all the way to the door and beyond. The store exhausted its supply of the new book, so Jeff signed bookmarks for the unfortunate ones who had to order theirs and wait several days. Maddie and I already had our own copies, and she'd read it twice.

Nancy caught up with us as Jeff was signing the last of the bookmarks. He hugged his sister and then bowed to us. "Thanks for coming, Family. Now I gotta run. I have another gig in the Valley tonight."

"What a grind," Nancy said. "The life of a famous author."

Jeff blew kisses to us as he hurried off.

"Want to grab an early bite?" I asked Nancy.

She pressed her lips together. As always, I was struck by her beauty, her thick, shoulder-length hair—red-brown as mine had been in my youth—and peaches and cream complexion. Maddie had inherited her father's blond hair and blue eyes, but otherwise she seemed a small carbon copy of her mother.

"Can't," she said. "We're leaving for Monterey tonight. Nick's on location up there and we're taking a long weekend. Maddie and I are playing hooky tomorrow, but don't tell." She seemed about to say something else but then turned her attention to Maddie.

"Gee, thanks for letting me know ahead of time," I said, the words coming out before I could stop them.

Nancy winced. "I'm sorry, Mom. You're right, it was inconsiderate. But I honestly didn't know until this afternoon if we'd be able to do it. You know how these out-of-town shoots are. If things weren't going well, then he couldn't be with us anyhow. It won't happen again, I promise."

My annoyance let up a little, although I knew it *would* happen again. Nancy's life was filled with challenges, and often she didn't think of anyone else's priorities.

Nick had once had a starring role in a hit TV series, but it had folded several years ago. His work was not as steady as either Nancy or I would have liked, but he'd just landed a recurring part on a cable drama, a family saga. The Monterey shoot was a five-episode arc, and I knew Nancy was relieved to have him bringing in a regular paycheck. She and Nick liked to live well, and I doubted they had much put aside for a rainy day.

"Besides," Nancy added with a funny little grin, "Maddie needs a rest. She's been having so much fun with you after school—the zoo was genius, by the way—but she's been falling asleep over dinner the past couple of weeks."

I glanced down at Maddie. She didn't look tired to me; she looked like a normal, happy, excited eight-year-old. But maybe I had been overdoing it, trying to keep her entertained and engaged with the world.

"I'll ease up a little," I told Nancy, but I winked at Maddie. "Have a fun trip. Email pictures."

"We will," Nancy replied. "Mom? You look... different. New makeup or something?"

I laughed. "Or something."

Maddie gave me a farewell hug before we went our separate ways, and her peppermint aura followed me into the car and all the way home.

* * *

Saturday morning, when Steven and I set out on our hike, I felt that same wild surge of energy, but I reined it in. From the pleasure on Steven's face when he reached the summit first, I figured he had no clue I'd let him "win."

The sensation of power stayed with me, however. It was weird, sure, but good-weird, and I decided I'd go with it and see what happened. I was delighted to roll out of bed in the morning without the usual stiff, sore joints, my spine more limber than it had been in years. I could put on socks and lace my sneakers without my hip burning its protest. And my reflection in the mirror—well, that looked different, too. Still me, only better. Younger. Maybe all those years of exercise were finally paying off, the way the magazines promised they would.

Steven hadn't seemed to notice yet, but when you see a person every day, things like that aren't obvious. Even I hadn't perceived them at first. Once I did notice, however, the changes moved to the front of my awareness and stayed there.

I didn't assume that what was happening to me was anything permanent. I enjoyed my rejuvenated body, but I really didn't believe it was mine to keep.

Chapter Three
Old Friends

My best friend Maura and I met for lunch the following Tuesday. We hadn't seen each other for over three weeks because she'd been wandering around Europe with Robert, the new man in her life. I didn't know how she'd react to the new and improved me—if she even noticed. I expected her to be wrapped up in a romantic haze that blocked out reality.

Despite differences in our backgrounds and politics, Maura and I became friends in college, bonding over love of the Eagles and Kurt Vonnegut, Jr. After graduation, our careers went in different directions. I took a secretarial job in a real estate office while figuring out what to do with my Liberal Arts degree. Maura's Business degree was more useful; she brought her skills and knowledge into the family business, a popular Mexican food joint in East Los Angeles. While I stayed single and played the dating field, Maura married long-time family friend Luis Salcedo. The marriage imploded a couple of years later, however, when Luis turned out to be a mean drunk who liked to use Maura as a punching bag when things didn't go his way. By then I was dating Steven Devlin and beginning to think I'd found Mr. Right, so I felt vaguely guilty as I held Maura's hand and soothed her tears during the anguished days when her rock-solid Catholic parents threatened to disown her and Luis raged at her for divorcing him.

When Steven proposed, Maura was happy to be matron of honor at my wedding. At least she pretended to be happy, which is sometimes the best a good friend can do.

We remained close over the years, although no friendship is flawless. I wondered if Maura sometimes resented my stable family life, the handsome lawyer husband and the two attractive, well-adjusted children.

If I'm being totally honest, there were days when I envied the hell out of Maura: her adventurous spirit, the guys she dated—usually upscale professionals who took her on glamorous trips like the one Robert had just underwritten. There were days when I wondered if Maura was hiding some imperfections from me the way I camouflaged a few in my own life. But maybe not; maybe it was all candlelight, roses, first-class airline tickets and five-star hotels.

* * *

She breezed through the door of Chez Reynard in her four-inch heels and wrapped me in a Chanel-scented embrace.

"You look terrific, Di," she said. Then she took a step back. "You had work done? And didn't tell me?"

I brushed a speck of lint off her navy blazer. "No, I didn't. You've been gone so long you forgot what I look like."

Maura scowled. "Been near a mirror lately?"

After the hostess seated us, we scanned the menu and ordered our usual salads. Then Maura added a bottle of chardonnay.

"I shouldn't," I protested. "I'll be useless the rest of the day."

"So? It's not like you have to get back to the office."

I flinched. "Don't remind me."

"You're missing Gardner? Hey, I just came from a meeting there—want me to share some of the latest horror stories to wipe out your regret?"

"Let's remember who got me in the door there."

"And there are times when I'm not sure I did you any favors."

The wine arrived, and we toasted our friendship.

Then I had to ask, "Okay, tell me one little horror story, so I won't miss being part of the action."

Maura laughed. "I see a lot of unhappy faces in what's left of your old department, and they've cut their marketing budget so deep it's bleeding. I don't know if they'll renew my contract next year."

* * *

When Maura's parents kicked her out of the family business, she started a catering company and eventually became a popular event planner, which led to a contract with Gardner Engineering.

Meanwhile, my life ambled along. I'd earned my real estate license before the kids were born, and I wasn't bad at selling houses, but I gave up the long hours and late-night phone calls when I got pregnant with Nancy. Eight years later, when Jeff started school, I started to miss the working world, but my real estate license had lapsed. Maura heard about a job in Gardner's relocation department, and my real estate experience, even without a license, suddenly became relevant.

Gardner sent their employees all over, and they provided generous relocation benefits, which had to satisfy employees—and their families —while keeping costs under control. The job had practically been tailor-made for me, and the hiring manager must have agreed. I started as an analyst, reviewing appraisals and approving marketing plans for the houses Gardner bought from employees. I had a knack for it, and one promotion led to another. I'd been department manager for several great years by the time the company started paring staff, outsourcing everything except what they deemed their "core business."

* * *

"For sure they'll renew your contract. Nobody can fill your stilettos."

Maura grinned at our running joke. Because she was only five foot three, Maura almost always wore impossibly high-heeled shoes.

"I wish I had your confidence, Di," she said. "Now, let's get back to what I really want to know: what's going on with you? Swear to God, you look ten years younger than the last time I saw you."

We were seated by the front window, and I glanced at my reflection in the glass. I *did* look perkier than my usual self.

"No big secret, pal. Just eating right and exercise. And water."

She frowned and set her glass down. "And maybe a little Botox on the side?"

I waved the suggestion away. "Nope."

The salads arrived, along with a slab of French bread. I tested the bread—still warm, so I pulled off a slice and handed the basket to Maura.

She wrinkled her nose and declined. "Diane, we've been friends forever, and I don't believe what you're telling me."

"I didn't—"

Maura traced squiggles in the condensation on her wine glass. "I know you've always obsessed about your looks—I do, too. But to have work done then deny it—to me, of all people."

My mouth was probably hanging open. I couldn't think what to say to her. So absurd!

"And it's not like you were turning into a wrinkled hag, Di. But I thought you had more perspective. I mean, there are things more important than superficial appearance."

My wine glass hit the table so hard a few drops splashed on my hand.

"Are you finished?" I asked when I could form words. My hands were shaking, and so was my voice. "First off, I haven't had a facelift, okay? Or Botox. No matter what you think. Second, we haven't seen each other for weeks, and you start in lecturing me about perspective, when you—"

I was going to finish with "jump in bed with any guy who looks twice at you," but I stopped myself. This was *Maura*. We'd gone through my marriage, her divorce, the birth of my kids, the deaths of our parents. She'd always been the kind of friend who, if you told her you'd just murdered six people with an ax, would have replied, "They must have had it coming." When did she turn so self-righteous?

As the angry haze cleared, I realized her demeanor had changed.

Tears glimmered in her big dark eyes. Sunlight shifted, and for a few seconds her normally cheerful face, in sharp focus, appeared frail and frightened. She wiped her cheeks, and her scarlet fingernails shone.

"I'm sorry, Di. I don't know what got into me. You're right—I'm the last person who should be lecturing *you*. My own life's a mess, so I guess I wanted to throw water on your party, too."

"A mess? After a trip to Europe with Mr. Right? What happened?" I'd been dying to ask about her trip.

She glanced away. "Mr. Wrong, you mean—which I discovered as we were sitting in a cute little café on the Place Madeleine. There was the Eiffel Tower, like on a postcard, and I was feeling so *immersed* in Paris. And then, right after they brought us these heavenly croissants, these two French women walk by, and his eyes practically fell out of his head. And he says to me, 'My God, French women are *so* classy.' Then he looks at me, and his lip curled—honestly, like in a bad movie, like I'm something a stray dog dragged in! And it's not like those women—girls, really—stepped out of a Saint Laurent ad. One had on this skimpy little sundress and the other one wore an ugly yellow tunic over faded jeans. And flats! Both of them in flats!"

"Incredible," I agreed.

Maura sipped her wine—actually it was more gulp than sip. "It got worse. When the bill for our food came, he told me to ask the waiter the best way to Notre Dame, and when I tried and fumbled, the waiter graciously started speaking perfect English. No big deal, right?"

"Doesn't sound like it."

"Exactly! But Robert says to me, 'I thought you knew enough French to get us around. I should have brought an interpreter.'"

"Was he joking?"

"Not hardly."

Outrage flooded me. "Then that was uncalled for!"

Maura nodded. "It's not like he was any great shakes with the language either. Besides, everybody there speaks English anyway. And even though he invited me on this trip, I did offer to split the cost, but he refused—then he kept handing me the check at a restaurant and asking if he'd left enough tip and telling me to go over the hotel bills to be sure they didn't add in any bogus charges."

"Maybe he really did need help with that."

Maura shook her head so hard her dark curls bounced. "I think he wanted to be sure I knew how much he was paying for stuff."

"Speaking of class, where's *his* class?"

"To put it mildly. There were other things, too—one night in a restaurant he says to me, 'You really don't appreciate French cuisine as much as I thought you would.' But when I asked him what he meant, he just said, 'I can tell.' Like there was some secret behavior I was supposed to know about. Then he adds, 'I'm disappointed. I thought you had more experience in European travel.' Right to my face he says this!"

"Did you tell him you've been to almost every country in Europe?"

"I mentioned it, sure."

"Good thing for him I wasn't there. I'd have clawed his eyes out."

She smiled at that. "I know you would have, Di. And it's not like I have trouble standing up for myself, you know that."

"Do I ever!"

"But I don't think it would have made any difference. It's like he started the trip with some preconceived idea of who I was, and I didn't measure up. I'm not hyper-sensitive; my skin is pretty damn thick. But he kept on like that, put-down after put-down, and never too subtle." She sighed. "Serves me right for going off with someone I barely knew." She took another hefty swallow of wine. "Although, I won't lie, the sex was fantastic, even with all that. This clearly wasn't his first rodeo. But by the time we got on the plane home, I could barely speak to him."

Her eyes misted over again, and I reached across the table and grabbed her hand.

"I'm so sorry, Maura."

She squeezed back. "Yeah. Me too."

Then she straightened. "But that's life, you know. Water under the bridge. At least I didn't fall in love with the bum."

"Right," I agreed. "You dodged a bullet."

"Damn straight. Men! You can't trust 'em not to hurt you one way or another, right?" She tilted her head. "Except Steven of course. He turned out to be a good one. Mostly."

I didn't know how to reply to that, and after a few seconds she went on, "Anyway, Di—you do whatever you need to do to make you feel good. Don't mind me. I'm just jealous, that's all."

"You'll find the one who's right for you, Maura. Don't give up."

She raised her napkin to her lips in an elegant way that only Maura could pull off. "Maybe. But I'm running out of time. I'm not getting any younger, y'know." Her dark eyes narrowed. "Unlike you, my friend. You really haven't had plastic surgery?"

I put my right hand over my heart. "Swear to God."

"Then what *is* going on with you, Di?"

I broke the gaze first. "Not what you think. I mean, I don't know *what* it is, but I'm loving it."

She leaned forward and listened intently as I filled her in on what little I knew: stronger muscles, more energy. Fewer wrinkles.

"And my hip! It hasn't hurt in days!"

* * *

When I'd told her I might need a hip replacement, Maura had protested that I just needed physical therapy and then went on to share some horror stories of people she'd known who went under the knife and ended up crippled. When I told Steven what she'd said, he got mad.

"That woman can find the black cloud in every silver lining. I don't know why you listen to her."

"She's a realist," I retorted. "And she cares about me."

"I don't?"

Our argument ended with nothing resolved. I told myself I'd consider hip surgery when the pain got really bad, without a clear definition of what "really bad" was. Some days I'd hurt so much I couldn't stand for more than twenty minutes without a burning in my hip and leg.

And now the pain was gone. Like magic.

* * *

Maura speared the last chunk of tomato on her plate. "That's great, Di. But why? Did you change vitamins or something?"

"Steven asked the same thing. No, I'm not doing anything different. This just started up, all on its own. All of a sudden."

"Maybe you should check with your doc."

"Why? I feel great. More than great!"

"I get that, Hon, but this isn't *normal*. I mean, you look fabulous, and I'm glad you *feel* fabulous, but…"

I pushed my salad plate away; it was empty except for one shred of lettuce, glistening with oil. "But what? Whatever this is, I don't want to stop it. I like it."

"Maybe you can bottle it and share with me." She cocked her head. "But, Di, what if it *doesn't* stop?"

I'd wondered that myself but had pushed the question away.

"It will. This is only temporary."

"Is it? What about that Fitzgerald story? Benjamin Button—see how *he* ended up."

"That was *fiction*."

"And you know the saying—life is stranger than fiction."

"Actually, the quote is '*Truth* is stranger than Fiction.' Mark Twain said that. And the rest of the sentence goes, 'but it is because Fiction is obliged to stick to possibilities; Truth isn't.' And I believe he was talking about writing, not aging."

Maura tossed her napkin on the table. "Do you ever lose an argument?"

"Only with Steven. And he taught me well."

Maura sniffed. "Did he ever! Now back to my original point—oh, yeah, nice try, but I still want you to check in with your doctor."

"Maura—"

"Do it for me. Pleeeeeeeeeeze."

Her voice rose to an ear-splitting pitch and a half-dozen people turned to stare at her.

I held up my hands in surrender. "I promise."

Maura giggled. "Okay, then we can share a dessert."

* * *

After lunch, still a little buzzed from the wine and the *crème brûlée* sugar rush, we wandered into the soft late-spring sunlight and cruised the boulevard on foot, window shopping and making snide remarks about some of the fashions on display. Then a new women's clothing store caught my eye. There was a dress in the window that reminded me of one I'd worn back in the 1990s, before age and gravity began having their way with me: shimmery black, with a tiny rose print and a flared skirt that would end a few inches above my knees.

I stopped mid-step and pointed. "We have to go in there," I said.

Maura was never one to turn down a shopping opportunity—one of the many things about her I loved—so we entered the shop, which smelled of jasmine while Enya's voice sang softly from invisible speakers. A smiling woman with spiky silver hair greeted us, and when I asked about the dress in the window, she whisked it off a rack, and it was exactly my size.

It fit like a dream. The dress wrapped around, the cap sleeves and hem hitting at exactly the right places, the V of the neckline stopping just short of my bra.

"You look stunning," the saleswoman gushed.

Maura whistled softly. "It's like it was made for you."

I had to have the dress, even though it was priced higher than I usually paid. I browsed the shop, which was filled with other temptations.

"How long have you been here?" I asked.

The saleswoman explained they'd just opened the month before; the owner was also a designer and had created much of the clothing. Whoever she was, it was like she'd fashioned dresses with me in mind. Me and Maura, because I saw a spiffy shirtwaist in bright magenta that was devastating on Maura. The dress would have ended up wearing *me*, but with her jet black hair and tawny skin, Maura owned it.

"I'm buying it for you," I told her when she flinched at the price tag. "A welcome-back present. A consolation prize for the trip with Robert not working out."

"I can't let you."

This was a familiar dance. Maura had plenty of money, but she also had trouble spending it on herself.

I put my fingers on her chest and gently pushed her away from the register. "Too late," I said. "I just gave them my card."

Back on the boulevard, other stores beckoned. How long since Maura and I had gone shopping together? And there were so many possibilities I hadn't noticed before. Had these shops all sprouted like mushrooms after a rain?

"Shoes," I said. "We need shoes."

Maura stopped walking. "But I'm paying this time."

I had to let her get even for the dress, now didn't I?

* * *

In the end, we both spent more than we probably should have, but I had some shiny new red pointy-toed pumps with heels as high as Maura's; they went perfectly with the dress. Maura found some bright green stilettos, too. We browsed a lingerie shop, and I found a blue negligée that I had to have. Next came the kitchen store, where Maura picked up some new wine glasses. After that, I pointed out another clothing store across the street, but Maura put her hand on my arm.

"Hon, I am wiped out! I don't know where you found all this energy, but you're leaving me in the dust. I gotta quit."

She lagged a little behind as we returned to Reynard's parking lot, and for an instant I flashed on Steven on the trail up Cardiac Hill. I felt fine, super-charged in fact. I could have kept going for hours. Clothes shopping usually gave me an adrenaline rush, but this was something else. Something wonderful but scary at the same time.

We stashed our loot—Maura's light blue Volvo coupe was right next to my Honda—and hugged goodbye. Then Maura stepped back and took another look at me.

"You're amazing, Di. Sure wish I had some of what you've got."

"And I wish I could give it to you, pal. Believe me, if I knew how to bottle this, you'd be the first one to share."

She tapped the back of my hand. "But I still want you to call your doctor. First thing tomorrow."

I blew her a kiss. "Okay. Promise."

* * *

That night I studied my reflection in the mirror after I'd washed off my makeup. The grooves around my eyes and mouth weren't as deep; the skin beneath my chin had firmed up, and so had the flesh on my upper arms—it hardly wobbled when I stretched toward the ceiling.

This is great, I assured my reflection. But Maura's words kept echoing in my head. It *wasn't* normal.

Okay, I told myself. *Let's humor Maura and find out what's going on. Maybe there actually is something new in my vitamins. And maybe I'll really get to stay this way.*

Chapter Four
Breakdown

I'd had my annual physical exam in January, and Dr. Dennis had pronounced me in very good health "for a woman your age."

We'd both laughed at that qualifier because Laura Dennis was only six months younger than I. Cheerful, calm, and no-nonsense, she'd been my primary care doctor for over fifteen years, and I liked her style. We trusted each other, too.

But when she entered the exam room, this time my doctor did a double take.

She recovered quickly and sat on the rolling stool across from me as I started talking.

"I know what it looks like," I told her, pointing to my face, "but this is no facelift. It happened all on its own."

She squinted and rolled the stool closer to me, put her hand under my chin and tilted my face toward the light. "Interesting," she said. "You do appear years younger than you did in January."

"So I've been told. But it's not normal. I know that. Please tell me it isn't some weird kind of disease."

That made her smile. "If it is, breathe on me because I'd like to catch it."

She ran her hand over my cheeks, and her expression turned serious. "This *is* unusual. I've never taken measurements of the fat layer under your skin, but it seems to have increased since I last saw you—it's smoothing out some of those wrinkles, making your face rounder." She lifted my right arm. "Same thing here—see how much firmer your skin feels?"

"Yeah—no more chicken wings."

Another smile. "So it appears."

I smirked. "All my life I've fought the fat battle. Then this happened—without me even trying."

Now she laughed. "Fat isn't a bad thing—in the right places. But I've never seen subcutaneous fat increase in an older person's *face*—not on its own."

"Then what's causing it?" I asked. "I feel fine. In fact, I have energy like I did in my forties. Maybe my thirties. I haven't done anything different. This just started… *happening*."

Dr. Dennis squatted and took hold of my left ankle. "Let's check a few more things. Try to push up."

I pushed. She was applying pressure, but my foot came up so fast it nearly knocked her over. She repeated the drill with my right ankle and raised her eyebrows when I lifted that one with even more force.

She sat back on the stool, rolled over to her computer and tapped a few keys. "You're not taking any new meds I don't know about?"

"Nope."

"No new exercise routines?"

"Not deliberately."

"Come again?"

I explained my new and improved workout at the Y and told her how easily I'd overtaken Steven on the hike, and how I'd rescued the puppy.

The doctor tapped a pen against her lip, a gesture I recognized as a sign she was puzzling something out.

"You haven't had any illness since you were here last?" she asked.

I shook my head. "It's like I woke up one morning and started getting younger."

"And you feel well?"

"Better than well."

She turned away from the computer and studied me again.

The exam room was one I'd been in probably fifty times, and it hadn't changed much over the years except for new paint and a couple of different watercolors on the wall. Hummingbirds. Dr. Dennis liked hummingbirds. So did I. And usually I felt comfortable in the exam room, and comfortable with Laura Dennis.

She didn't wear a white lab coat, that was part of it. She dressed very stylishly, right down to her shoes—always fashionable yet comfy-looking. That morning she wore dark brown tweed slacks and a brown and orange silk blouse. And a hummingbird pendant hanging from a gold chain; I'd never seen her without that necklace. She had soft, intelligent gray eyes and chestnut hair that, like mine, got some help from a bottle. I knew because one time she hadn't done a touch-up, and gray roots were showing around the crown. She was an attractive woman with a warm, alert manner.

She reached for some forms beside the computer monitor. "I don't think we need to worry at this point, Diane. I admit this has me baffled, but let's run some blood tests and see if anything turns up. And let's do another EKG for comparison. I'm pretty sure I know what it will say, but I want to double-check."

She handed me the blood work orders for the lab and then grasped my shoulders. "We'll get to the bottom of this, Diane."

Dr. Dennis had always worked hard at keeping her face neutral, and that morning she'd done a good job, but there was something in her demeanor that made me wonder if maybe I *should* be worrying.

* * *

All the blood tests came back normal. Better than normal. My blood glucose level was lower. So was my LDL cholesterol, and the HDL cholesterol, the good kind, had gone *up*. The EKG was fine, just as it had been in January. And Dr. Dennis had run an extra test: something called a Glomerular Filtration Rate—a test of my kidney function, she explained. It was totally normal. My doctor remarked how rare that was in a person my age. "I'd trade lab results with you any day," she said.

After a brief pause, she added, "I wish I had more to tell you. And I still don't think this is any cause for concern, but it certainly has me puzzled."

Dr. Dennis was a curious woman, and I knew she wouldn't stop until she'd solved the puzzle, so I wasn't surprised when she added, "At this point, we need to send you to a specialist. I know a fellow who might be able to help. He's an endocrinologist, and I'm going to work on the premise this is somehow hormone related."

"Hormones? At my age?"

"At any age they can wreak havoc. You're lucky the effects are so benign in your case. I believe there *is* a logical explanation for what you're experiencing, and if anyone can find it, Charles can."

* * *

Dr. Dennis gave me a referral slip for Charles St. Onge, M.D, a board-certified internist with a specialty in endocrinology, but I put off phoning for an appointment. I wanted an answer, and I was afraid of that answer. I tucked the paper in a desk drawer with a silent promise to make an appointment "soon."

I'd mentioned my doctor visit to Steven in an offhanded way, saying we were doing a midyear follow-up on some of my lab tests from January. He still hadn't remarked on the changes in my appearance, and I didn't bring it up. The copyright case claimed most of his attention, and I was used to that. The price of being a successful attorney's wife was small in comparison to the benefits. He did ask if everything was okay, and I assured him I was fine.

Maura bristled with curiosity over Dr. Dennis' findings, and when I confessed I hadn't contacted the specialist, I heard her huff of annoyance over the phone.

"This isn't like you, Di," she said.

I resisted an urge to point out that nothing going on was like Old Diane.

"There's no rush," I replied. "The tests were all normal. I'm fine. Better than fine."

"I noticed," Maura said. "You like it, don't you? Feeling younger. Looking younger."

"Naturally I do! Wouldn't you? Wouldn't anyone?"

"Maybe. But you know what I always say. If it seems too good to be true…"

"It probably is," I finished for her.

"And I know that better than anyone," Maura added. "Like with Robert."

"I get it. But for the first time in ages I don't hate looking in the mirror. I missed this face."

"You're more than a pretty face, Di. Always have been. I wish you believed that."

"You make me sound so…"

I was going to say "superficial," but I trailed off because it may have been true. Was I a vain, superficial woman who measured my own worth in terms of appearance? Had I always been? Or was this the New Diane?

"I don't mean to," Maura said, mind-reading as she often did. "And you're not. Listen, you're right. I'd feel the same way if this happened to me. But, Di, you have to find out what's going on. What if whatever this thing is changes its mind? What if you start getting older again? What if you start getting *older* than you are?"

I shuddered. That idea hadn't occurred to me. "Gee, thanks, Maura."

"Sorry—I'm not trying to scare you, honest"

"But you are."

"Okay," she said. "We'll put this on hold for now. Temporarily. Hey, let's have a Girls Day Out tomorrow. There's a movie I'm dying to see."

"Um, don't you have a company to run?"

"I can leave Yvette in charge. She did fine when I was in Europe. There's only one event going on anyway."

"Promise you won't bug me about seeing any more doctors."

"You know I don't make promises I can't keep."

I agreed anyway. Nancy was off work for the summer and hardly ever needed my help with Maddie, so a diversion was ever so appealing.

* * *

We met up at our favorite art-house theater in Pasadena for a film about vampires in Detroit, and despite the white subtitles against a snowy background, I was enthralled by the story.

When we walked out into the bright June afternoon, I realized with a jolt that spring had ended. Where had the time gone? I stopped to study the poster for the film, which featured the lead actress leaning against a muscle car, her leather jacket zipped halfway up, and, apparently, nothing underneath it. Despite being a vampire, she hadn't opted for perpetual youth but had let her hair gray, and her face had the lines of a woman well past middle age. Yet she carried herself with total confidence.

"That was great," Maura said, and I murmured agreement.

"She sure has an *interesting* face," Maura added, and I saw her glance at me.

"Yes, Maura, I get the point."

She pointed to a florist shop on the corner. "Can we dash in there? I want to ask them about doing some centerpieces for a client's wedding. His fourth," she said with a giggle.

"Sure, I love flowers."

The shop's interior was lush with the scent of roses and honeysuckle, almost too much to take in. While Maura chatted with the shop's manager, I browsed the arrangements, thinking I might pick up a centerpiece for our dining room table. The price tags changed my mind, but it was fun to browse. And smell.

After a few minutes, however, the mingling fragrances began to bother me, as if they'd taken physical form and were overwhelming my senses. Even my vision was affected.

Then I realized what was happening, as a scalding zig-zag of light flared across my field of vision. A migraine aura. I hadn't had one of those in years. Fortunately for me, the auras had never been accompanied by the pain and nausea so many migraine-sufferers experience, but the aura was pretty damn debilitating for as long as it lasted. And this one seemed to be making up for lost time. I could barely make out a padded bench near the entrance and wobbled over to it, where I sat and closed my eyes.

"Di?"

I hadn't heard Maura approach. I opened my eyes but quickly had to shut them again. The light was excruciating, and now my temples began to throb. *Oh swell. Now I get the pain.*

"Sorry," I muttered, and pointed to my head. "Migraine ambushed me."

"Oh, hon," Maura said, sinking down next to me.

At least I didn't feel the need to throw up, but I had to sit on the bench for twenty minutes before the jagged line of light began to fade. The headache itself was still going strong, but I'd had worse from a night of swilling Cosmopolitans.

Maura sat stroking my hand the whole time, as I filled my lungs, exhaled, and tried to will the aura away. They always came on unexpectedly like that, and I'd never found a particular trigger. I'd gotten them on and off ever since my early twenties, and doctor after doctor had explained they were mostly benign as long as the vision impairment was "bilateral." They speculated on causes, and we tried various remedies, but none worked. It was, everyone concluded, probably hormone related. As long as they didn't become totally disabling—and a mere thirty minutes of not being able to see didn't count—they were nothing to worry about.

Hormone related. *Okay, world, you win. I'll call Dr. St. Onge.*

* * *

But first I decided to do some grocery shopping on the way home from my date with Maura. I didn't have a list with me, but I could visualize it sitting on the counter at home as I filled the cart and waited in line to pay, caught in the evening rush that clogged everything from freeways to checkout lines. The market had posters promising to open additional check stands if more than three people waited in line, but they never did, and the crowd around me was sullen and fidgety.

I finally made it out of the store, loaded my groceries into the car, and was thinking about what to make for dinner as I pressed the Honda's start button. Nothing happened. The car had always been reliable, from the moment I drove it off the dealer's lot four years before, and I couldn't believe it was letting me down.

I gave it a few more tries, then got out my phone and called the Auto Club, which gave me an estimated wait time of forty-five minutes. Shit. I had that trunk full of groceries, including some perishables, and the sun was nowhere near setting. I phoned Steven to see if he could break off work and rescue the groceries.

When he answered, he was already fighting his way out of downtown Los Angeles, so we figured he might arrive before Triple A.

We figured wrong, or the Auto Club dispatcher did, because the repair truck showed up twenty minutes later.

The serviceman, a genial fellow with "Jack" embroidered on his work shirt, diagnosed a dead battery—my first guess as well—and said he could replace it on the spot.

I pulled out my credit card. "It didn't give me any warning."

"These newer ones don't. One minute they're fine, and the next—ka-blam. Dead as a doornail."

It took Jack less than five minutes to install the new battery, and as I scribbled my signature on the work order, Steven arrived. Even though the situation was under control, relief washed over me as I saw his familiar shape loping toward us. He hugged me, kissed my forehead, and thanked Jack for his help.

"That was sure sudden," he remarked about the battery's failure.

Jack grinned. "Your daughter said so too. Like I told her, these new ones don't warn ya. One minute they're fine, and the next—ka-blam. Dead as a doornail."

And off he went, humming what sounded like the theme from *Dragnet*.

Your daughter.

I'd heard it—had it registered with Steven? Yes. He didn't move as he watched Jack get in his truck and drive off, but outrage—and pain —clouded his expression.

I tugged at his arm. "Can you believe that old goat? I didn't know Auto Club hired blind men."

Steven's mouth opened and closed, but no words came out. He turned to me, his gaze moving up and down my face as tiny furrows deepened across his forehead. He'd loosened his tie but still wore his suit jacket—his armor, I often thought of it—and he appeared incredibly attractive and pulled-together. Cars rumbled past us, spewing exhaust and rap music.

"Diane," he said softly. "That *is* you, isn't it?"

I stretched up and kissed his lips. "Who else would it be, silly man?"

"You look so… different. Am I losing my mind? You do look young enough to be my daughter."

"Not by a long shot, Buster," I replied, poking his ribs gently. "I tell you, that guy needs his eyes examined. And maybe his head."

He didn't budge.

"Well," I said, "may as well leave the groceries in the trunk now. Steven? Thank you for coming. I felt better knowing you'd be here for reinforcement."

He turned away. "See you at home."

* * *

I poured a glass of chardonnay for each of us before I started dinner. Steven changed into jeans and went to his workshop in the garage, where he was building a bookcase for Maddie. The girl did like to read, and Nancy had good-naturedly complained that Maddie's library was outgrowing their storage space.

Steven's dad, a master carpenter, had taught his son a lot of tricks of the trade. In fact, Steven could probably have made a living as a carpenter if he'd been so inclined. I envied him having a fallback career. I'd put all my eggs in one basket at Gardner, never moving out of my comfortable niche. None of the other work had really interested me, but in hindsight I regretted my lack of ambition. They wouldn't have been able to push me out the door so easily if I'd had other skills —even if I was sixty-five years old, and looked it.

One memory in particular still hurt. I'd created a detailed procedures manual over the years, to help my assistants understand how the job was done and fill in during my vacations. Standard practice back in the day. When my departure was imminent, I'd taken the manual to George Sessions, the VP of Human Resources.

Sessions had studied it like it might bite him—the cover was slightly frayed because people had *used* it, including myself from time to time. Finally, he'd held out his hand for the manual, and I saw him trying to conceal a smirk.

"Very conscientious, Diane—as always. I'm sure the management company has their own job description in place, but I'll pass this along."

"It's more than a job description, George—it explains how things work, has sample forms, mailing addresses and—"

George waved his free hand like he was swatting a fly. "I'm sure it's very complete, Diane. You've always been most thorough." He paused and then his condescending smile widened. "I'll pass this along. Thank you."

He spoke as if addressing a child, and as I left his office for the last time, I thought I heard my procedures manual hit his metal wastebasket.

* * *

Steven kept studying me during dinner, and I finally put down my fork and stared back.

"You're staring at me like I'm some kind of freak," I said. "And it's making me nervous."

"I'm sorry. I can't help it. You look so different. How did I not see it before? When did this happen? Did you… ?"

"Have plastic surgery? You know better! When would I have done that? I'm here every single day. Steven, this is me, all me, all the original equipment."

"But you look—"

"I know. I was wondering when you'd notice. I can't explain it—it's like my body stopped aging, like it's moving backward in time."

Recognition must have dawned then—that time in the park, the way I'd stopped asking him to open stubborn jars of mayonnaise, the fact that a few strands of auburn were appearing among my gray hairs.

"My God, Diane—what's happening to you?"

He seemed so terrified that I got up and went to him, eased into his lap and stroked his hair. "Whatever it is, Steven, don't worry. Dr. Dennis says I'm perfectly healthy."

I described my conversations with Dr. Dennis and the utter normality of all the lab tests.

When I mentioned her referral to a specialist, Steven broke in. "When is your appointment?"

I winced. "I haven't made one yet."

"Why on earth not?"

He'd demolish my flimsy excuses in seconds. No sense even trying. "I will. I promise."

"How about right now?"

This was the Steven I knew. This Steven took charge, made things happen, got things done. Won his battles.

"His office will be closed now. It's almost nine o'clock."

"Tomorrow morning then. First thing. And Diane—I want to come with you when you see him."

"What if you're in court?"

"You let me work that out. First thing tomorrow, you call. Promise."

I knew better than to try and negotiate with a lawyer like Steven, so I gave him a three-fingered salute.

"Now, how about dessert?" I asked, and he let me off the hook because he'd seen those plump red strawberries when he helped me put away the groceries.

Chapter Five
Mysteries

Steven fidgeted and checked his watch. "Why do they always overbook?"

We'd been in Dr. St. Onge's waiting room for over thirty minutes, and of the six people ahead of us, only four had been called. Another couple came in not long after we did, both of them looking as apprehensive as I felt.

I rubbed Steven's arm. "I'm sorry. You need to get back to the office. I can take Uber home."

"No way," he said. "I need to be with you for this."

Although I appreciated him being there, his bristling impatience was contagious. Fortunately, the nurse called us in a few minutes later, just as I was going to *order* Steven to leave.

After another fifteen-minute wait, Dr. Charles St. Onge breezed into the examining room. He was a bear of a man with curly auburn hair and a great bushy beard. Without apologizing for the delay, he held out his immense hand, which practically swallowed mine, his grip warm and friendly, and then shook Steven's.

As he reviewed the lab tests Dr. Dennis had ordered, his deep baritone filled the room with questions.

Some of them worried me. Did thyroid disease run in my family?

Any history of immune disorders? Other questions were more routine. Had I traveled outside the U.S. recently? Had I changed my diet?

As I answered, he would study my face, as if judging the truth of my words. Then he'd shake his head and key the information into his computer. Eventually he sat back from the monitor and looked at me again. His direct stare made me uncomfortable, and I shifted in my chair.

"Do you have any theories about what's going on?" he asked.

I sat up straight. "I—we—were hoping you could tell us."

Dr. St. Onge peered at Steven over the top of his eyeglasses. "How about you, Mr. Devlin?"

Steven shrugged. "It's baffling. And I'm worried about what it all means."

"You're not happy to suddenly have a younger wife? Some men fantasize about that."

I sensed Steven's growing annoyance by the way his eyebrows pinched together.

"Not me," he said. "I'm concerned for Diane's health."

Dr. St. Onge continued to gaze at Steven, as if expecting more. Finally, he turned to the computer and typed a few more notes. Then he pushed back and stood.

"Let's check out your muscle strength first," he said, and motioned for me to stand too.

Then he asked me to walk, turn, touch the floor, and resist as he pushed against me. He grabbed my right wrist and tugged, and instinctively I pulled back.

The doctor's eyes widened. "Impressive," he said, and somehow it sounded like a criticism.

"I work out at the Y," I said.

Steven cleared his throat. "Fitness is important to Diane—to both of us."

Dr. St. Onge smiled for the first time. "I can tell that."

He sat and squinted at his computer screen again and the smile faded. "I wish I had an answer for you, Mrs. Devlin, but I don't."

I must have looked disappointed, for he quickly continued. "At least not yet. There are so many variables. Let's get some more tests and see if they give us a clue. All right?"

My mouth was so dry I could only nod.

He wrote up orders for additional blood work, a bone density test and a "muscle strength evaluation."

"You get these done, and we'll talk again soon."

* * *

Since none of the blood tests required fasting, we stopped at the lab on the building's ground floor, where an Asian man in white scrubs quickly—and almost painlessly—filled four vials with my blood, pressed a piece of cotton to the puncture site, and wrapped a fabric bandage around my arm.

"What did you make of all that?" I asked Steven as we walked back to the car.

Summer was pushing its way in, and the mid-afternoon sun sharpened our shadows on the parking lot asphalt.

"Not much," he acknowledged. "He didn't even have a theory. But maybe these new tests will show something."

"Maybe," I said, but I had my doubts.

Steven checked his watch again before he opened the passenger door for me.

"You should get to the office," I said. "You were so sweet to come with me, but I know you'll pay for it."

"It doesn't matter. I'll drop you off and go on in to work." He patted my back. "Are you okay?"

"I think so."

He looked at me like he didn't believe me, so I worked up a smile and said, "Take me home and I'll prove it."

His concern morphed into surprise, and I was a little shocked myself at that offhand remark. But Nancy was on summer break, and the rest of my day was free, so why the heck not. *Because you're not a hormonal teenager, that's why not!*

"I'm kidding," I said as I slid into the passenger seat.

Steven's shoulders slumped. "Well, you've not lost your sense of humor, I see."

* * *

After Steven dropped me off, I checked the laundry hamper (not quite enough to make up a full load), traced a finger over the coffee table to check for dust (there was none), and tried to recall when I'd last vacuumed the carpet (three days ago, I decided.) An itchy restlessness settled in as I paced the kitchen floor and wondered what I should do with this free afternoon. I had plenty of energy, but I didn't feel like spending it on chores.

Then I phoned Maura, since I'd promised her a report on the results of the exam, such as they were.

"That's it?" she demanded. "More tests?"

I pulled the bandage and cotton off my arm—a tiny speck of dried blood my only reminder of the recent procedure—and tossed it in the kitchen wastebasket.

"Modern medicine," I muttered.

"What are you doing now?"

"Trying not to crawl out of my skin. I'm bored, and I'm disappointed, and Steven went back to work. He'll probably be home late since he spent all that time at the doctor's with me."

"I have two words for you, Diane. Happy hour."

My mood brightened immediately. "Wayward Vine?"

* * *

Wayward Vine had an awesome happy hour from four to six p.m., and Maura and I went there often after we'd discovered the place in Atwater Village. From the outside it didn't look like much, but on the inside, Wonderland awaited. Tiny colored lights glimmered from the ceiling and around the twelve-foot mirror behind the bar, and the mirror reflected a silhouette of Downtown Los Angeles painted on the opposite wall. The Vine's happy hour menu featured popcorn shrimp, chicken wings and calamari, along with inspired quesadillas and incredibly delicious breadsticks. Their wine list was impressive, and the prices were reasonable—for Los Angeles anyway. Maura and I usually split a couple of appetizers and washed them down with a glass or two of wine, and the total tab was never more than fifteen dollars. We would have paid more because the food and drink were so good.

Maura's Volvo was already at the curb half a block up from the Vine, and I found an open spot nearby—a small miracle. Before I left the house, on impulse I'd slipped into the red patent stilettos I bought on our recent shopping spree. They were as comfortable as my sneakers as I sashayed up the sidewalk to the Vine's entrance.

As I stood in the doorway and let my eyes adjust to the darkened interior, Barbra Streisand's voice serenaded me. Jordy, the Vine's owner and chief bartender, was a big Streisand fan. Maura waved to me from the far end of the bar, and as I slid onto the stool next to her, Jordy placed a glass of chardonnay in front of me. He winked at me, and for the first time I was struck by how incredibly handsome he was. Jordy was maybe fifty, tops, with a weathered complexion that suggested he didn't spend *all* his time in dimly lit bars. As usual, he wore a sleeveless white t-shirt top that displayed some well-developed biceps: proof of how he spent that time away from the bar. A few minutes later he returned with an appetizer sampler plate and another wink.

Maura and I clinked glasses, and even that first sip of wine loosened some of the knots in my nerves.

"I Googled your new doctor," Maura began, "and he's got more credentials and testimonials than all of my doctors put together."

"You Googled him? I never thought to do that."

"You wouldn't—you're so trusting, Di. But he looks like the real deal. So, if anyone can figure this out, I bet he's the guy."

Her concern—and thoroughness—reminded me of why we'd been friends all these years.

"Thanks, Maura. When you start dating again, I'll remember to check out your latest victim online too."

Maura grinned. "You better get busy then, girl."

"Seriously? Already?"

"Why not? I needed an antidote to *Robert*." Maura crunched down on a popcorn shrimp and closed her eyes for a second.

"Tell me more." As if she wouldn't do that without urging.

"His name's Neil. He's a chef. At the Envy."

Ah, the Envy—a hip new West L.A. bistro that catered some of the trendier celebrations in town. Even I knew about it because the *Los Angeles Times* had run a glowing review several months ago.

"Wow," I said. "He must be good." I tried the shrimp too—almost as delicious as Maura's intriguing news.

"Oh, he's good all right," Maura murmured. "Incredibly good."

I poked her gently. "I meant his cooking."

Maura wiggled her eyebrows. "So did I." She took a deep drink of her chardonnay. "I was checking the place out for a client dinner next month, and the seared Ahi was so delicious it made me want to cry. So, I had to meet the chef. Naturally."

"Naturally," I echoed. "And?"

"And it was chemistry at first sight." She twirled her wine glass. "He's a little younger than I am... all right, so he's fifty-one—but he's an old fifty-one."

"And you're a young sixty-five."

"Sixty-four, Di. Why do you always forget I'm a year younger than you?"

"Oops," I said. "Sixty-four. That makes it perfect."

Maura narrowed her eyes. "Sarcasm does not become you."

"No, I'm happy for you. Really. So, what's he like, Cougar?"

"Very funny. He's divorced, has been for about six years, no kids, the ex moved to New York so she won't be stalking us like... what was her name?"

I shuddered at the memory of one flame's vengeful ex-wife.

"Anyway, he's educated, cultured, likes to read, and..." she broke off, smiling at something, and I could only guess what.

"Let me fill in the rest," I said, ticking off points on my fingers. "Walks on the beach, puppies, good wine, travel, cozy dinners with friends, women who know their own mind..."

Maura burst out laughing. "You've met him, then."

We made short work of the nachos, and I passed on the quesadilla. At this rate, I'd be too full for dinner, and I owed Steven a decent meal when he got home.

"He sounds great, Maura. And as your friend I feel compelled to remind you to take it easy this time."

"This time? I always do. It's just that I'm a lousy judge of character. That's why I want you to meet Neil."

I raised my glass to her. "Gladly. But he'll think you're too serious if you drag in the best friend."

"I know. So not yet. But soon."

"Soon," I agreed.

"Although," Maura added, "as foxy as you're looking these days, maybe I shouldn't risk it."

"Ha."

We left it at that and went on to talk of other subjects. Maura wanted to know what Jeff and Nancy thought about their newly-youthful mom, and I replied truthfully that they sensed something was going on but hadn't asked any questions. Yet.

"And Steven?" she asked.

I told her about the mechanic mistaking me for Steven's daughter, and that brought on a fit of giggles from Maura.

"It's not funny!" I protested. "He was so hurt. If you'd seen him…"

Maura wiped her eyes. "I'm sorry. It's just that he's always so Mr. Perfect, Mr. I'm-so-much-smarter-than-you."

"He is not! Honestly, I wish the two of you would call a truce someday."

Steven and Maura had never hit it off, to my eternal mystification. They had a lot in common, besides me—they liked the same books and music, not to mention food. But dinners with the two of them were often a strain, with Maura proclaiming the beef overcooked and Steven arguing that it was perfect, or Steven relating a work-related story and Maura's eyes glazing over. Circumstances had thrown them together now and then, especially when the kids were little, but I always breathed easier when they parted company.

"He's always hated me because I knew you first," Maura said, and sniffed. She drained her glass and checked the time. "Anyway, I better get going before total gridlock sets in. Have to be in Long Beach for dinner."

"Long Beach? Neil lives in Long Beach?"

"You'd love his place! It's on Ocean Boulevard—you can walk to the beach."

"Safe travels, pal."

I grabbed the check. "My treat this time—get going."

I put a twenty on the bar for Jordy, and when he reached for it, his hand grazed mine and held onto it for a couple of heartbeats. His skin was smoother than it looked, and warm. We made eye contact as Neil Diamond serenaded Sweet Caroline, and something in Jordy's dark gaze sent my heart into overdrive. *What would it be like?* I wondered. I hadn't touched another man that way besides Steven in all my married life. In that instant, however, I wanted to. I wanted to run my hands down Jordy's well-muscled arms, I wanted to take in his scent, which I knew would be equal parts sunshine and salsa, I wanted to taste him— beer and cilantro and something else: danger. It may have been my imagination, but I thought I saw desire in his deep brown eyes as well.

I pulled away first.

"Thanks, Jordy," I said, waving farewell as I picked up my purse and went back into daylight.

* * *

Two weeks later, Steven and I were back in Dr. St. Onge's office with a view of the San Gabriel Mountains.

"You are a mystery, Mrs. Devlin," said the doctor as he flipped through the test results. His immense desk was covered with tidy stacks of papers. An impressive display of medical books filled shelves on two walls.

A mystery. Swell. When I was eighteen, I thought it was cool to act mysterious, but I never wanted to *be* a mystery.

Dr. St. Onge went on to talk about low inflammatory markers, the mild increase in my bone density T Scores, and the "explosive power" of my muscles.

But he was as clueless as Dr. Dennis about the cause for all this good news.

"So, where does that leave me?" I asked, biting back frustration that was near its boiling point.

Steven sat quietly next to me, but his placid façade, I knew, was deceptive. If he'd been given to yelling, which he wasn't, he'd be ready to unload on the doctor for having nothing to offer after all this time, all these tests.

Dr. St. Onge rubbed his chin and then jotted some notes on a pad of white paper. "I have a friend who does aging research and teaches at Wallace Taylor," he told me. "He doesn't see patients often, but Lewis owes me a favor."

Even civilians like me knew of Wallace Taylor University. Its School of Biological Science was second to none in prestige, and I'd seen it cited in *The Wall Street Journal* for breakthroughs in cancer research and treatments for immune disorders. If Dr. St. Onge's friend taught there, maybe he *could* solve the mystery. Maybe.

"Oh great," I muttered to Steven on the way home. "More needles and poking and probably more baffled looks."

He patted my hand. "Maybe not. Maybe this will actually give us some answers. Besides, what choice do we have?"

We could leave well enough alone, I thought. But that was not really an option. By that point I realized something bizarre was happening to me, and no one, not even these smart doctors, knew what had caused it or what the outcome would be. Sure, it was fun to see a younger face in the mirror, to feel energy and strength I thought were gone for good. But I'd lived long enough to know that few good things came without a price tag, and I had no idea what this one would be. I needed to learn more, even though I dreaded going through more doctor visits, and more painful needle pokes.

At least I had Steven alongside me. We were in this together, as we'd almost always been.

Chapter Six
"Rejuvenation"

Taking a cue from Maura, I'd researched Dr. Lewis Banks online. He was a board-certified internist, in addition to being a gerontologist, and had been a professor at Wallace Taylor for eleven years. Graduated from Stanford with some post-graduate training at USC. He'd written or co-written a long list of articles in his field for publications like *Nature* and *Frontiers in Biology.* I read a few abstracts, but their complex terminology left me dizzy. No complaints had been lodged against him on any of the physician-rating sites.

Dr. Banks had a pretty swanky office suite in a five-story building near Huntington Hospital—high rent territory, especially for someone who supposedly didn't see all that many patients. I'd assumed Steven and I would find another crowded waiting room, but I assumed wrong. The room was softly lit and full of nicely padded chairs, and classical music played in the background, but unlike Dr. St. Onge's crowded reception space, Steven and I were the only ones there. No other signs of life, unless you counted the tall Ficus in one corner, and it might have been fake.

"This is weird," I said quietly. Something about the place seemed to demand whispering. "I wonder where everyone is."

Steven nodded. "Eerie. Maybe we walked into the Twilight Zone."
"Very funny."

But he was right; the atmosphere was downright spooky.

The window at the reception desk was closed, and I almost jumped out of my skin when the partition shot up and a woman called out, "Good morning!"

I grabbed Steven's hand. "Good morning."

The woman glanced at the file she was holding. "Mrs. Devlin? I have some papers for you to fill out."

No surprise there. She handed me the papers on a clipboard, and I started writing, while Steven tapped his foot against the chair leg and checked his phone for messages.

The usual batch of questionnaires and releases went quickly, but Dr. Banks wanted another form signed, a new one for me: I showed it to Steven for a translation. He scowled as he read.

"Essentially," he told me, "this says that all discoveries made as a result of your treatment will remain the property of Wallace Taylor University."

"Discoveries? What discoveries?"

He drummed his fingers on the clipboard. "I suppose if they learn you have a rare condition that turns out to be a cure for some disease, they can patent it. The cure. It would probably be worth a lot of money for them."

"Should I sign it?"

He frowned. "I tell my clients never to sign anything they don't have to."

"But what if he won't see me unless I do?"

The receptionist must have tuned in to our discussion. "It's just standard procedure, Mrs. Devlin," she said. "Like the privacy disclosure."

Before Steven could stop me, I scribbled my signature on the bottom. What choice did I have, anyway? I turned in the forms and handed over my insurance cards to be copied.

After what felt like an hour but was probably closer to fifteen minutes, a door opened, and a slender blond woman in pale blue scrubs came out. "Diane Devlin?"

Steven rose when I did and started to put his arm around my waist, then let go. We followed the woman as she moved briskly down a quiet corridor and ushered us into an exam room. Unlike the reception area, this room looked exactly like every other one I'd been in: exam table, rolling stool, counter with shiny instruments, two visitor chairs, and the inevitable computer. I caught a faint whiff of rubbing alcohol.

Although her name tag already told us that she was "Lucy Gervais, R.N.," the woman introduced herself and gestured to the visitor chairs. "I need to check your vitals before you see Dr. Banks."

And there we went again. Lucy measured my blood pressure, heart rate and temperature, height and weight. Nothing had changed since the last time I'd been evaluated except I'd gained a quarter inch in height.

After entering the information into the computer, Lucy stood and opened the exam room door. "Let's go see Dr. Banks, shall we?"

Dr. Banks's internet photo hadn't prepared me for the man who rose from behind a large wooden desk as we entered his office. Tall, pale and hollow-faced, he looked at least two decades older than he appeared online. Another surprise: there was a second man in the office, much younger, with dark hair and wire-rimmed glasses. Unlike Dr. Banks, who was dressed in a gray business suit, the younger man wore a white lab coat over black trousers.

Dr. Banks's voice quavered. "Mr. and Mrs. Devlin, welcome. This is Dr. Peter Willis, a colleague of mine. I invited him to join us this morning because Peter and I have been collaborating on a study of age disruption—a field that may pertain to your situation. His input will be helpful."

He and Dr. Willis held out their hands at the same time, and I shook Dr. Banks's first; his flesh was dry, almost scratchy; Willis's, however, was warm and moist. He hadn't spoken beyond "Hello," but he had a smile I found comforting. After handshakes with Steven, we all sat, Dr. Banks on one side of the desk, and the three of us opposite. Something about Dr. Banks's demeanor—maybe it was the suit—made me feel like I was on a job interview.

His wood-paneled office didn't have much in the way of décor except a large sculpture on the credenza behind him: a bronze of a soldier on a galloping pony. Remington, maybe, and possibly an original; I couldn't tell.

Dr. Banks opened a slim file and glanced at it, then looked at me with utter seriousness.

"I've been reviewing Dr. St. Onge's notes," he said. "Most intriguing. I gather that, until recently, the effects of this phenomenon have been benign, correct?"

I sat up a little straighter. "Until that migraine last month."

"Anything since then?"

"Nothing bad, just… you know, getting… younger." I spread my fingers on my thighs. "I guess that's the best description."

Dr. Banks didn't take notes, but Dr. Willis opened a laptop computer and typed as we spoke. The clicking keys formed soft background noise, and I concentrated on giving complete answers to Dr. Banks's questions. We went over my history—again—and the tests that had already been done. I described my increased energy and the physical changes I'd noticed.

"Then this is not your normal appearance?" Dr. Banks asked.

"No. This isn't the face, or the body, I'd gotten used to seeing in the mirror."

Steven leaned forward. "Diane's always been pretty—no one knows that better than I—but she's sixty-five years old. Show me another sixty-five-year-old who looks that good without help."

"Ah, to be sixty-five again," Dr. Banks said, with a wistful expression that quickly turned serious. "And both of you are displeased with this development?"

"Concerned," I replied. "I confess I'm enjoying the effects, but—"

"But we're both worried about what might happen next," Steven said. "I'm sure you'll agree that this is not normal."

Dr. Banks rolled a shiny silver pen between his hands. "And you have no idea what might have precipitated it?"

"Not a clue," I said.

"And you're retired now, correct?"

"Yes," I said. "It wasn't my idea, but my job was eliminated. And it *is* nice, in a lot of ways, no fighting rush hour traffic, no stress, no deadlines."

"But it was unexpected?" Dr. Willis asked. It was the first time he'd spoken.

"It was," I replied. "I didn't see it coming."

"And what are you doing to fill the time now?" Dr. Banks asked.

This *was* like a job interview. The question sounded like a challenge, and I fought off a wave of defensiveness. Why did I need to justify my free time to him? And what difference did it make what I did? None of it had anything to do with this suddenly growing younger. Or did it?

"I look after my granddaughter—she's eight, and smart as a whip. She keeps me busy. She keeps me young." I paused. "Maybe I'm around her too much."

I laughed after I said it, but the notion made me wonder. Could my time with Maddie be contributing to this unexpected change?

Dr. Banks didn't even crack a smile, however. "And nothing like this has ever happened to anyone else in your family? Parents, siblings?"

"Nope. No brothers or sisters. My parents are gone now, but they both aged like anyone else."

I cringed at the memory. Neither Mom nor Dad had been blessed with a quick or painless death.

"Any recent travel outside the U.S.?"

I shook my head.

"Vaccinations?"

"Not since my flu shot last fall."

Dr. Willis coughed softly. "Have you had contact with anyone with an unusual illness?"

The hairs on my arms stiffened as I thought that one over. Had I? I never avoided crowds, but I was a regular user of soap and water, or at least hand sanitizer. There were so many new diseases out there—not just the flu now, but also a surge in measles, plus hepatitis and TB, not to mention Ebola and even more recently, COVID-19. Dr. Banks's office became unnaturally quiet, and the paneling seemed to press in on me, squeezing my lungs. Light glinted from Dr. Willis's eyeglasses.

"No," I replied.

"Visited any medical labs?" Willis asked.

I gestured toward the file on Dr. Banks's desk. "Only to have my blood drawn, and those other tests."

Dr. Banks peered at me over his dark-framed glasses. "You haven't walked through any radioactive fields, have you?"

"Not that I know of," I said as calmly as I could. Where were these questions coming from? For the first time, real fear nudged into my thoughts. Could I have been accidentally radiated somewhere? Did that kind of thing actually happen?

Banks finally smiled. "I wasn't serious. I'm just stalling for time, trying to think." He turned to the younger doctor. "Peter? You thinking what I'm thinking?"

Hope stirred. Maybe they had a clue after all. Maybe they'd be able to explain.

Dr. Willis looked away from the laptop. "Cytokine panel. Definitely."

What the hell was a cytokine panel? I didn't like the way the doctors were studying me, like I was some kind of interesting but alien specimen, ready to be dissected in the name of science. I shifted in my chair and reached for Steven's hand. He squeezed mine a little too tightly, but I drew reassurance from the slight pain. He and I were both real. The chair I sat in was real. The waistband of my skirt, digging into my flesh, was real.

Dr. Banks took off his glasses, picked up a cloth, and rubbed the lenses. "Another blood test, Mrs. Devlin. Cytokines are proteins that modulate the inflammatory response, and while *some* inflammation is important for a healthy immune response, the cytokines themselves have the potential for inducing damage. This panel is used to identify elevated levels of specific cytokines. It may not give us the complete answer, but it will help us rule out some possible sources of this rejuvenation you're experiencing."

The eyeglasses went back on, and he pushed on the bridge to adjust them. The same way I did. The same way Steven did.

Rejuvenation. He made it sound so simple, so benign. So desirable. Not to experience the insults of aging. To have energy again, and strength. And, I had to admit… to feel more alluring. I let the word whisper in my mind. *Rejuvenation.* I loved the sound of it.

Dr. Willis stood. "I'll write up the order for the test. You can use the lab downstairs; in fact, you can stop by on your way out if you like. The test doesn't require fasting."

Swell. I was becoming a human pincushion.

Chapter Seven
Family Secrets

Steven took me home after our stop at the lab. He had a partners' meeting, so I thanked him again for going with me and kissed him goodbye. Then I had a quick snack and drove to Nancy's.

She wanted to spend part of her summer break doing something creative, or, as she put it, "I need an antidote to all these weeks trying to convince a bunch of cell-phone-addicted high school juniors that history is relevant."

Nancy found that creative outlet/antidote in an afternoon photography class, and she recruited me to look after Maddie on the days when she was learning how to use a digital single-lens reflex camera.

Steven wasn't too keen on my commitment, but he'd be at work anyway, so what did it matter to him?

When I asked him that question and I reminded him this was my life, my time to spend as I chose, he simply said, "As long as it's *your* choice."

* * *

That afternoon, still rattled by the doctors' inability to explain what was happening to me, or to reassure me it was harmless, I was especially grateful for Maddie's cheerful company.

"Ow, Grandma—what happened?" Maddie asked as I took off my sweater.

She was pointing at the bandage the lab tech had wrapped around the crook of my left elbow after the blood draw; I'd forgotten it.

I took off the bandage and tossed it in the kitchen trash can. Then I showed Maddie my arm, where the puncture wasn't even visible.

"Nothing, darling—see? Grandma's fine. She had to have a blood test done this morning. No big deal."

"No big deal," Maddie echoed. She turned to her mother, who was searching for something in her purse. When she noticed Maddie's intense gaze, Nancy stopped and focused on me.

"Mom, is everything okay? If you're sick, I can always—"

"I'm fine—just a little blood test."

Relief flooded her face, either from my reassurance or from not having to skip her class on my account. Or maybe both.

She grabbed her camera from the counter and slipped her mobile phone into the back pocket of her jeans. "You've got her schedule, right?"

"Right," I told her. Ballet class, then art, then whatever I chose to keep Maddie entertained until Nancy got home.

"I'm off then. Thanks, Mom."

She gave us both goodbye kisses and ruffled Maddie's golden hair. "Be a good girl."

As if she could be anything else.

* * *

At Maddie's ballet class, I sank onto a folding chair along the back wall and watched my graceful girl run through the pliés and jetés, then leap through the air like a featherweight bird. She was born for dancing, I thought. Unlike myself. Unlike poor Nancy, who'd inherited my lack of grace.

My phone buzzed. I pulled it from my purse and saw Jeff's picture on the screen. As quietly as I could, I rose and backed out the door to take the call.

"Hey, Moms," said Jeff. "How's my best girl?"

"Elsa's fine, darling."

"Funny, Moms." A pause. "Will Dad be home tonight?"

"Later on, sure. What's up?"

"I need to pick his brains about something—nothing bad, a licensing thing. Thought maybe he could look at this contract I'm supposed to sign."

"He'd be thrilled. Why don't you come for dinner then?"

He didn't answer right away, so I added, "I'll make vegetarian chili."

Jeff could never turn that down.

I slipped the phone back in my bag and tiptoed into the classroom, where my absence apparently hadn't been noticed. So Jeff needed Steven's help, and Nancy needed mine. It was good to still be useful to the children.

* * *

Ballet class ended with a *reverence*, where the girls curtsied to thank their teacher, Ms. Aubrey. Then they scampered off to the dressing room to change clothes.

Ms. Aubrey approached me with a somber face, which was unusual. We'd chatted after class several times when I'd subbed for Nancy, and she always complimented me on my talented granddaughter. Today, however, no compliments were forthcoming.

"I'm glad to see you, Mrs. Devlin. I'm a bit concerned about something, and I hope I'm not overstepping, but I didn't feel quite comfortable asking Mrs. Ross." She paused, gnawed her lip, and lowered her voice. "Is everything all right with Madison at home?"

I didn't know how to answer—that was the last thing I expected her to ask. *Was* everything all right at home? It appeared to be, especially with Nancy getting a break from the stresses of teaching, and Nick fully employed for at least a few weeks.

"Certainly," I replied, with more assurance than I felt. "Why? Is

Maddie having trouble? I'm sure she's been practicing—my daughter is very strict about that."

Ms. Aubrey stroked her throat. She was a slender woman with a ballerina's practiced grace that had always made her seem confident, but the distressed furrows on her forehead alarmed me.

"There was an... incident in the dressing room last week."

She gestured toward the folding chairs and turned one to face another. We sat.

"An *incident?*" I repeated.

Distress was obvious in Mrs. Aubrey's demeanor. "Yes. I don't know exactly how to describe it, but..."

She broke off, and I leaned forward, motioning for her to go on.

"...Madison and three of her friends were... well, 'teasing' is too mild a word for it, actually. I heard a commotion, and when I came in, Madison was holding another girl's necklace just out of her reach and taunting her with it, and the other three were egging her on."

I straightened my back. "Maddie? My Maddie?"

"I know—it was so out of character that at first I thought they were playing a game, but Olivia, the girl reaching for her necklace, had tears streaming down her face." Ms. Aubrey took a deep breath, as if she was reliving the scene. "I put a stop to it immediately, needless to say. I gave them a stern talk about respecting their classmates and made all four of them apologize to Olivia.

I nodded. "Exactly what I would have done."

Mrs. Aubrey's right hand was clenched in a fist. "Thank you. But I could tell from their faces that none of them felt contrite. It was as if the whole thing was a joke to them."

I was having trouble picturing my sweet granddaughter bullying anyone, much less one of her classmates from ballet.

"You should have discussed this with my daughter," I told the teacher.

Now she was actually wringing her hands. "I tried! But Mrs. Devlin... now I know I *am* overstepping, but Mrs. Ross—she became angry with *me* and implied I was not properly supervising the students. She was quite argumentative, unlike the other parents when I spoke with them. They all assured me they'd talk to their daughters about bullying, but Mrs. Ross… I wonder if perhaps her own profession might make her more sensitive to this, and…"

She broke off, and I put a consoling hand on her shoulder.

"Thank you for telling me, Ms. Aubrey. I had no idea this happened, and I'm frankly shocked. It's so out of character for Maddie."

"It is!" she quickly agreed. "Madison—Maddie has always been a darling, an angel. That's why I was so stunned when I saw her misbehaving like that."

"I'm pretty shocked, too," I said. "I just can't get over it."

"Yes. I understand. And I kept thinking about it, trying to figure out what would have caused such behavior. That's when I began to wonder if perhaps something in her home environment has shifted recently, and she might be reacting to that."

"As far as I know, things are fine," I said. "Her father's been gone on location, but that's nothing new."

Ms. Aubrey pressed her lips together and seemed on the verge of saying something else, but she didn't. I thanked her again and assured her I'd talk with Maddie and with Nancy too.

* * *

The conversation with Ms. Aubrey kept replaying in my mind on the way to Maddie's art lesson, but I forced myself to put it aside and focus on driving. *Besides*, I told myself, *Maddie's very perceptive. She'll sense if something's wrong, and you don't know the whole story yet.*

I watched Maddie intensely during art class, where the students were working on pastel drawings of animals. Maddie had created a wonderful likeness of Elsa, and from memory. I felt a flush of pride that vanished when the teacher approached. I braced for another complaint, but instead he smiled and whispered, "Your granddaughter has a gift." I was so relieved, and grateful, that I wanted to hug him, but I merely murmured my thanks.

We had another hour together before Nancy would return, and Maddie was full of energy. Mindful of Nancy's request not to tire her, however, I took her home with me, and we took Elsa for a walk. The late July afternoon was unseasonably cool—perfect for a stroll around the neighborhood.

Maddie loved Elsa almost as much as I did, and the sentiment was clearly mutual as Elsa greeted her with yips of pleasure and bestowed big sloppy dog kisses on my giggling granddaughter.

I let Maddie hold the leash as we set off; in truth, Elsa was so docile at that point she could have walked without one, but I thought it would make Maddie feel grown-up and responsible.

"Elsa's slowing down, isn't she?" I asked as we turned the corner.

Maddie stroked Elsa's back. "She's old, huh?"

"Yes, she is. And she can't take care of herself like she used to. She needs us to watch out for her."

"I know. We protect her."

"That's right. We do. We protect anyone who can't protect themselves, don't we?"

"I think so."

We walked in silence for a few minutes, and then I decided to chance it. "Maddie, Ms. Aubrey and I are concerned about something."

"I know. It's about Olivia, isn't it?"

"It is. Maddie, what happened? Ms. Aubrey told me what she saw, but I'd like to hear it from your viewpoint."

Maddie stopped and put her arms around Elsa's neck. "That Olivia is a bitch," she muttered.

The word hit me like a slap in the face. Not that I hadn't used it myself, but from my eight-year-old granddaughter? "Madison, that's a bad word to use."

"It's true, though," Maddie said. She released Elsa but kept the leash in her hand as she started walking again, head down. "Olivia's always showing off. Her parents are rich, and she has all this jewelry, and these fancy shoes, and she acts like she's better than everyone else. Cindy and Rachel and Emma and I decided to teach her a lesson."

"But it sounds as if you made her feel really bad."

"She makes us feel bad! I just wanted her to know what it's like to want something you can't have."

"Was it the necklace you wanted? Maddie, if there's something special like that and you really want it, we can talk about it. I didn't know you wanted anything bad enough to hurt someone else."

"I didn't hurt her! I wanted to, though. I wanted to punch her."

"Madison!"

She stopped and looked up at me, that beautiful angel face, her hair lifting like golden silk in the summer breeze, blue eyes so open and trusting. I calmed myself by thinking back on times when either Jeff or Nancy had done something completely out of character with what I knew their true nature to be. *Normal childhood upsets, that's all,* I told myself. *No, this was more extreme.*

"Maddie, I'm sure your mom has explained to you that violence is—"

"I know it's wrong," Maddie said in a sing-song voice. She stopped walking and put her head down. "But I still wanted to."

I patted her back. "The main thing is that you didn't, though. I'm proud of you for that, darling."

She seemed satisfied with our conversation and went on to tell me about an elaborate game she and her best friend Brianna had created; it involved levitation and magic spells, and after what we'd just discussed, I welcomed a trace of the supernatural.

* * *

Nancy was supposed to be back from class by four, but she wasn't.

"Hmmm," I said to Maddie, "Mommy must have gotten stuck in traffic."

"Rush hour," Maddie said in an eerily adult voice.

Since I dreaded the discussion I had to have with Nancy about Maddie's recent bad behavior, I was in no hurry to see her, but I did need to get home in time to cook dinner for Steven and Jeff. Maddie went to her room to put away her ballet outfit, and I made myself a cup of tea while I waited and considered whether there *was* something going on in Maddie's home life that would make her act out as she had.

As far as I knew, Nancy and Nick had a solid marriage, but was it really? Things may have appeared fine from the outside, but...

The sound of a car door slamming brought me back to the present. I glanced at my watch: almost five o'clock.

Nancy rushed in the back door, breathless and flushed. "Sorry! I hung around after class to take some shots, and the time got away from me."

I stood and hugged her, but she pulled away quickly. "Where's Maddie?"

"In her room, probably reading. You said not to tire her out, so I got her to rest."

Nancy seemed distracted. "Oh, right. Well, thanks, Mom. I'm sorry I'm late."

"Me too. I have to get going, but we need to talk for a minute first. Put your things down and—"

"Mommy!"

Maddie burst into the kitchen, a little blond hurricane.

"Hi, baby. Did you have a good afternoon with Grandma?"

"We did! I got to take Elsa for a walk."

"That's nice."

I put a hand on Maddie's head. "Maddie, your mom and I need to talk for a minute. Can you go and read your book while we do?"

Maddie nodded sagely. "Grown-up talk."

"It is," I agreed, and I was pretty sure she already knew the subject.

Maddie hesitated a moment and then scurried back to her room.

Nancy put her camera on the counter and crossed her arms. Impatience radiated from her like heat off a car hood in full sun. "What's up, Mom?"

I worked up my courage and summarized what Ms. Aubrey had told me, adding my own concern over Maddie's atypical behavior.

Nancy rolled her eyes as I finished. "Really, Mom. That old hen blew it all out of proportion."

"That's not all," I said, and went on to tell her what Maddie had said about Olivia and how she wanted to "punch her."

Nancy waved her hand dismissively. "She's a kid. Kids say stuff. Mom, compared to those hoodlums I deal with every day, Maddie's an angel. It's normal kid behavior, and if you make a big deal out of it, she'll just—"

"I didn't make a big deal out of it! Not with her anyway. But it *is* a big deal to me. Or it might be, if this kind of thing goes on."

"It won't! It was one little incident, and she didn't hurt the other girl. She apologized. She knows it was wrong. Honestly, Mom, when did you get to be such a worrywart about every little misstep? Good God, if you'd been this uptight about Jeff and me, we'd have grown up little robots who never did *anything* wrong."

No sense in discussing it further. And maybe I wouldn't have to.

* * *

At home, as I chopped and sautéed zucchini and onion and bell pepper, I put aside my worries about Maddie and my frustration with Nancy. Instead I focused on the pleasure of fixing a meal for someone other than Steven and myself. Steven was never an enthusiastic eater, and when we were first married, I thought he was dissatisfied with my cooking—until his mother assured me he'd always been like that.

I dumped canned tomatoes into a pot with the veggies and then realized we were out of tortillas. It was six-thirty, and Steven would probably be packing up his briefcase, so I phoned him to ask if he'd buy some tortillas on the way home.

The call went to voicemail, so I tried Susie Chen, his assistant, who answered on the first ring. After a few pleasantries, I asked if Steven had left yet.

Susie sounded wary when she answered. "He left after the partners' meeting, Diane." However, my imagination may have concocted the undertone of *You didn't know?*

"Oh," I said. My cheeks were on fire. "Right. He probably told me, and I forgot."

"You must have a lot on your mind these days. Steven mentioned your doctor's appointment this morning. I hope everything's okay."

"It is, Susie. Thanks."

After I disconnected, I fought an unexpected urge to throw the phone across the room. Then I remembered Maddie saying how she wanted to hit Olivia. Maybe these violent urges were hereditary.

Maddie overcame hers, and if an eight-year-old could do it, so could her sixty-five-year-old grandmother.

The market was only half a mile away, so I made a quick trip while the chili simmered, and when I got back Steven was changing out of his business suit.

He didn't explain where he'd been, and neither did I.

"Jeff's coming for dinner," I told him.

Steven's eyebrows rose. "That's a surprise."

"He needs your advice on some kind of licensing contract."

"Really?"

"Yes. Don't look so skeptical. You're not only his father, you're the best lawyer any of us knows. Besides, it'll be nice, the three of us having dinner together."

Where were you, Steven? It was probably something innocent. Surely not like that other time.

"Yes," he agreed. "It will be."

He hung his tie in the closet and rolled up his shirt sleeves. I'd always found that look appealing, and as he traded his business slacks for jeans, casually balancing on one leg and then the other, I lingered for an admiring glance at his legs, which were firm and toned. Thank goodness he didn't have those stick-thin legs so many men his age developed. His middle might be softening, but not those legs. I wanted to grab hold of him for a long, deep kiss, but a ruckus in the kitchen announced Jeff's arrival.

With a wisp of regret, I left Steven to finish changing and went to greet my son, who was wrestling with Elsa on the kitchen floor.

As Elsa squirmed in Jeff's bear hug, her thrashing tail and happy whimpers were as vigorous as they'd always been, but when she stood I noticed her back legs quivering. Had we taken her on too long a walk earlier? Jeff rose and went to search for Steven, and I bent and massaged Elsa's back. She turned her white muzzle toward me in what looked like gratitude. *Oh, Elsa, I'm so sorry this is happening. I wish I could make it stop.*

Elsa was our third German shepherd. Steven had found her as a half-starved puppy, wandering along a freeway off-ramp. We'd been temporarily dog-less at the time, and Elsa settled into our household like she'd always lived there. Jeff had recently moved to his own apartment, and the house echoed with ghosts of his voice and footsteps. Elsa chased away the echoes, and she grew into the most beautiful dog I'd ever seen. She was fierce, my big furry girl, and I always felt safe with her beside me.

* * *

My meal did not go unappreciated that night, thanks to Jeff. Steven cleaned his plate, too, and complimented the chili. Almost like he was trying to make up for something. I shoved that notion aside and cleared the table while Jeff got out the contract to discuss with his father. Steven poured each of them two fingers of Crown Royal—his usual after-dinner drink—and the two went to his office to go over the contract.

Their voices drifted into the kitchen, a comforting backdrop as I loaded the dishwasher and washed up the pot I'd used for the chili. Judging by the laughter that punctuated their discussion, the two were having a fine time. It cheered me to see the two of them getting along so well. It hadn't always been like that.

Jeff went home a little after ten, and as we stood waving goodbye from the front window, Steven put his arm around my waist and pulled me close.

"Our son's going to be a millionaire by the time he's forty," he whispered in my ear. His breath was warm and tinged with whiskey.

"Good," I replied. "He can provide for us in our old age."

He drew back. "You don't think I'll be able to?"

"I didn't mean it that way. But someday you're going to retire, right? No more late hours. More time for us to spend together."

Steven stroked a lock of hair from my forehead. "I've been thinking about that," he said. He picked up his glass and took a sip of Crown Royal. "I went to see Vic DeWitt this afternoon."

Relief, mingled with curiosity, flooded me. Victor DeWitt, one of the founding partners of Steven's law firm, had been on medical leave for several months. Lung cancer.

"How's he doing?" I asked.

Steven pressed his lips into a thin line. "He's in bad shape, Diane. The chemo's wiped him out. You wouldn't recognize him."

"That's so sad. I like Victor."

"So do I. And he's still fighting. He's hanging on to the chance he'll recover."

"That was kind of you, to go see him."

"I'd put it off far too long." He took another drink of whiskey and then held me so tight I could hardly breathe. "I don't know what I'd do without you."

"You won't have to," I said.

"Life is so precious, Diane. So…" He paused and looked down at me. "…Vic told me his one regret—aside from smoking all those years —was not spending more time with Alice and the kids."

"But he was building the firm," I reminded Steven. "We all have to make hard choices."

"I know, and I suppose it's natural when death's staring you in the face to look back at what you did wrong, and what you failed to do. It made me think, though. We still have time, you and I. But we're not getting any younger—well, *I'm* not."

He broke off and laughed, but it didn't sound like a happy sound.

"Steven, I'm not sick. I'm not dying."

"I know you're not. But this has made me realize—we don't know how much time we have left, either of us. If there's something, anything, you've been wanting to do, let's not put it off. Let's do it *now*."

I promised Steven I'd think about what else I wanted to do, but I honestly had no clue where to start, so instead I went to wash my face and brush my teeth, that comforting nighttime routine.

Steven was reading a Lee Child novel when I came back to the bedroom and peeled off my t-shirt and jeans. I glanced at the mirror over the bureau and for an instant didn't recognize myself. My biceps and triceps were noticeable, but the flab on the underside of my arms —which had become an unwelcome sight over the past decade—was not. The flesh jiggled only a little as I raised my arms.

Steven was staring at me with a puzzled expression, like he, too, was trying to figure out who I was.

I took out the blue negligée I'd bought on my shopping spree with Maura. For some reason, I'd never worn it, but that night I wanted to.

"What's Jack Reacher up to tonight?" I asked as I slid into bed.

Steven didn't answer, but he put the book aside and removed his reading glasses. The gesture, familiar after decades of marriage, suddenly seemed so appealing to me. So *sexy*. Desire for him surprised me like a rogue wave on the ocean, and I didn't even try to resist.

I turned off the lamp on my side of the bed and then leaned over him to extinguish the other one. His skin smelled so clean, so enticing, and his lips were soft and warm when we kissed. That kiss made me dizzy. I wanted him, in a way I hadn't for years, and to my surprise and delight, he wanted me too. I fell into that wave of desire and let it carry me away, with no fear of drowning, only the wanting of Steven, more of his hands and his body, more of all of him. And when that wave crested and crashed back onto shore, for both of us at the same time, it felt like it had when we were young.

Chapter Eight
"Ouch!"

Dr. Banks telephoned after what seemed like an eternity but was only a week—a week of wondering, a week of waking up without stiffness in my back and legs, a week of thinking, *whatever this thing is, it's great.*

"The cytokine panel results are very… interesting, Mrs. Devlin. Your levels are not what we'd expect in a woman your age. It doesn't explain the cause, but it does confirm that you are in fact experiencing some type of physical age reversal. Most intriguing."

In other circumstances I'd have been flattered by the term "intriguing," but right then it made me want to cry in frustration.

"Is there a next step?" I asked.

"Yes. It won't be pleasant I'm afraid, but Dr. Willis and I agree that we need to collect a bone marrow sample."

"A bone marrow sample?" *What the hell?* "That sounds painful."

"It is," Dr. Banks assured me cheerfully. "But you'll be anesthetized. It will be uncomfortable, but not excruciating."

"Promise?"

"They'll do their best."

Dr. Banks explained the extraction and said it could be done that Friday. He didn't ask if the timing was all right with me, and let's face it, I would have switched around other plans so I could get it over with. I'd have to undergo the procedure on an empty stomach, and I'd need someone to drive me home, because of the anesthesia. I scheduled it without checking with Steven to see if he could take more time off—if not, I could ask Maura, or even one of the kids.

The kids! I still hadn't talked to them about what was going on. Aside from Nancy's question about the blood test and Jeff's glib remarks about my appearance, they hadn't noticed anything unusual about me yet. To them, I was good old reliable Mom—had always been there, always would be.

I decided to keep it that way until I had more information.

* * *

Dr. Yamada, the hematologist, had an office in the same building as Dr. Banks, one floor above him. As Steven and I entered the elevator, I felt the beginnings of a caffeine withdrawal headache. No breakfast also meant no coffee, and that I missed. At least it was "only" a normal headache—no light shows, no migraine. So far.

Steven squeezed my hand. "It'll be over soon," he said, with an encouraging smile. Sure, he could be optimistic—he'd had his coffee, and they weren't sticking a needle into *his* bone. I banished my uncharitable thoughts with a reminder that he hadn't hesitated to take more time off work to accompany me to and from the hematologist's.

Dr. Yamada's waiting room was as bright and cheerful as Banks's was subdued, and several of the chairs were occupied. I signed in and handed over the batch of forms I'd downloaded and completed the day before—including one where I promised not to sue if the procedure killed me. I'd done the paperwork while Steven was still at work, because I figured that, as usual, he'd find something to object to.

A few minutes later, a chipper young brunette in pink scrubs called my name. We already knew Steven couldn't accompany me into the room for the actual procedure—something about maintaining a sterile environment. Along with all the forms I'd found on the hematologist's website were documents to prepare me for the marrow extraction: common sense stuff like leaving my valuables at home and having someone to drive me home, picking up the prescription pain meds right away and taking as directed. Kind of like having oral surgery, except for the caution that "some pain may occur during and following the procedure."

I undressed and put on a gown—cloth, not paper, for which I was thankful—and sat on a cold table while the lady in pink checked my blood pressure and other vital signs. Then she gave me a shot "to help you relax," but I don't think it worked very well.

Dr. Yamada breezed into the room to introduce himself, this man who was going to poke a hole in my bone and pull some marrow out. I only saw him briefly that one time, and I was lying on my side, looking up at him silhouetted against the light, so all I had was an impression of a tall man with shiny black hair and frameless eyeglasses. In a monotone, he explained they were going to anesthetize "the site." Something cold and wet moved across my right hip, and then came a sharp pinch.

I closed my eyes and tried to visualize myself in a lovely green meadow studded with wildflowers, but pain reared its fiery head a minute later. *"Some pain" my ass.* The worst was an impression of pressure quickly followed by a burning sensation, as if they had shoved a red-hot poker into my pelvic bone. Then a terrible sucking feeling, presumably as they withdrew the marrow. The pressure stopped, but not the pain.

"We are done," Dr. Yamada murmured. "You were very good."

He actually patted my shoulder before he left the room.

The woman in pink bandaged my hip and let me rest for a few minutes—not that rest was possible with that fiery ache gnawing at me. Then she came back, helped me sit and gave me a pain pill to swallow. I didn't refuse.

I was a little woozy but managed to get back into my clothes and hobble out to the waiting room where Steven rose and put his arms around me. He kissed the top of my head.

"You okay?"

I couldn't answer.

Somehow, I made it to the car. I dreaded sitting down, but the pain pill must have kicked in because the ache lessened by then. I leaned my head back, closed my eyes, and let Steven take us home.

I slept the rest of the day, except for the times when I inadvertently turned on my right side. Steven went to the pharmacy and got the pain meds, and as soon as allowed, I swallowed one like a crack addict going through withdrawal. I don't know what was in those little tablets, but they did the job.

* * *

While I waited for the results of the bone marrow extraction, I tried to keep busy and not think about it—although for the first few days, the pain from the incision was a continuing reminder; and I felt exhausted, like they'd drained a few pints of my blood when they took that tiny bit of marrow.

With school back in session and Nancy back at work, I managed to keep up my duties with Maddie. Fortunately, the most I had to do was drive the car or sit and cheer when her team won at volleyball.

I skipped my gym workouts and instead walked the neighborhood with Elsa—two old girls out for morning strolls. Elsa kept sniffing my hip; her nose no doubt picked up scents even under the bandage. And I probably seemed different as well. I know I was *feeling* different.

* * *

I made a remarkably fast recovery, however. By Thursday, I didn't need to cover the puncture site; it had almost completely healed and hardly hurt. When Nancy invited me to go shopping with her and Maddie that night, I felt peppy enough to accept.

Maddie needed some horseback riding gear because, after months of pleading, she'd persuaded her parents to sign her up for riding lessons at a stable in Sunland. I had agreed with some misgivings, because the responsibility for transporting and watching over her would fall to me, naturally. The lessons would start in a week, right after Maddie's school day ended, while Nancy was still at work.

Maddie was beyond excited. Nick had grown up in Wyoming and

was an experienced horseman—although he'd only needed the skill for one film in his entire career. All it took was a visit to that movie set when Maddie was six, and she fell in love with the big animals. She badgered her father constantly to take her riding, and he did, showing her the basics. But Maddie craved more than he had time to give her.

Therefore, Grandma would take up the reins—but only figuratively speaking. I liked horses well enough, but their size intimidated me—so *big*. I was not looking forward to watching, my heart in my throat, as Maddie sat astride a galloping horse. God forbid they'd be jumping hurdles too.

Before her lessons started, Maddie needed proper clothes. Apparently, jeans and sneakers weren't sufficient.

Hillcrest Saddlery smelled of leather and, oddly, of hay—even though the closest stable was a mile away. Track lighting reflected off wide-planked hardwood floors, and racks of saddles served as room dividers. Maddie skipped through the display of jodhpurs and breeches, tried on riding helmets, and grinned the entire time we were in the store. She narrowed down her choices of outfits and insisted on going into the dressing room alone to try them on. Nancy and I sat nearby and waited.

"Our little girl is growing up so fast," I said.

Nancy shifted in her chair. "Too fast."

When I turned toward her to reply, I noticed how the overhead lights threw shadows on her face, emphasizing tiny wrinkles around her eyes. I hadn't noticed them before.

As if reading my mind, Nancy jabbed a finger at the full-length mirror across from us. "Good grief, Mom. It's like we've switched places. You're all perky and rosy-cheeked, and I look like a dried-up old hag."

"You do not! You're beautiful, but you do look tired. You need a good night's sleep."

"How am I supposed to get that? All the work I bring home, I have to shortchange Maddie to get everything done." She rubbed her right arm. "I hate having a part-time husband."

I patted her hand. "I know, darling. I'm sorry."

"So am I," Nancy said. "He finishes filming next week, so at least he'll be around for a while. But there's nothing lined up for him after, so we'll be watching every penny. Again."

"He'll find something. He always does."

"You don't know that," she said. "And then I'll go back to worrying about him being surrounded by all those predatory women, and not knowing how good he is at resisting temptation."

I didn't have any reassurance to offer because Nick didn't seem the type to resist.

Nancy ran her fingers through her hair. "I need to start coloring my hair. Do you still go to Zola's? He's doing something different—I like the way he's letting a little gray show up. It looks so natural. Not that it looked fake before, but—"

"This looks natural because it is," I told her.

Nancy glared at me with disbelief written on her face, and I thought maybe it was the right moment to explain what was going on.

Maddie popped out to model one of the riding outfits she liked, and as she pirouetted in front of the three-way mirror, I decided it was *not* the moment.

"That's a nice one," Nancy said. "Let's see the next."

As Maddie danced her way back to the dressing room, Nancy gave me a sidelong glance.

"I probably couldn't afford Zola anyway. That's what you're thinking, isn't it?"

"Of course not. He isn't that expensive, and besides—"

"I should have married someone like Daddy. Steady income. No fooling around. Do they even make men like Daddy anymore?"

Oh, darling, if you only knew. I kept my voice neutral. "Nick has so many good points. And he obviously loves you. And *Maddie.* Give him a little credit."

Not that *I* did, but she needed to hear that.

"I'm trying."

Nancy's pity party was in full swing, and I did sympathize—no mother wants her daughter to suffer. But she was ignoring the advantages she did have—like a career and quality childcare whenever she needed it.

"Sometimes it's hard living with the consequences of our choices, Nancy. But we all have to do it."

Nancy narrowed her eyes. "And what are you living with, Mom? You have it pretty easy."

"I didn't always. I had my share of hard times. But I protected you and your brother from knowing about them. As I'm sure you do for Maddie."

She looked away.

"And at least you have me to help out."

"I know, Mom, and I'm sorry if I don't go around thanking you every five minutes." She bit off every word, every syllable.

I was about to snap back and remind her that I might have better things to do with my life than be her on-call nanny. If I didn't have the responsibility for Maddie, I could do all those things I'd wanted to do when I quit working. The thoughts sprang up on their own, but they felt true. There were even opportunities for another career, paid or unpaid, if I had the time. If I didn't have every weekday afternoon committed to Maddie.

The universe was protecting us all, because Maddie burst from the dressing room before I spoke, and I shuddered to think what she might have overheard otherwise. How could I even think those things?

I found a smile for Maddie. "You look beautiful. Which outfit is your favorite?"

"I don't know, Grandma. I like this one, but that blue one is nice, too."

Nancy stood and picked up her handbag. "You need to choose, Maddie." She emphasized "choose" and glanced at me. "We can only buy one."

I rose and touched her arm. "Let me help. I'll buy the second one as an early birthday present."

The joy on Maddie's face wiped away the bad emotions that hung between Nancy and me. As Maddie went to change into her own clothes, I turned to apologize to Nancy and saw tears in her eyes. She swiped them away. "Thanks, Mom. For everything."

I moved to kiss her cheek, but a painful spasm gripped my right leg—*the world's worst Charley Horse* was my first thought as I bent to rub those rock-hard calf muscles. I almost fell over, because another spasm seized my left calf, and I shrieked from the pain and surprise. I'd had my share of nighttime leg cramps, but this was ten times worse, and in both legs. I hobbled to a chair and sat.

"Mom?"

Maddie paled, her eyes wide and fearful. "Grandma?"

I couldn't speak to reassure them I was all right, because I wasn't. I couldn't even talk, and for a horrible minute feared I'd pass out.

"Leg cramps," I finally gasped, and Nancy knelt and began rubbing my calves for me.

The spasms finally subsided, and I drew in enough breath to be able to speak.

"I'm okay," I told Maddie. Then I patted Nancy's shoulder. "Thanks, darling. That helped." Nancy didn't take her eyes off me as she stood, concern in every line of her face. "That was scary! Mom, what's going on with you? Those blood tests, the way you look…"

I saw her putting two and two together.

"Mom, have you had some kind of operation?"

"No. Really—I did not. This is something else. It's hard to explain." I put my hand on Maddie's upturned head. "Grandma's fine, precious. I've had some tests done just to make sure, and we're waiting for the results. But it's nothing bad. I promise."

I only hoped I could keep that promise.

Chapter Nine
"A Simple Procedure"

Dr. Willis telephoned me the next morning, and I heard something in his voice that I didn't like—a new uncertainty.

"The results are… interesting," he began.

Why do you doctors always use that line? What the hell does "interesting" mean this time?

"Is that right?" I replied as mildly as I could manage. "Interesting how?"

"We did discover some abnormalities in your hematopoietic stem cells, Mrs. Devlin. However, it's nothing to be alarmed about."

His matter-of-fact tone didn't reassure me.

"Abnormalities? What abnormalities? And what are hema… whatever… stem cells?"

Oh, what I'd have given to have Steven there with me for this conversation. Questions swirled in my brain, moving so fast I couldn't hang on to them.

"Hematopoietic stem cells—let's call them HSCs for short. They're cells in your bone marrow that regenerate your blood, and they make different kinds of other cells." He paused. "We need to do one more test to quantify the results."

He hadn't really answered all my questions, but the word "test" snagged my attention.

"Another test?" I heard the whine in my voice, and he probably did too.

"Yes. I'm sorry, but we really do need this, Mrs. Devlin. I hope it will provide the final piece in the puzzle."

"What is it this time? Will it hurt, too?"

"Not like the marrow extraction, I assure you. We need a sample of your muscle cells."

"My muscle cells?" I repeated as I tried to make sense of this new development.

"Yes—it will be quick. You can have it done right in Dr. Banks's office. Unfortunately, the specimen must go to a special lab back east, and it will take about three weeks for the results. But I'm confident it will be worth the wait."

Well, goody for you.

"I don't understand, Dr. Willis. What will this tell you that the bone marrow didn't?"

I imagined him drawing in a long, patient breath.

"It's rather complicated to explain, but… the cells produced by our HSCs are of the *lymphoid* or *myeloid* type. Lymphoid cells are either B cells or T cells, which are the active cells in our immune system and protect us from infection and disease. Myeloid cells include a cell called a macrophage, which goes around and scavenges cell debris and secretes cytokines that help boost the immune system. The right number of macrophages is very healthy and important. However, as we age, our HSCs start producing too many myeloids, so that we have too many macrophages, and they infiltrate every organ of our body, like our muscle and kidney cells. When there are too many macrophages, they make too many cytokines, and they in turn recruit T cells to the area. The T cells begin to attack local, normal cells even if there is no infection—this is what we call chronic inflammation. Bottom line, since chronic inflammation goes steadily up with age, it's a hallmark of aging. One of the fundamental causes of chronic inflammation is that HSCs in older patients produce too many myeloid cells instead of lymphoid cells."

Thank goodness he had to stop for air. My head was spinning, and my right hand was cramping up as I scribbled notes.

"Although that's a very simplified explanation," Dr. Willis continued after too brief a pause, "it may be meaningless to you. But the main thing to understand is that, as we age, we have less lymphoid and more myeloid cells. And this results in a change in the growth factors in our blood. However, in your case, Mrs. Devlin, you are now producing *more* lymphoid cells and *fewer* myeloid cells, as if you were decades younger than your real age."

"I see," I replied, although I really didn't. Maybe if I kept him talking, he might eventually come to something I did understand.

Dr. Willis continued, speaking slowly but not entirely masking the enthusiasm in his voice. "Besides the inflammatory cytokines that I just talked about, there are other cytokines that are good for us. One is called Growth Differentiation Factor-Eleven, and it's remarkable. When we're young, we produce high levels of GDF-Eleven, but we gradually lose it as we age. The job of GDF-Eleven is to maintain the function for a wide array of organs, like our heart, lungs and brain. As we age, low levels of GDF-Eleven appear to be part of the cause for diminishing function of these organs. It seems too good to be true, but when scientists injected synthetic GDF-Eleven into the blood of old mice, the old mice showed significant rejuvenation of a number of their organ systems."

"You're kidding."

"I'm not. But you see, the change in the ratio of lymphoid to myeloid cells affects the ratio of good to bad cytokines. I think that changes in *your* stem cells are the underlying cause for lower levels of inflammatory cytokines and higher levels of GDF-Eleven. We would not expect to see this in a person of your age. That's why we performed the marrow analysis, and it confirmed that your HSCs are producing a surprisingly high level of lymphoid cells."

Damned if it all didn't start to make sense to me, in a fuzzily abstract way.

"I think I understand. But you don't know *why* this is happening, do you?"

I heard another long inhale. "Not yet. But we've found some encouraging clues. And that's why we need the muscle biopsy."

The word "biopsy" sent ice down my spine.

"Biopsy? As in cancer?"

"No, nothing like that. Biopsies are done for other purposes, Mrs. Devlin. In fact, the bone marrow extraction is a kind of biopsy as well. Taking the muscle sample will allow us to sequence tissue that isn't from your blood and compare it to the HSCs. That, we hope, will yield an explanation."

I didn't believe him. They'd find another "abnormality" and request another test, and soon there wouldn't be a single part of me that hadn't been sliced and diced in the name of medical science.

This discussion of my muscle cells triggered a memory of the agonizing leg cramps that had attacked me the night before. I told Dr. Willis about them.

"Do you think they're connected?" I asked when I finished. "I mean, if you're checking out my muscle cells—do you think there's something going on there?"

He took a minute to reply, and I imagined him jotting notes of this development. "It's possible," he said at last, and I was relieved he didn't use the word "interesting" again. "It may be a side effect of the rejuvenation, but until we get this last bit of information, we won't be able to tell for certain."

"Fine," I said. "Let's do it. Let's do it right away."

"Good. I'm glad you agree. Can you come in this afternoon?"

I hesitated. "I'm supposed to pick my granddaughter up after school. Will I be able to do that?"

"Definitely. This is a simple procedure, Mrs. Devlin. We'll use a local anesthetic. You won't feel a thing. A tiny bandage and you'll be on your way. I promise."

And he told the truth. I walked out of Dr. Banks's office an hour after I arrived, with a small bandage on my left bicep and a mild throbbing where the needle had gone in. Lucy Gervais, his attractive blond nurse, offered two Tylenols to ease the discomfort, and by the time Maddie bounced into the car's back seat, full of stories about her day's adventures, I felt fine.

* * *

That night when I told Steven about the biopsy, he looked stricken. "I should have been there with you! Why didn't you call?"

"It was a really tiny needle, and it hardly hurt. Dr. Willis said it was nothing, and he was right. I've taken you away from work enough."

He caressed my arm, where the puncture was barely visible. "Tell me again about this cell thing. I didn't quite follow."

As I set the dinner table, I went over Dr. Willis's explanation of cell functions again, as clearly as I could remember it. Steven's pinched lips and furrowed forehead, however, told me I wasn't getting through. I showed him the notes I'd scribbled, which were probably illegible to anyone but me. He pored over them and pressed his lips together.

"Cytokines… lymphoid… myeloid. It's like another language."

"It is," I agreed. "And I don't pretend to understand half of it. But something in my cells is out of whack, and they need this last test to try and figure out why."

"Tell me again why they're focusing on your muscles."

I forced myself to relax my hands because my fingernails were biting into my palms. Steven's mind was usually razor-sharp, and he could grasp concepts that left me floundering. When did I suddenly get to be the biology expert?

"They need something that isn't a blood cell, Steven. Don't ask me why, because I don't understand that part either. It's all so complicated."

Steven rubbed his temples. "Too complicated for me. And it takes three weeks to get the results?"

"Three very long weeks," I replied.

He tossed my notes across the table; some of them skittered to the floor, but he made no move to retrieve them. "Why does it take so damned long? Why is this all so fucking complicated?"

Steven seldom swore unless he was righteously furious, and his reaction surprised me. Was he trying to start a fight? Blaming me for all the complex technicalities? I concentrated on aligning the silverware, giving him time to collect himself, but his flushed face and rumpled hair told me he had a way to go. He still wore his business suit, tie loosened as usual by the end of the workday. The aroma of roast beef wafted in from the kitchen, softening the tension in the dining room only slightly.

I retrieved the scattered papers. "I don't know, Steven. It's not like I want it this way. I didn't cause this, and all I can do is wait it out and see what they say. I only hope it'll be worth the wait."

He turned to pour himself a drink.

I patted his back. "Dinner's almost ready. Go change clothes."

He took the glass of whiskey with him and went upstairs while I dished up our meal.

* * *

Dinner table conversation was neutral enough, as he filled me in on the events at the office. Victor DeWitt seemed to have turned the corner in his cancer treatment, and his outlook was encouraging, for now. I was glad for Steven's sake because I knew how much he liked Vic.

Afterward, Steven helped me clear the table.

As he carried the last of the dishes into the kitchen, he said, "When you get those test results, I want to be there to discuss them with the doctors."

I wiped my hands on a towel and hugged him. "I promise. I won't let them say a word to me until you're there to hold my hand."

He rubbed my back. "You don't need hand-holding, Diane. But I want to come with you anyway."

"You can come with me any time," I said and then giggled at the double entendre.

An unexpected wave of desire washed over me. Had he suddenly grown more attractive to me, or was it all part of this strange "rejuvenation" I was experiencing? Whatever it was, I welcomed this renewed appetite for sex, and evidently so did Steven.

* * *

Before I knew it, we were in bed, our naked bodies moving with a passion I thought had long abandoned me. I surrendered to the delicious sensation of Steven's flesh, so warm and solid, against mine. His cheeks bore a trace of stubble as they grazed mine, and his mouth tasted faintly of whiskey. The undeniable male-ness of him made me dizzy with wanting, so much I would have done anything, anything at all, to seize that exquisite release I knew he would give me. And he did. The world fell away, and it was just Steven and me, alone in the universe, defying age and gravity, the weight of our everyday lives. Steven climaxed an instant later, and I held onto him fiercely as his moan of pleasure filled my ears.

Pleasure. Such a mild word for what I felt, but there is none stronger.

* * *

Afterward we lay in each other's arms, still panting, satiated and content. Steven stroked my bare leg.

"That was nice," he whispered.

"It was," I agreed.

Why had we let the fires of our passion dim? Was it a natural consequence of growing older, or something I'd come to believe was "expected" as we aged?

I'd always enjoyed sex with Steven, and he was a thoughtful lover who always tried to be sure I had as much fun as he did. How had I let that pleasure slip away?

* * *

Later, as we were getting ready for sleep, Steven switched on the bedside lamp. "Let me get another look at you."

"Here I am," I said, puzzled.

He brushed my hair away from my face. "You are so lovely. I can't imagine anyone more beautiful. Or desirable."

"You're making me blush. Turn off the light, Steven."

He kissed me again before he complied, and before long I heard his deep, regular breathing. I, however, had trouble getting to sleep as I relived the wave of desire that had swept me away—one good effect of the rejuvenation. That led me to ponder what Dr. Willis had told me, and the bit about myeloid cells and lymphoid cells and how mine were behaving abnormally.

I made myself stop thinking. My brain had absorbed all it could for one day, and I was finally able to give it a rest as I fell into the mercy of sleep.

Chapter Ten
"A Mutant?"

By the time we saw Drs. Banks and Willis again, my nerves were tingling. Three weeks was a long time to wait, and to speculate on the results of the muscle biopsy. I started picturing all kinds of weird outcomes, like a rare disease, with this rejuvenation being an early symptom that would turn ugly. What if the rejuvenation stopped, or reversed itself? I tried to block those thoughts, but they crept in whenever my brain wasn't busy.

Finally, the morning of my appointment came, and maybe I imagined the undercurrent of excitement in Dr. Banks's book-lined office as he and Dr. Willis greeted Steven and me. Maybe not. I scanned the framed certificates on the wall behind Dr. Banks's desk. He was surely an accomplished doctor; he had to have found a clue about what was happening to me.

Steven and I sat, facing Dr. Banks's big desk.

He leaned forward. "I'm sure you're anxious to hear what we've found."

Now, that's an understatement. Come on, will you? I leaned forward and realized I was holding my purse strap so tight that my hands hurt.

I flexed my fingers. "We certainly are."

Dr. Banks swiveled the computer monitor so that it faced us. "Then let's get to it. Peter, why don't you start?"

Dr. Willis dimmed the room lights. The monitor's screen saver showed a soothing ocean scene, blue waves lapping a sandy shore.

"How much do you know about genetics?" asked the younger doctor as he rested one hip on the desk.

Steven spoke first. "Genetics? Like DNA and heredity and all that?"

Dr. Willis nodded.

"I remember a little from high school biology," I told him. "But not much."

"No worries," said Dr. Willis. "We'll sketch out the basics for you."

Oh, no, I thought. *Here we go again. I hope this isn't as complicated as the cell biology.*

Dr. Banks tapped a computer key, and the monitor lit up with a drawing I recognized: the "Double Helix"—a strand of DNA.

"Deoxyribonucleic Acid," I said aloud. "It carries our genetic code, right?"

Dr. Willis grinned. "Exactly. Now, to get you both oriented, here's a simplified explanation of how this all fits together. Our bodies are composed of about thirty-seven trillion cells, and every one of those cells—except the red blood cells—has a nucleus. The nucleus contains chromosomes." He paused. "You with me so far?"

I motioned him to continue, although Steven seemed less clear on the subject so far.

"Great. Now the chromosomes carry genes, which in turn are composed of DNA." He pointed to the graphic on the computer screen. "And every strand of DNA—as Diane has rightly noted—contains a person's genetic code: who we are, who we were, who we will be—and how we will age."

Steven and I looked at each other. Now we were getting somewhere, although I still wondered what it had to do with the HSCs and the lymphoid and myeloid cells Dr. Willis had described before the muscle biopsy.

"Go on," Steven said.

Dr. Willis did. "Our cells are constantly dividing and replicating, and they also change as we age. Diane and I discussed some of this after the bone marrow analysis. Hair turns gray, muscles go slack, and so on." He pointed at me. "But in Diane's case, these aspects of aging are reversing themselves."

"That's not news," Steven said. "That's the *what*. We're here to find out the *why*."

His tone and body language practically shouted "Get to the point."

So I wasn't the only one getting impatient. *Thank you, Steven!*

"Yes," Dr. Banks replied. "And we've come up with a theory."

Dr. Willis cleared his throat. "This may sound a little far-fetched, Diane," he began, "but we believe you have experienced a spontaneous genetic mutation."

I think I stopped breathing for a few seconds. A shiver rippled through me. *What the hell? How can that be? I'm a mutant?*

"A *what*?" Steven and I said at almost the same time.

Dr. Willis held up his hand, palm out, like he was reading my thoughts and trying to derail them. "It's not as uncommon as you might think. As our cells divide, there is always an opportunity for something to change within the DNA molecule—for something in its composition to get switched around. In the majority of cases, the change is so small that it goes unnoticed. Its effect is neutral, even benign."

He paused, and I nodded to show I was with him so far, even though I wasn't really. I was still in shock over what he'd just told me.

"There are some mutations, however, that aren't benign," he continued. "Cancer being one of them."

"But we're not talking about cancer here," Dr. Banks quickly interrupted. "Your health is *excellent*, Mrs. Devlin."

"Absolutely," said Dr. Willis.

"What makes you think this is some kind of mutation?" asked Steven.

I was glad he still had the ability to talk, because I didn't.

"Diane's bone marrow sample revealed some very interesting chemistry, as she and I discussed," he replied. Then he hesitated. "This gets a bit technical, but I'll try to stick with plain English when I can. You're familiar with stem cells?"

"I am," said Steven. "They can become any kind of cell, right? And they usually come from embryos as I understand it."

"You're right about their capabilities, but actually adults have stem cells in their bone marrow, although they're usually not very active. One type of stem cell—the hematopoietic stem cell—regenerates our blood."

"Hematopoietic," Steven echoed. "Hema—as in blood." He glanced at me. "Those are the HSCs you told me about."

I squeezed his hand. "Right."

"Exactly," Dr. Willis looked at me. "Shall I do a quick recap for Steven's benefit?"

Come on, Diane—focus! Think of questions! Find out what this means.

"Please," I replied. Maybe if he kept talking, this would sink in, start to make sense—to both of us.

Dr. Willis went over the things we'd discussed before the muscle biopsy: the cytokines and lymphoid cells and myeloid cells and growth factors. The words were becoming old friends to me by then, but Steven's puzzled expression showed that he hadn't reached that point yet. And to me they were still only words, overshadowed by that other word: mutation.

"And the bad cytokines… well, they cause things like chronic inflammation," Dr. Willis explained. "As we age, the ratio of good to bad cytokines changes. And the change is not in our favor, as you might imagine."

Steven stared at him blankly.

Dr. Willis held up a thick file folder. "It's a lot to take in. That's why I've printed out the most pertinent information for your review. This morning I'm merely giving you an overview."

"A crash course," Steven muttered.

Dr. Willis set the folder gently in front of me and patted Steven's shoulder. "We're almost done. Now, the good news for Diane is that her level of lymphoid cells is much higher than one would expect—thereby raising the ratio of good cytokines, including one: Growth Differential Factor Eleven. GDF-Eleven is rather like the Fountain of Youth, and Diane's GDF-Eleven level is similar to that of a much younger person.'"

I was getting annoyed at the repetition of what he'd told me three weeks earlier, even though it was for Steven's benefit.

My own thoughts bounced all over the place, and I had to speak up. "I still don't understand how this mutation happened. And why."

Dr. Willis picked up a pen and pointed to a section of the DNA diagram on the computer screen. "First, let me explain *where*." He motioned to Dr. Banks, who brought up another image on the monitor. "Right here. This is a gene called Sirtuin-Three—a master regulator that controls the switch from lymphoid to myeloid HSCs. Sirtuin-Three causes your HSCs to become lymphoid rather than myeloid, and thus high levels of Sirtuin-Three lead to more lymphoid HSCs and low levels lead to more myeloid HSCs. Normally, as you age, your levels of Sirtuin-Three go down, which is why people make more myeloid cells and less lymphoid cells."

The picture on the screen resembled a tangle of curly gift-wrap ribbon in many different colors. It was labeled SIRT3, and none of it helped me understand what Dr. Willis was talking about.

He must have noticed my confusion.

"You seem to have a mutation in Sirtuin-Three that activates it," he continued, slowing the pace of his words, "so you always have high levels of it, just like you did when you were young. You were not born with this mutation—it must have occurred sometime during your adulthood, in one of your stem cells. Activated Sirtuin-Three could explain how your HSCs became rejuvenated."

I didn't know where to begin asking questions, and Steven was silent as well. Was his head spinning as much as mine?

"The part that I could not understand," Dr. Willis went on, "is why you see benefits in all of your organs—like your muscle strength, your skin rejuvenation and your mental acuity. Just like HSCs, there are other stem cells for the other organs. Satellite cells are the stem cells for muscles, neural stem cells regenerate neural cells, and so on.

"From your muscle biopsy sample, I found the Sirtuin-Three mutation in the muscle satellite cells. So, both your muscle *and* blood stem cells seem to be rejuvenated from the same Sirtuin-Three mutation. How can the same mutation appear in both muscle and blood stem cells?"

He paused and looked at Steven and me as if expecting an answer.

When neither of us spoke, he continued, "There is no precedent for this occurrence. Dr. Banks and I discussed it between ourselves and among some colleagues at the University. We concluded—and this is only a theory, and a radical one—that the Sirtuin-Three mutation happened in the 'mother of all stem cells.'"

"The *what*?" Steven posed the question that I was still forming.

Dr. Willis raised his palm again. "Yes, I know it's a strange concept. But you see, scientists have long wondered if there is such a 'super' stem cell, one that not only makes specific organ cells but that also makes the stem cell for multiple stem cells. Before you are born, you have such a 'super' stem cell called an embryonic stem cell—which Steven mentioned—that can make every cell in your body. It's just that no one has ever found a 'super' stem cell in an adult before. Perhaps there are 'super' stem cells in adults, and miraculously Diane's Sirtuin-Three activation occurred in this 'super' stem cell. The result is that she seems to be reaping the benefits of youthful stem cell activity in virtually all parts of her body.

"The part we can't explain is the 'why' of it. But I can tell you that somewhere in the process of cell replication, Diane, *your* Sirtuin-Three has mutated and has, in effect, reset your biological clock."

"And you think this is a spontaneous thing? It wasn't inherited?"

I was thinking out loud. Of course it wasn't inherited. My parents had died in their eighties, Mom from a stroke and Dad from stomach cancer. Both had aged normally until then.

"Definitely," Dr. Willis replied. "The muscle biopsy confirmed that."

"We don't know how precisely," Dr. Banks said, "but something happened to 'flip the switch' and activate the mutation. Perhaps it was reaching a certain age, or something stressed your body, or... simply the passage of time."

The room was silent for a moment, except for the hum of the computer processor. I had so many questions I couldn't speak because they were crowding their way around my brain like a panicked crowd in a movie theater when someone yelled, "*Fire!*"

Steven apparently organized his thoughts more quickly than I did.

"That *is* good news—about resetting the clock. But what happens next? Does Diane keep getting younger? Forever? What if she doesn't want to?" I saw panic in his eyes. "Can this be stopped?"

Dr. Banks's silvery eyebrows rose. "Stopped? Why on earth would you want to do that?"

"Isn't it obvious?" Steven said, his voice rising sharply in the silence. "To begin with, this is not normal. And if it continues, Diane could end up..."

He waved his hand as if that gesture could convey all the appalling possibilities, the ones I hadn't dare think about.

I joined the argument. "Yes, and what about these weird things that have been happening? The migraines and muscle cramps—will they get worse?"

The two doctors looked at each other, and then Dr. Banks spoke. "We don't know. Not yet. But the implications of this discovery are staggering, Mr. and Mrs. Devlin. What if we could somehow share this miracle with others? Could Mrs. Devlin's body possibly yield the actual Fountain of Youth?"

I didn't like the way he said "Mrs. Devlin's body," and I saw Steven tense up, too.

"You mean use her as a guinea pig," Steven said. "That's what you're talking about, isn't it?"

Dr. Banks shook his head. "Not at all."

Even in that dimly lit office, I thought I detected an eagerness in his eyes. He was what—sixty-five? Seventy? Facing the same age-related failings I had been experiencing before this mutation intervened. Did he hope "Mrs. Devlin's body" could somehow save him from that? I wanted to give him the benefit of the doubt; perhaps he hoped to save all humanity from the ravages of age.

"You obviously haven't considered the downside," Steven said. "Not for Diane. Not for anyone else."

Dr. Willis seemed uncomfortable with the conversation's direction.

He twisted the computer monitor away from us and turned the lights up.

"Aside from the muscle pains and the migraines you've described," Dr. Banks said, his tone as soothing as a spoon of honey in warm tea, "have you been feeling well?"

"Absolutely," I said. "Better than ever. It's as if I shaved ten years off my age, maybe even twenty. That part is very enjoyable, no matter what caused it."

"No other adverse effects?" Dr. Banks asked. "Anything in your… personality?"

What a question! I frowned. "Nope. Why? Is that something you might expect?"

"Excuse me," Steven said, "but I have noticed a certain—I guess you'd call it impatience—in you, Diane. More than your normal self."

Well, now's a fine time to bring it up!

I glared at him. "For instance?"

He pressed his lips together, and I got it. My very tone of voice sounded pissy and defensive.

Dr. Willis broke the tension. "I realize this is a lot to absorb all at one time. Let's call a time out, shall we? Here, take this file home, study it, and discuss what we've shown you today. We should meet again after you've had a chance to take it all in."

Steven scowled. "I don't see the point. What good will going over all this scientific jargon do?"

I reached for the file. "Let's at least look it over and see. Maybe it will help us understand our options." I tried to keep my tone placating, since he'd accused me of being "impatient."

"As if we have any," Steven said. He pursed his lips as he opened the calendar on his phone. "Fine. When do you want us to come in again?"

Now who's being impatient?

Dr. Willis's posture relaxed. "Two weeks? There's a lot to absorb, and comprehension won't come overnight."

"Don't I know it," I said.

With the appointment set, we rose and left the office. I didn't know what Steven was feeling, but I was sure perplexed and disappointed.

I don't remember if I even thanked the doctors. I probably did; good manners don't go out the door just because you've learned you're a mutant.

Steven pushed the down arrow for the elevator, and while we waited for it, I had time to mentally replay the conversation with the doctors. The more I thought about it, the madder I got.

"Don't those two have human emotions?" I said out loud, even though I wasn't really asking Steven. "Whatever happened to breaking news gently? This is a huge thing, and they just laid it on me like I should be happy about it. God! All they care about is their big scientific discovery. Not what it means for me."

Steven put his arm around me. "I guess we should be grateful they at least have an explanation for you."

"Some explanation! They can't even answer our questions! Will I keep getting younger and younger? Where will it end?"

Steven released me as the elevator bell chimed. "And they didn't tell us if they can stop it."

We got into the elevator, and I shook the thick folder Willis had given me. "We're supposed to read through *this* and figure it all out. And how do I know I even want to stop it? I mean, if it's not going any further, if I can stay like this—Steven, I wouldn't mind that. Wouldn't you love to shave ten years off your age?"

He didn't answer. It was a ridiculous question—how could he say anything but "yes?"

Why didn't he?

Chapter Eleven
Blackout

As soon as Steven left for work the next day, I started on the file Dr. Willis had given me. By mid-morning, scientific articles and scribbled notes covered the dining table, but I was no closer to understanding what was happening inside my own body. Terms like "nucleotides" and "base pairs" danced past my eyes but refused to explain themselves. I'd had four cups of coffee and nothing to show for my efforts but a caffeine buzz. Elsa nudged my elbow to remind me I'd neglected our walk, and I gladly set aside the reports and graphs.

While we walked, I wrestled with the concepts swirling in my brain. As soon as I grasped one notion, however, it merged with another, and then both evaporated like cigarette smoke. How had this happened to me? And *why*? Did I somehow bring it on myself?

Sure, I'd resented the way I'd been aging, the slack skin and wrinkles, the fading energy. But I knew a lot of people with those same complaints, and *they* didn't mutate into some kind of freak.

Freak: that's what I was. Until recently, I'd simply been a wife, mother, grandmother—and a retiree figuring out her changed life. Oh, how I wished I could turn back time and wake up that normal, slightly decrepit woman who was aging just like everyone else.

Or did I? *Come on, Diane,* I thought, *you have to admit it feels pretty damned good not to wake up with stiff joints and muscles every morning. Not to cringe at the face in the mirror. Not to need help lifting a twenty-five-pound bag of dog food into the shopping cart.*

Naturally I wanted my younger self back, the pretty one, the woman with self-confidence to spare. That's only human. I used to enjoy looking good, doing a little harmless flirting, getting admiring glances, even from strangers. I remember one time I was checking out my reflection in a shop window, and I bumped into a man walking in the other direction. When I apologized, he said, "Hey, pretty lady, I'd take a second look too." How could I not miss times like that?

* * *

Elsa had no answers for me. She moseyed along, stopping to sniff spots that interested her, big pointy ears swiveling to take in birdsong and traffic sounds. Her coat gleamed in shafts of sunlight, and I realized I was caressing my own hair, my own noticeably thicker hair, as I watched her.

The day was September-mild; a few clouds blunted the sun's strength, and our street was well shaded. Nevertheless, Elsa's sides began to heave, and her rear right leg started to drag, nails scraping the sidewalk. I stopped to rub her hip and stroke her velvety fur. She licked my hand, and I hugged her.

"You're such a good girl, Elsa," I whispered. "I wish you didn't have to slow down. I wish you didn't hurt. I love you, big girl."

Elsa's tail wagged in reply.

"Come on, baby. Let's get you home. I'm sorry I took you too far."

I winced and consciously slowed my every step as I watched her limp toward home.

Elsa's days were coming to an end, much as I tried to deny it. I urgently hoped that when the time came, her death would be quick, in her sleep. I hoped Steven and I wouldn't have to make the choice for her, although we'd done it before, for other pets over the years. It never came easy or without a lot of second-guessing and tears.

At least we had the option of saving them from suffering. Unlike my poor father. Despite the amazing compassion of the hospice workers, he thrashed and moaned and begged for death at the end. One especially bad day he clutched my hand and muttered, "I didn't know it would be this horrible."

No, Elsa wouldn't have to endure that. Small comfort, though.

* * *

I needed a distraction from those morbid thoughts, and an excuse to avoid Dr. Willis's headache-inducing reports and studies—even though I hoped to find answers in them. I needed to burn off some nervous energy, so I got out my garden gloves and pruning shears. I'd neglected the Double Delight roses that Steven and I had planted in the back yard. I loved those roses, and they lived up to their name: creamy blossoms and sweet, rich fragrance, guaranteed to lift a gloomy mood.

Elsa joined me, and now that we were home, she seemed fine, slurping her water and even rolling on the lawn, groaning with pleasure as she twisted left and right.

Roses are very ungrateful to their caretakers, however. Despite my best efforts to be careful as I snipped away shriveled blooms and dead canes, I managed to pierce my thumb on a thorn. The pain was immediate and sharp. I yanked off my glove; the thorn had ripped a chunk out of my thumb, and drops of bright red blood began running down my hand. Time for a bandage.

Elsa followed me into the house and watched with her ears perked as I gasped at the shock of cold water on my thumb. As I wrestled with a bandage—normally a simple task—a migraine zig-zag chose to appear, and it came on fast. It didn't bring pain this time, but the aura itself was hell-bent on disabling me. It morphed into a wide black band and began to block my whole field of vision, like someone was pulling a window shade down over my eyes.

I groped for the edge of the bathtub and eased onto the floor. I don't remember being frightened, because I assumed it would clear up, the way the auras always did after they'd had their fun, but I did start thinking about what I would do if I'd suddenly gone blind.

Elsa, meanwhile, decided it was big fun for me to be at ground level with her. I heard her nails click on the tile floor and felt her big sloppy tongue on my face. I grabbed onto her and held tight, wondering if I could find my way to a phone to call for help. Then I guess I passed out.

When I came to, I don't think much time had elapsed. I was lying on my back on the hard tile floor. My back hurt, and I was woozy and disoriented—and a little scared until I realized I could see again. I let out a big relieved exhale, then pushed myself into a sit and leaned against the side of the tub. My thumb still throbbed, but the bandage wasn't soaked with blood. Elsa crouched beside me, and if a dog could look worried, she did.

"It's okay, Elsa," I said. "Mom's still alive."

She cocked her head, like she was trying to judge if I was telling her the truth.

Then, very carefully, I stood; my legs shook, and my back ached like it did after a few hours of yard work, but the only thing that really hurt was my thumb. Even it was feeling better. I checked my reflection in the mirror—no visible harm, no blood or bruises. My hair was tangled, and my eyes were dark and scared-looking, but the rest of me seemed all right.

"Well, Elsa," I said, "that was pretty interesting, huh?"

One more thing to add to the list for the doctors—not that they'd be able to explain it, any more than they could the other "adverse effects." I considered calling Dr. Willis right then, but he'd probably want more tests, and I was done with those. Every answer raised a bunch of new questions anyway.

Neck-deep in denial, I had a burst of insight: the old migraine auras, I'd been assured, were hormone-related. This last episode had merely been an aura on steroids, and it made sense that my hormones were reviving along with everything else, which probably meant that the migraines were also getting stronger. So, nothing to worry about. Oh, sure. But that raised a new concern: how much stronger would they get? Would I end up permanently blind next time?

At the moment, safe in my brightly-lit bathroom with my less-wrinkled face staring at me from the mirror, that awful possibility seemed as far away as the planet Jupiter. I pushed the worry to the back of my thoughts.

Then I took a shower, ate lunch, and spent another two hours on Dr. Willis's file. In the end, however, I was still baffled by all the scientific verbiage. And nowhere in all that jumble of words did I see "migraine aura."

My brain, and my eyes, had just about given out by the time I left to pick Maddie up at school. I was otherwise feeling pretty good by then, however, as if that blinding migraine aura had never happened.

This was a rare afternoon when Maddie had no after-school activities, so I took her to the local Barnes & Noble. She loved to read, and Nancy and I encouraged her. This was one part of parenting that we agreed on; neither of us wanted her to be one of those kids so addicted to electronic devices that she lost the joy of imagination. Maddie's current favorite author had written a series about a ten-year-old girl "detective," and the latest release had just hit the shelves. I told her I'd buy it for her as an early birthday present, since she'd soon be turning nine, and the smile she gave me could have lit up the bookstore on its own.

I inhaled some of my favorite smells as we entered the store—all that clean new paper and freshly dried ink. The promise of so much knowledge, packaged and waiting on the shelves, had always intoxicated me, and Maddie shared my enthusiasm—so much like her mother that way.

I pointed down the row of children's books to a cluster of Jeff's *Defender Dog* series.

"Your uncle is well represented," I said.

Maddie wrinkled her nose. "Yeah. But that last one was kinda juvenile, didn't you think?"

I couldn't suppress a giggle. "Yes, darling—but isn't that the point?"

Maddie and I took our time browsing through the store, and when a handsome young staffer approached us, smiling, I assumed he was drawn to Maddie, who tended to attract people to her, as if she generated a kind of magnetic field.

He was looking at me, however.

"May I help you?" he asked.

My hand went to my throat, and I smiled back. "Why yes, you certainly may." I paused while I worked out what to say next. I didn't really need help, but I wanted him to linger. He was so handsome! "Do you perhaps have a book that explains genetics in simplified terms?"

Now where had that question come from? It was a good one, but I hadn't intended to ask it.

The young man fingered the ID badge hanging from a lanyard around his neck—his name was Ryan—and considered my question. Then he snapped his fingers. "We have just the thing: *Genetics for Dummies!*"

Then he flushed. "Not that you're a dummy, but it might be—"

He was so flustered that I almost patted his hand. But I didn't. "No offense taken, honestly. It sounds perfect."

Whose voice was that, so low and throaty? My God, I was practically batting my eyelashes at him!

Apparently, Ryan didn't mind, however. "Let me show you where it is. This is such a strange coincidence, but I actually noticed it the other day, and I don't know why."

He led me through the aisles to the "Diet, Health and Fitness" section, where I'd never have thought to look, and there it was. He pulled the book out and handed it to me like the prize in a raffle and stood nearby as I thumbed through the pages—close enough that I caught a whiff of his cologne. He smelled like the ocean, cool and blue.

"Getting your DNA tested?" he asked.

"No," I said, "just trying to understand some technical papers I'm reading. It's like they're in a foreign language."

He laughed. "I know what you mean. Some of the bulletins we get from upper management are incomprehensible—like they've been written by monkeys."

"An infinite number of monkeys," I said, looking up from the book. "If you put them in a room with an infinite number of type-writers…"

He snapped his fingers again. "They could write the works of Shakespeare!"

My turn to laugh. "Now, you are much too young to have heard about that."

He cocked his head. "How young do you think I am?"

Oh, dear God, how to answer that?

"That is a loaded question, Ryan."

I think I made him blush, and I pretended to study the book so he could recover, which he did very quickly.

"Your daughter is so cute," he said.

Now I had to make eye contact, to see if he was joking. He seemed sincere.

"You mean my granddaughter? Yes, she's adorable. Watch out— she'll have you wrapped around her little finger soon."

"No way! You're not possibly old enough to have a granddaughter!"

I mirrored the head-tilt. "And how *old* do you think I am?"

He wagged his index finger at me. "Oh, no you don't! Now, that *is* a loaded question."

By habit I reached for Maddie, and my hand closed on empty space. I turned to where I thought she'd been standing, but she wasn't there. Hadn't she followed us? Had I even been paying attention?

Maddie! A reel of horrid stories unspooled in my thoughts—chil-dren being snatched from under their parents' noses while they shopped, or chatted with friends. And idiot me had let that happen, flirting with a stranger while some evil person grabbed my precious Maddie.

I fought the panic, reminded myself to breathe, and looked around. There were a few customers browsing, but no golden-haired little girl.

"Did you see where she went?" I asked, amazed at how calm I sounded.

Ryan shook his head. "I thought she came with us, but maybe not. Let's check back in Children's."

And there she was. I had never been that relieved and delighted to see my beautiful Maddie. She was sitting cross-legged on the floor, caught up in her girl-detective book, and it was all I could do to stop myself from scooping her up in my arms. She heard us coming and looked up.

"This is the best one yet," she told me.

* * *

Nick's car was in the driveway when I took Maddie home.

"Daddy!" she exclaimed as we entered the house. She launched herself at him.

"Hey, pumpkin! How's my girl?"

His girl was tickled to see her dad, that was for sure.

"Thanks, Diane," Nick said to me. Then he did a double-take, and his expression clearly said, "What the hell is going on with you?"

I didn't even try to explain. "Maddie told me she got an A on her spelling test today." I stroked my granddaughter's golden hair. "She's a smart one, our Maddie."

Nick chuckled. "Must've gotten Nancy's brains—and yours."

He stood in the middle of the kitchen, hands in his pockets, looking like he wanted to talk more.

"How's the filming going?" I asked.

"Ah, you know. The director had a family emergency so they canceled the shoot today and tomorrow." He grinned down at Maddie. "And I hightailed it back here to spend time with the family."

"You'll be around tomorrow then?"

"Yep."

"Excellent. Maddie starts her horseback riding lessons after school. And I'm sure she would love for you to be there."

He seemed surprised. "Horseback riding?"

Maddie's head jiggled up and down. "Yeah, Daddy. Real horses!"

"Nancy didn't mention it?" I asked.

He looked away. "We haven't had much of a chance to talk this week. But that's great, sure, I'll be tickled to take her. See my little equestrienne in action." He snapped his fingers. "Hey, forgive my manners. Would you like a drink or something? Hang around and chat a while? Maybe bring me up to speed on what Maddie's been doing, since Nance obviously doesn't tell me much."

My new genetics book beckoned, but Nick's blue eyes met mine with something that felt like urgency. Did Nancy intentionally withhold information from him?

"She's got her hands full with work and keeping up with Maddie," I replied.

Nick flinched. "I know, and I'm a selfish bas—"

I glanced at Maddie and interrupted. "You're earning a living too, Nick. No blame on you."

He kissed the top of Maddie's head. "Whatcha got there?"

Maddie giggled and showed him the book. "Grandma bought it for me. It's good."

He ruffled her hair. "Okay, little bookworm. I can tell you'd rather be reading it than listening to us grownups."

She scampered toward her room, clutching the book with as much tenderness as if she held a new puppy.

"Now," Nick continued, "That drink?"

I checked my watch. Steven wouldn't be home for at least an hour, and we were eating leftovers anyway.

"Just one," I said.

The kitchen was large and bright, the place where everyone hung out because it had a wide granite breakfast bar with comfortable upholstered stools. I claimed my usual spot while Nick opened a cabinet above the refrigerator. Nancy and I needed a stepstool to reach the liquor, but Nick didn't even have to stand on tiptoe.

"What's your poison?" he asked.

I hesitated a second and then said "Scotch." When was the last time I'd drunk hard liquor? Couldn't remember.

Nick whistled and produced a bottle of Johnnie Walker Black Label—almost full, I noticed. "A serious drinker. Me too."

"Not usually," I replied. "And hardly ever during the week."

He turned those blue eyes on me again. "I didn't upset you, did I? I didn't mean to badmouth your daughter."

I smiled. "I know. No worries, Nick. Sometimes she gets on my nerves, too."

He dumped some ice cubes into two highball glasses before he poured the clear golden-brown liquid over them. Somehow being with Nick made me feel like I was part of a movie, but that was probably my overactive imagination.

We clinked glasses and both said "Cheers" at the same time.

He slid onto the bar stool across from me. "So, Maddie's doing well in school?"

I sipped the drink and grimaced. Why had I asked for scotch instead of my usual wine? Nancy always had a bottle of chardonnay in the fridge.

"More than well." I swirled the liquor around the ice to dilute it. "She *is* very smart, Nick. I know I sound like a doting grandmother, but I swear she understands things my own kids didn't get until they were much older."

He nodded. The overhead light threw gold sparkles in his hair. No wonder Maddie was such a beautiful child. Her parents both looked like they'd stepped out of magazine ads.

"Sometimes I worry kids today grow up too fast," Nick said. "I don't know if it's the TV, or so many of 'em with cell phones and computers..." He paused. "Maddie doesn't have a cell phone, does she?"

"Certainly not. Nancy won't allow that until she's much older."

"That's one thing we agree on," Nick muttered. He cocked his head. "But I bet she knows how to use one, right?"

I bit my lip. "That's my fault, Nick. I taught her how to make calls on mine—in case of emergency, you know?"

"Guess I can't argue with that."

"And Nancy is very strict about her TV watching. She's probably less permissive than most parents—teachers often are."

Nick took a swig of his drink. "That's my wife. And I'm grateful."

He studied my face again, long enough to make me self-conscious.

I took too big a pull on my scotch, and it burned the back of my throat.

"Diane, don't mind me asking—but you look so *different* from the last time I saw you. Years younger." He bit his lower lip. "Hell, it's none of my business, and God knows in my line of work you see plenty of facelifts and whatever. I'm just sayin', if you did have work done—nothing wrong with that, and you sure as hell got your money's worth."

A nervous giggle escaped, dammit. "No plastic surgery, honest."

There was nothing to do then but summarize, as clearly as I could, what I'd learned so far from Drs. Willis and Banks.

While I was talking, Nick drained his glass and refilled it almost without looking. I declined his offer of more; his rapt attention unnerved me, and my thoughts were turning fuzzy around the edges.

"That's the gist of it," I concluded.

He ran his fingers through that thick, curly hair. "Genetic mutation. That is wild, Diane. Just fantastic. Man, I wish it was happening to *me.*"

The image of Nancy's tired, worn face in the mirror at Hillcrest Saddlery flickered to life. She was the one who needed rejuvenation.

"Don't be too sure, Nick. No one understands how this happened, or how long it will continue, or if it can be stopped."

"Stopped? Why the hell would you want to stop it? You should ride it, Diane, as long as you can. To be young again? Who wouldn't want that? I mean, look at you—you've always been a handsome woman, but now you are drop-dead gorgeous."

At that moment, the connecting door from the garage opened, and Nancy walked in, grocery bags hanging from both hands. I hadn't heard the garage door grind open, but Maddie must have, because she came running.

"Mommy! Daddy's home."

"I see that," Nancy said, her gaze moving from Nick to me and back again. "I wasn't expecting you."

The grocery bags looked heavy as she eased them onto the counter. Nick hadn't risen to welcome her, but I shook off a momentary paralysis and went to help put the food away.

She kissed my cheek. "Thanks, Mom." Then she knelt and hugged Maddie, whose enthusiastic greeting had faded into uncertainty.

"Grandma bought me the new Sally Sherman book," Maddie said.

"Did she?" Nancy's smile seemed forced. "Mom, you're spoiling her."

"If I can't spoil my only grandchild, who will?" I replied.

"I suppose you're right." She stroked her daughter's blond curls. "Is it as good as the last one?" she asked Maddie.

"Better!"

"Don't let me keep you from Sally then. You can go read a little more before dinner."

Maddie scampered off, and the tension in the room rose as she left.

"Hey, hon," Nick said after another swallow of scotch, "you've been holding out on me. Riding lessons for Maddie? And this mutation thing with your mom? Incredible!"

Nancy almost dropped the head of lettuce she was handing me to put in the fridge. "Mutation?"

She scrutinized me more closely, and her expression—a mixture of shock, curiosity, and a smidgen of horror—just let me say, you never want to see your daughter look at you that way.

"The doctors got back those test results I mentioned," I told Nancy, and then summarized what I'd told Nick a few minutes earlier. While I was talking, I emptied one of the grocery bags and put its contents away, but Nancy stood where she was, her mouth hanging open.

"Mom, that is the spookiest thing I've ever heard," she said when I finished. "Are you going to be okay? Why are you just now telling me?"

"I only found out yesterday, darling. And don't worry, I'm fine. At least I *feel* fine. For now. I'm still learning about genetics and mutations, so this is all new to me, too."

"What's going to happen? Will you keep getting younger? Will you end up younger than *me*?"

"We don't know yet. That's why I'm reading up on it." I sighed. "But the material the doctors gave me is awfully technical—it's hard to understand. In fact, I just bought a book called *Genetics for Dummies*. I hope it'll help."

The concern on Nancy's face deepened. "Did I inherit it too? Did Maddie?"

"No—and remember, your grandparents aged normally. This is what the doctors call a spontaneous mutation, meaning *I* didn't inherit it. It just *happened*, and only to me."

The lines on her face didn't ease. "Can they undo it?"

I winced. "Darling, I don't know. I doubt if even the doctors know. I told you, we're in a learning mode right now. When I know more, I'll tell you. I promise."

Nancy hugged me. "I'm scared for you, Mom."

I patted her back. "Don't be. I'm sure once I wade through *Genetics for Dummies*, I'll know enough to make us all feel better about this."

She pulled away and picked up her cell phone, thumbs dancing over the screen. "I'm texting June—she teaches the class next door to mine, and her sister's a nurse at Alta Vista. June's son has chronic allergy trouble, and her sister told her about Alta Vista's medical library, said they're incredibly helpful. June went there to study up on treatments."

Alta Vista Hospital—one of the best in the county, in my opinion. I'd had my hysterectomy there, Maddie had been born there, Jeff had been a patient when he broke his arm in eleventh grade. But I didn't know about their library.

"I bet they can help you research this stuff," Nancy said as she put down the phone. "I'll let you know what she says."

Nancy's concern, so unexpected, made me want to cry—or maybe it was the scotch. I swallowed the last of it and rinsed the glass.

"I have to go," I said. "Dad will be home soon and expecting dinner on the table."

Nancy pointed to the empty glass. "You shouldn't be driving, Mom."

I patted her arm. "I'm fine, darling. I hardly had any—honestly, I didn't try to keep up with Nick."

"Few of us can," Nancy said, with a laugh that held shards of glass.

Nick looked uneasy. "She's right, Nance. Her drink was mostly melted ice. But if you'd rather, I can drive her home."

"That's silly," I told both of them. "Then Dad would have to bring me back later to get the car, and I'd have to explain why, and... really, I'm perfectly fine to drive."

I wasn't as fine as I told them, but it was still daylight, and I drove very cautiously, sticking to surface streets, conscious of the liquor singing in my blood.

Steven pulled into the garage moments after I did. After he kissed me hello, he frowned.

"You've been drinking," he said. "Bad day?"

"Not exactly, although reading through that doorstop of a file from Dr. Willis is enough to drive anyone to drink. No, Nick was home when I dropped Maddie off, so I stayed to chat for a while, and he offered me a drink. Scotch."

"Scotch, eh? Not enough that he led our daughter astray, now he has to corrupt you?"

"Says the whiskey drinker."

"And you just got home? You drove?"

"I did. Don't start on me, Steven. It was stupid, but I knew you'd worry if I wasn't here when you got home, and—"

"That's what cell phones are for, Diane. To call if you're running late." He shook his head. "Now this rejuvenation thing has you acting like an irresponsible teenager."

"I am not! But you're acting like a judgmental old geezer!"

It was a low blow, and the "old" was probably what caused the angry flush on Steven's face.

"At least I come by it naturally."

Jaw clenched, he stomped upstairs and slammed the bedroom door.

* * *

Steven had calmed down by the time I had dinner on the table, and we kept our conversation to neutral topics, except when he asked if Nick was unemployed again. I explained the unexpected halt to filming, and Steven merely grunted, as if the delay were Nick's fault.

Steven barely concealed his dislike for Nick when Nancy or Maddie was around, and he didn't even bother to with me. It wasn't only Nick's lack of a steady income; I doubted that Steven would find *any* man worthy of his daughter.

As I lay in bed that night, however, I kept seeing the admiring look in Nick's sparkling blue eyes *"…but now you are drop-dead gorgeous."*

What woman wouldn't want to hear those words from a handsome TV star? Even if he was married to her daughter.

Chapter Twelve
Genetics for Non-Dummies

Alta Vista Hospital stashed its Medical Library in the East Tower basement. I learned that it was intended primarily for staff, students and patients, but according to Nancy's friend June, anyone with a twenty-dollar membership fee could use its resources.

I'd searched the internet for hours, following a tangled trail of links when I typed "genetic mutation in humans" in the search box. Although familiar with some of the conditions—like cystic fibrosis and progeria—that came up in my search, I didn't know they were caused by mutation. As my knowledge grew, so did my alarm and confusion. There were a lot of dreadful afflictions out there that were caused by a glitch in someone's genetic code. My own situation seemed benign in comparison. Some false leads popped up, but the information worth printing began to fill a cardboard file box. What I didn't find there, or in *Genetics for Dummies*, was a single example of someone whose stem cells had spontaneously begun to rejuvenate.

Dr. Willis's folder of technical information included some lovely illustrations of a cell nucleus, a chromosome, and a strand of DNA, along with an explanation of the nucleotides contained within the strand. He'd also provided an article detailing the characteristics of

SIRT3, and terms like "mitochondrial DNA" and "protein deacetylation" became as familiar as my own name.

None of it, however, helped me understand a mutation like mine, or reassured me that I was not unique. I therefore figured I had little to lose except twenty bucks by visiting the Alta Vista library. Nancy's friend told her that the reference librarian *might* be able to help me find relevant material. My hopes weren't high, but I was ready to try anything.

* * *

The hospital basement, three stories underground, was quiet but brightly lit, which offset the lack of windows. The librarian who greeted me was an attractive young man named Luke, according to the ID badge clipped to his shirt pocket. Tall and trim, with wavy brown hair and a friendly demeanor, he looked more like an athlete or an actor than my vision of a librarian.

I signed up for a membership, handed over the fee, and explained I was trying to find information on genetic mutations in humans. When I complained about the confusing amount of information I'd already found on the internet, he smiled knowingly.

"It can be overwhelming," he said, and I half-expected him to pat my hand sympathetically, as if I were a doddering old aunt who had trouble even remembering what she ate for breakfast.

Then his manner shifted. "What specifically are you trying to find, Mrs. Devlin?"

I stalled for a minute because I wasn't sure how much I should say. *What the hell,* I decided. *You won't learn anything by being evasive.*

Two men in white lab coats came in, nodded to Luke and kept walking, their voices low and urgent. I waited until they'd moved into the stacks before I began explaining to Luke, as briefly as possible, how I was experiencing a weird genetic mutation that had interfered with my aging, and I was, in fact, growing younger.

His brown eyes widened in what I assumed was interest and perhaps delight: here was a challenge for his research skills.

"Fascinating," he said. "Just fascinating. How much information have your doctors given you?"

I sighed. "I can tell you more than any lay person around about cytokines and hematopoietic stem cells. I even sort of understand that part, but I'm trying to learn whether this has happened to anyone else, and so far, I haven't found anything remotely similar."

"Mmmm hmmm," Luke murmured. He tapped a pen on the countertop for a moment and then his face brightened. "Tell you what: I'll set you up at a computer terminal and give you some search terms to use with our literature data base. Meanwhile—and lucky for us it's a quiet day here—I can go on some of our specialized data bases and do my own search. Then we'll compare notes and see what we've found."

I loved his use of "we." Luke probably had a better chance than I did of unearthing relevant information.

"Great! Thank you so much."

At the well-lit computer station, I eased into a surprisingly comfortable chair that even had padded arm rests, braced myself for a flood of new information, and typed one of Luke's parameters into the search box. Up came a lot of articles I'd already seen, read, and filed away. I scanned new ones, disappointed but not surprised to find that none of them addressed anything like my situation. I was the oddball exception—and that was a very lonely sensation.

Why was this happening to me? Was it a good thing, or as dangerous as Steven and Maura believed? Should I worry too? Was it wrong to enjoy feeling younger again? If only I knew what had caused the mutation. But the big "why?" remained a mystery—to me, and even to smart doctors like Willis and Banks.

"It's not like I wished this on myself," I muttered as I followed another cluster of hyperlinks.

Is that right? The voice sounded real enough that I jerked my head around to see if anyone was watching me. Luke was a good forty feet away at the reference desk, staring at the computer monitor as he worked the keyboard—presumably prowling those online data bases he mentioned. The other two visitors had seemingly found what they wanted and left.

Great; now I was imagining voices. The question was legitimate, though. I had been griping about the effects of aging—pain and stiffness, flabby skin, gray roots that sprouted way too soon after I'd had my hair colored. Wrinkles. Fatigue so strong I usually craved an afternoon nap. It sucked, and hundreds, maybe thousands of times I *had* wished I wasn't feeling my age as much as I did.

* * *

Only one other time in my life had I wished something away, and then the doctors had assured me the miscarriage had been inevitable, that I'd done nothing to bring it on. Oh sure, nothing except regret the baby growing inside me every minute of its brief life. No, that's not true. When I felt that first thrilling stir, I'd accepted the reality of another round of child-rearing. Except I wasn't ready to face it again, so soon.

Jeff had started first grade, and half of each day was mine again, after almost ten years. I'd loved being home with Nancy and Jeff, watching them learn and develop personalities. But I'd missed the working world and wanted to go back to adult conversations and a different sense of purpose. I was *not* looking forward to diapers and sleepless nights and the incessant worrying over fevers and stomach upsets. Well, Fate, you got me good that time, didn't you?

Miscarriage—such a tidy word for so much blood and pain. They had to remove my uterus too, and I presumed it was my punishment for not wanting that baby. It was *not* my fault, though. I'd done everything right—right food, right rest, right activity level. It was *not* my fault. I only wished I believed that.

* * *

So maybe Fate was playing a practical joke at my expense. I pushed the notion aside and clicked another link on the computer screen.

The more I read, the more the terminology began to make sense. I could sketch a DNA molecule in my sleep by then, and I knew about cell replication and the difference between DNA and RNA. I scanned several articles describing ever more bizarre genetic mutations, and the mechanisms behind them became understandable—and totally irrelevant to my situation.

The library was even quieter than the ones in the outside world. Three more visitors came and left. A woman in blue surgical scrubs entered and stopped to talk with Luke. They both kept their voices so low I couldn't overhear what they were discussing, but then she laughed—a sound like wind chimes on a breezy afternoon—and I glanced over. She was leaning on the reference desk, head tilted to one side flirtatiously.

Hmmm, I thought, *so Luke isn't all business.*

The woman slapped her hand on the desk gently and then left, and I watched Luke watch *her* as she sauntered away.

After that, no more visitors. The library was silent except for the soft hiss of conditioned air flowing from overhead vents, and the sound of Luke's fingers on the keyboard. We were sealed away in our own private world, Luke and I.

My eyes began to burn from the glare of the computer monitor, and my arm and neck muscles ached. I pushed away from the monitor and rubbed my temples.

Luke looked my way. "Any luck?"

I stretched the kinks out of my back. "Not really. What amazes me is how many different *kinds* of mutations there are. Things I'd never even dreamed of, like the guy who's immune to HIV, or the woman who can thrive on four hours of sleep."

Luke brought some papers over and pulled up a chair next to me. "The human body is an amazing mechanism."

As he said that, I became aware of his very attractive human body just inches from mine. I imagined its warmth. Yes, amazing—that strong, smooth flesh. What would it feel like? What would he do if I reached over and caressed that firm young arm? My right hand, all on its own, moved to the top button on my blouse; my fingers stroked its smooth surface.

Stop it!

I forced myself to put both hands on the chair arms. My fingers dug into the padding as I tried to slow my fluttering heartbeat.

Evidently oblivious to my arousal, Luke handed me a printout and pointed to the top page. "This one isn't exactly like yours, but it's related."

The article's title—"Chromothriptic Cure of WHIM Syndrome"— might have given the Old Diane a headache. The New and Improved Diane was curious, however, and I welcomed the distraction from my salacious thoughts.

"It's about a woman with an inherited immune deficiency," Luke explained. "A serious one that caused all kinds of nasty infections. Then in her late thirties, the condition spontaneously disappeared. The doctors believe it was because one of her chromosomes shattered, rearranged itself, and deleted the defective gene. Her body cured itself."

"I didn't know that could happen," I said.

"It's rare—but our bodies do all sorts of miraculous things. Your mutation is more obvious than some, but you're not the only one."

There he went talking about bodies again. I kept my thoughts in line, mostly because the word "mutation" still felt like a needle in my skin.

I scanned the printout. "Is the woman still alive?"

He shrugged. "As far as I know. They don't identify her by name so I can't do a Google search to confirm, but there's no mention of her death."

He held up a second set of papers. "This might answer some of your questions. You've probably already learned about CRISPR."

I had.

"Clustered Regularly Interspaced Short Palindromic Repeats," I recited. "That's about all I know, however. Except it's some kind of gene-editing tool, right?"

He pressed his lips together. "Yes, and what a tool. It can go into a gene, identify a flawed segment of DNA, and snip it out, or even replace it with a healthy segment. Pretty amazing stuff."

"It is," I agreed, as my mind whipped through the implications.

"This won't explain why your genes mutated," Luke continued, "but your doctors might be able to use CRISPR to remove your mutation."

"And I'd stop getting younger?"

"In theory anyway." Luke paused. "It might also be used to replicate the mutation in a lab, and then share it with others."

I shuddered. "That's what Dr. Banks wants to do."

"Dr. Banks? Lewis Banks?"

"Right—you know him?"

"I know *of* him. He's very well thought of. If he's treating you, I'm surprised he hasn't explained what CRISPR could do in your situation. Your mutation is a potential gold mine if they can replicate it."

"I bet it is. I should have pressed Dr. Banks for more information. I was just so stunned when he said 'mutation' that my brain froze up. I hadn't even thought of *that* upside." I grinned for the first time. "Hey, maybe I'll be young and *rich*."

Luke didn't smile back. In fact, I think I saw a flash of sympathy on that handsome young face.

"I didn't know Dr. Banks was still practicing medicine," he said.

"He isn't, much. He took me on as a favor for another doctor. And he has an associate—Dr. Willis. Do you know him too?"

"Nope. But I don't deal with the docs that much." He gestured toward the stacks. "They don't usually come down here in person. And I only know Dr. Banks by reputation."

He's so handsome. What a shame to keep him buried down here.

"How do you like working here? Doesn't it get a little lonely?"

He turned his brown eyes on me. "It can get busy at times. And I enjoy helping people find what they're searching for."

I couldn't stop gazing at him. *So good-looking.* "I bet you do."

He stared back at me so long that I felt a blush warm my cheeks. Was he attracted to me as much as I was to him? *We're alone down here. No one would ever know if...*

If what? If I started undoing the buttons on his crisp white shirt? If he leaned over and kissed me? What would those lips feel like? How would he taste?

Luke broke the spell when he glanced at his watch. What time was it anyway? I checked my own watch and realized it was almost one in the afternoon.

"I bet you're starving," I said. "Do you get to close for lunch?

Could I bring you a sandwich or something—to thank you for all your help?"

Ah yes, we could share a bite to eat here among the stacks, and maybe share something else.

"Thanks," Luke said, "but my wife made me a sandwich."

Had he emphasized the word "wife?"

I gathered up my notes and the articles he'd printed for me. "I think I've gotten all I can for now, Luke. Thank you."

He stood. Maybe he was relieved to be rid of this old woman and her bizarre quest.

"I enjoyed meeting you, Mrs. Devlin. Your request has been the most interesting project I've had in days. I hope you find what you're looking for."

I shook his hand. "Me too. More than you know. And call me Diane. All my friends do."

I was halfway out the door when he called out to me. "Take care, Diane."

"Always," I replied, tipping an imaginary hat.

As the elevator rumbled up to the main floor, I thought about what I'd learned, and Luke's remark about a "potential gold mine." What if Dr. Banks could somehow capture the mutation and mass produce it? Give other people the benefits I was experiencing?

But no one, not even legendary Dr. Banks, knew how long the rejuvenation would last, let alone if or how it could be stopped.

And I still wasn't sure I wanted to stop it. Part of me wanted to hang on to this miracle. I loved having energy, my joints didn't ache, my brain felt sharper. Even my libido had come back to life. Yeah, there was that—and it wasn't exactly a good thing. I'd probably made a fool of myself with Luke, fantasizing about what he looked like under that prim white shirt, what it would be like to have his arms around me. What was going on? First the guy at Barnes & Noble, now Luke. I hadn't felt urges like that in years, except occasionally with Steven—and even those hardly ever anymore.

This getting-younger thing had some unexpected side effects. What else would I start thinking and feeling?

* * *

That night I showed Steven the printouts from the library. His forehead puckered over the "Chromothriptic Cure" article, his lips forming the words like a toddler learning to read.

"I don't understand," he said as he scanned the pages. "How can a chromosome shatter? Wouldn't that hurt?"

My jaw muscles clenched. "That's not the point," I snapped. "What's important is that I'm not the only one this kind of thing happens to. Maybe somewhere a scientist is—"

"What difference does it make?" Steven sounded like a little kid who'd been told to eat his broccoli before he could have dessert. He rattled the pages of the WHIMS article. "How can this possibly help *you*?"

Easy, Diane. He hasn't had all day to absorb this stuff.

I thumbed through the printouts until I found the article about CRISPR. "Maybe it won't, but *this* might." I handed it to Steven.

His scowl vanished as he read. "I was going to tell you about this."

"You know what it is?"

He nodded. "I stumbled across it a couple of days ago. I didn't tell you because I wanted to learn more, about how it's done and the long-term effects."

"You've been doing research too?"

"Of course I have, Diane. I told you, we are in this together."

My earlier annoyance washed away in a tide of shame. The dear man was doing his best to help me.

"Not that I've been much help I'm afraid," Steven continued. He jabbed his finger at the printed pages. "I've read it three times, and I still can't comprehend how it works. My brain seizes up."

He tapped the pages into a tidy stack and handed them back to me. "It's like these articles are written in a foreign language. It's taking me forever to understand them."

I kissed the back of his neck. "I felt that way earlier, Steven. But the more I read, the more sense it made, so between the two of us we'll figure it out. And meanwhile, there's something else to think about. The librarian at the hospital suggested Dr. Banks might be able to, in his words, 'replicate the mutation.' As in give it to other people—or more likely, find a way to *market* it. It might be worth a *lot* of money."

Steven's eyes narrowed. "How would they do that? Do you mean sell little pieces of *you*?"

"No! But maybe they could extract the mutation with this CRISPR and then reproduce it in a laboratory."

His expression told me he was nowhere near comprehension yet.

What had happened to us? Steven was the smartest person I knew. When did I suddenly become smarter?

Chapter Thirteen
Patent Confrontation

Dr. Banks raised his eyebrows when I mentioned CRISPR. "You *have* been doing your homework. Yes, it's quite a remarkable tool."

Steven and I had gone over the articles about CRISPR again and again and again. I'd squashed my impatience, and it was worth the effort to see his triumphant grin when he finally put the pieces together. A line from "My Fair Lady" flashed through my mind— "By George, I think she's got it!" Then I wondered if many people would still get that cultural reference. My body might be growing younger, but my memories stayed sixty-five years old. I pushed the thought away; I had more important things to worry about.

"So we surmised," Steven replied, narrowing his eyes at Dr. Banks. "And we think it might be a way to control Diane's reverse-aging. To stop it."

Despite the migraines, despite the bone pain, I still wasn't sure I *wanted* to stop the rejuvenation. Maybe, I'd tried to persuade myself, those things were worth the price of a second chance at youth. Besides, I'd reasoned, two weeks had passed without anything bothersome happening; maybe it had all merely been a phase.

Dr. Willis had been uncharacteristically silent, avoiding eye contact during Steven's verbal tennis match with Dr. Banks.

Finally, he spoke up. "We don't know enough about the long-term effects of altering the human genome," he said. "In theory, it might do exactly what you suggest. But the technique hasn't been studied long enough for anyone to—"

"It's been studied long enough to generate a lawsuit over the patent for it," Steven said. "I may not be a scientist, but I know enough about patent law to understand this means there's a known financial gain, which means the practical application is imminent. Otherwise no one would take the trouble to try and patent it."

Banks and Willis seemed startled by his outburst, and it surprised me too that he'd gone far beyond what I'd learned about CRISPR.

"You have a valid point, Mr. Devlin," Dr. Banks said. He glared at Dr. Willis. "It's true that experiments on human germ cells are prohibited, at least in this country. There are dangers if the altered gene is passed down to future generations without a clear understanding of the consequences. But that is beyond the scope of what we're contemplating. CRISPR *has* been used, quite auspiciously, with some devastating human conditions, such as Bubble Boy Syndrome."

A jittery current went through me.

Banks smiled benignly. "By altering a single gene in the patient's DNA, CRISPR can, in effect, cure it. The potential for use with other diseases, even cancer, is staggering."

Everyone was silent for a moment.

"The other magnificent aspect," Dr. Banks continued, "is that we already know the mutation in SIRT3 that is responsible for your rejuvenation, Mrs. Devlin. CRISPR could possibly be used to edit that mutation in the lab and study it in more detail." He paused and looked straight at me before he went on. "Or even to insert it into the stem cells of others so that they might share your gift."

Dr. Willis stood abruptly. "It's too soon to discuss that premise, Lewis. Our first concern should be treating Diane. She's already experiencing some adverse effects, and I don't want her to endure more."

"Actually," I began, and my throat felt thick as I choked out the word, ready to tell them about the blackout, "a couple of things have—"

Steven interrupted me. "What sort of adverse effects?"

Dr. Willis glanced at his shiny silver watch. "At this time, I have no idea. I only know the risk is there." He picked up his briefcase. "My next class starts in less than an hour. Cross-town traffic will be horrendous this time of day. I have to go."

"Wait a minute," Steven said. "I thought the purpose of this meeting was to discuss Diane's options for dealing with this... this rejuvenation. And the one thing we've found that might apply, you don't want to discuss? What the hell is going on here?"

Banks frowned at Willis, who suddenly appeared fascinated by a stack of books on the older doctor's desk. Finally, he looked up.

"We've had a bit of a philosophical difference of opinion," he said. "And I must bow out of your case. I'm very sorry."

He hurried from the room, shutting the door firmly behind him.

I turned to Dr. Banks. "What *is* going on? What aren't you telling us?"

He seemed to wither as the door closed behind Dr. Willis. His hollow cheeks and the shadows beneath his eyes grew more apparent. "I'm sorry you had to witness that. It's very unprofessional of Dr. Willis and myself. But he told the truth: he and I disagree, very vigorously, on what our course of action should be. Quite frankly, it ambushed me this morning, before you arrived, when he told me how strongly he felt. I'd hoped a rational discussion would get him back on board, but apparently not. I do have other associates I can bring in, but I need a few days to regroup."

More waiting?

"Dr. Banks," I said, "what about the study you and Dr. Willis are doing? I thought the two of you were on the same page."

Dr. Banks rubbed his long, tapered fingers. "Mrs. Devlin, I'll be candid. I strongly believe this discovery of your mutation is too important for us to keep for ourselves. Dr. Willis disagrees."

"What do you mean?" Steven demanded.

Dr. Banks's slumped shoulders reminded me of my father's in those last years of his life when I caught him smoking.

"I plan to patent your mutation," he began, but he didn't get far because Steven stood, his jaw clenched.

I knew that posture. *Watch out, Dr. Banks!*

"Wait a damned minute," Steven said. "You're not patenting my wife's *body*! Don't you even try."

Dr. Banks's hands went up, like he expected Steven to punch him. "Certainly not. Merely the mutation."

"You'll do no such thing! I'll have you in court before you even file a patent application."

Dr. Banks's look could only be described as pity. "I'm afraid you're too late for that, Mr. Devlin. The paperwork has been filed."

Steven and I stared at one another as he sank back into his chair, and I'm sure he realized the same thing I did: the release I had signed before meeting with Dr. Banks. It gave him *carte blanche* to do whatever he chose with his discovery.

I couldn't believe what I heard. "So that's it? You're going to sell the mutation, make a lot of money, and leave me dealing with this condition on my own? Not even try to help?"

Dr. Banks reached across his desk and clasped my hand; his skin was cold, and I pulled away.

"Definitely not!" he replied. "I intend to pursue a way to halt your rejuvenation, if that's truly what you want. Actually, I doubt that CRISPR is the answer, but there *is* an answer out there. However, as I'm sure you're well aware, your condition is unique, and there is no precedent for it. Dr. Willis was leading the research team, and, unfortunately, I let him proceed for the most part on his own, my schedule being what it is. Had I known this would happen, obviously I would have been more deeply involved."

"Obviously," Steven said, his voice oozing skepticism.

Dr. Banks ignored it. "In any event, be assured I'm fully engaged now, and I intend to involve other colleagues who have the background and resources to seek answers for you. For us."

I wasn't sure I could trust him. If he already had what he wanted from "Mrs. Devlin's body" and thought it was some kind of miracle cure for aging, what motivation did he have to try and find a way to stop the miracle? Maybe I was being unfair, but I was too stunned by the morning's events to think clearly.

"And in the meantime," Steven said, "you naturally plan to keep Diane under observation and see what other effects this rejuvenation might have, right? That would clearly be to your advantage when you try and market this *mutation.*"

Dr. Banks drew back and sat up straight. "Well, of course we'll want to watch out for her, and be wary of any adverse consequences."

I stared at him. "Like Dr. Willis mentioned. That scares me."

"Peter is something of an alarmist, Mrs. Devlin. I'm aware that you've had a few unpleasant experiences—that is actually understandable, given your body's rejuvenation. Your cells are changing, and rather rapidly. But as your muscles and blood chemistry adapt, I'm confidence these incidents will resolve, and you will continue to enjoy the beneficial effects of growing younger."

"So you're in no hurry to try and stop it," Steven said. "You have no idea how far it will go—just *how* young she might become. You're using her as a human guinea pig."

That hadn't occurred to me, and I couldn't control a gasp, which I know they both heard. I dug my nails into the soft fabric of my purse.

"I most certainly am *not!*" Dr. Banks said. "I swore an oath to help the sick and abstain from any wrongdoing! What you suggest is unbelievably insulting!"

I recovered from my shock in time to interrupt them before things got even uglier. I couldn't know for sure that Steven was wrong, but it made no sense to alienate Dr. Banks when he was the only person who had a chance of unlocking the mystery. And while I loved feeling better than I had in a decade, the prospect of reverting into a drooling infant, however remote, was enough to make me want that answer.

"My husband didn't mean to question your ethics, Dr. Banks. But I hope you understand how much of a shock all this is to both of us, and we haven't had a chance to absorb it all."

I squeezed Steven's hand, and he kept silent.

"I do understand, Mrs. Devlin. It is a lot to take in." He tapped his silver pen on the desktop. "I suggest you book an appointment next week, after I've consulted with some colleagues, and you've had a chance to reflect on these developments. I hope to have some good news for you by then."

* * *

We didn't speak as we walked to the car. Ever polite, Steven held the passenger door open for me. Bright sunlight emphasized the lines on his face—they looked like canyons—and his sandy-gray hair showed small patches of scalp.

Inside the car, I sank into the cushy leather seat. The Lexus had been an extravagance, but one we could afford, although I had to nudge Steven into buying it—a good car for a successful attorney. The Lexus was reliable, safe, and oh-so-comfortable. A faint trace of Steven's Old Spice always lingered, and that shred of familiarity comforted me as the engine purred to life.

Steven slid the gearshift into Drive, and off we went, still not talking. There was too much to say, and I didn't know where to begin. Steven was a very focused driver, one of the world's safest, and I didn't want to disturb his concentration. Once we got on the freeway toward home, with traffic unusually light, he finally spoke up.

"Are you hungry?"

The question seemed too complicated to answer. Was I hungry? I could hardly feel my own body. And what could we do about it? Choosing a restaurant was next to impossible with all the other decisions I faced.

"A little," I replied. "Are you?"

"Not really." Steven glanced over his shoulder to the right and flicked on the turn signal. "But I think we should eat. And I could use a cup of coffee. Hell, I could use a drink, but it's not even noon."

"Happy Hour somewhere," I said—our standard joke when one of us proposed an early cocktail.

I almost suggested stopping at the Wayward Vine, but the memory of Jordy's smooth, warm hand against mine was enough to keep me from bringing Steven there.

"Let's just go home," I told him. "I'll fix you a sandwich—and a drink if you want it."

Steven flicked off the turn signal. "Fair enough."

Outside the Lexus, late-summer brown landscape flowed past, and heat waves rippled up from the asphalt. Sunlight was beginning to show the pale quality of light that foretold cold weather to come, but for now, that promise lurked out of sight.

* * *

Elsa greeted us with yips of pleasure, her big plumed tail thrashing side to side. In the old days she might have reared up to lick my face, no matter how much I'd tried to discourage that behavior with a stern "no jump!" Even the obedience teacher hadn't been able to extinguish Elsa's wild enthusiasm for greeting those she loved. But Elsa couldn't rear up anymore. *Be careful what you wish for.* I knelt and hugged her, and her whole body quivered—whether from pleasure or pain I couldn't tell, and I didn't want to.

I put down my purse, washed my hands, and got out the bread and sliced turkey for Steven's sandwich. While I was at it, I decided to make one for myself. Elsa could take care of any leftovers.

Safe inside our home, I could finally let my emotions out, but I didn't know whether to cry or laugh or scream.

"Maybe we could reach out to Dr. Willis anyway," I said as I spread mustard on slabs of sourdough.

Steven took sliced mozzarella from the fridge and layered it on top of the bread. "I suppose it's worth a try. He may not be able to talk to us though. I don't know how these arrangements are structured."

"Me neither. It's all so weird. Like something out of a sci fi movie."

I laid turkey slices atop the cheese, then lettuce and tomato, and added a couple of pickle chips for Steven. He cut the sandwiches on the diagonal and kissed my cheek. The contrast between what we were doing—the mundane normality of it all—and the subject we were discussing, stunned me.

I reached into the fridge for a bowl of green grapes to round out our meal, and a searing pain flared up my right leg. I dropped the bowl and despite the agony, my first thought was, *Thank goodness it's plastic.*

"Oh!" I cried as I hobbled to the closest chair. Elsa whimpered and followed me.

"What is it?" Steven asked as he crouched beside me.

Pain kept me from speaking as I rubbed my leg. My bones were on fire, like a tree burning from the inside out.

Steven's hands, so much stronger than mine, kneaded my leg.

"Muscle cramp?" he asked.

I could only shake my head at first, then the spasm subsided enough for me to form words. "It's in my *bones*. I've never felt anything like it."

He started to get up. "I'm calling nine-one-one."

I clutched his arm, although the movement made me dizzy. "No. It's getting better." I made myself smile. "There. Almost gone now."

Elsa relaxed, too.

"Are you sure?" asked Steven, his face still scrunched in concern.

"I think so."

"We should get you to a doctor anyway," Steven said. "This isn't normal."

"Duh," I replied, with a little laugh. "I'll tell Dr. Banks next week. I'm sure he'll find it *interesting*."

Steven stood and rubbed his back. "We shouldn't wait that long, Diane. This could be serious."

I rose and did a little dance step to reassure him. And myself. "Don't be silly. If you rushed me to the ER, what would we say? My leg hurt a lot, and now it doesn't. If there's nothing to show them, how can they know what to do?"

Steven rubbed his chin. "I suppose you're right. Damn those doctors anyway! I should never have let you sign that release."

"What difference does it make? Banks wouldn't have let me in the door if I hadn't."

He ran his fingers through his thinning hair. "I hope he really *is* seeking a way to stop this, Diane. Who knows what other side effects will show up. They might not be as transient as that one."

I hadn't told Steven about the migraine and the muscle spasms. Neither had recurred, so what was the point?

"I feel fine now," I said. And I did. I'd probably just turned my leg the wrong way. Or something. I retrieved the grapes before Elsa got any; grapes are bad for dogs. My quick recovery reminded me of the benefits of this so-called rejuvenation. Nothing got me down for long, not like it used to. "And Steven? I'm not sure I want to stop this reverse-aging anyway."

His eyes widened. "You're joking."

"I'm not."

"Diane, this thing is dangerous. Don't let vanity cloud your common sense."

"Vanity? Don't be ridiculous. It's not vanity to want my body to work again, to be able to—"

"I understand, Diane, more than you might realize. But the potential cost… listen, I'm not crazy about getting older myself, but it's *natural*. I'm trying to accept it with as much grace as I can."

"Well, I'm not! I want to fight back, however I can, not just sit back and let my body and my brain fall apart."

Steven stared at me for what felt like eternity. Then he turned away.

"You may get your wish, Diane. Dr. Banks has no motive to hurry and find a cure, so we'll—"

"It's not a cure! It's not like I have a disease!"

"Are you sure? I think it's affected your normal good judgment. As I was trying to say, I believe he wants to watch you and see what else happens before he uses the mutation on himself."

He might as well have slapped me, and in fact, my hand went to my cheek.

"Where did you come up with that? You're making him sound like Dr. Frankenstein."

Steven opened a drawer and took out a sandwich bag. "For all I know, he is. I don't believe a word that man says. He has no reason not to sit back and see what happens to you."

"But he's a *doctor*! He's sworn to help his patients."

"I hope you're right, Diane. For all our sakes."

He shoved his sandwich into the plastic bag and checked his cell phone. "I need to get to the office. I'll take this food with me—it'll be lunch *and* dinner. Don't wait up."

"Don't leave angry, please."

Suddenly the idea of being left alone terrified me. I went to him for a hug, grateful no shards of pain stopped me.

He kissed the top of my head. "I'm not angry. Just out of my mind with worry and trying to deal with something so far out of my experience that I don't know what to do."

"We'll figure it out."

"Right. We will."

Did either of us really believe that?

Chapter Fourteen
"Hello, Stranger"

I stood on the front porch and watched the silver Lexus disappear down the street. Then I phoned Maura.

"Steven and I had a big fight," I told her, and before I could continue, I realized there were voices murmuring in the background. "Oh, you're in a meeting. I didn't mean to interrupt."

"It's fine, hon. I'm in Gardner's conference room but they're not listening to me anyway." She lowered her voice. "They hired Sessions's kid and she thinks she knows how to stage an awards banquet. And maybe she does—after all, as she informed me, she's thrown birthday parties for her daughter for five years. Yeah, that's a lot like a dinner for a hundred adult VIPS."

"Maura, be careful! They'll hear you!"

"Nah, she and the comptroller are trading USC stories, since they both went there, about a hundred years apart. So what was the fight about?"

I poured it all out to her as concisely as I could: the scene in Dr. Banks's office, how Dr. Willis had practically stormed out, and how Steven talked about finding a "cure" for my rejuvenation, even though I wasn't certain I wanted to be "cured." It felt good to tell my side of the story to somebody who would understand.

Maura was silent for a moment, and a woman's muffled cackle filled the void. That would be George Sessions's daughter.

"I hate to side with Steven," Maura said at last, "because we never agree on anything, but this time, I think he's right. You do look years younger—and what woman our age wouldn't get a kick out of that? But you don't know how far this will go, and if that migraine you had at the florist's is a sample of the downside, Di, you're playing with fire."

Fire. Ouch. And she didn't even know about the latest "adverse consequence." But, damn it, Maura was supposed to take my side, no matter what! Why did she have to get all rational when I needed her to tell me I was right?

All I could think was that everyone seemed against me, and nobody was happy for the *good* changes I'd been experiencing. Nobody but me, and even I was less sure than I'd been that morning.

I made my fists unclench, but it wasn't easy. "We don't have many options yet, pal—not until I see Dr. Banks again. After that I'll have to decide—at least I hope I'll have something to decide about."

"Me, too, kiddo. Me too."

The other voices grew louder.

"I'm being summoned," Maura said. "*Now* they want my opinion. Talk later?"

"Sure thing."

"I'm worried about you, Di."

"I know. I am, too."

* * *

I hung up, even more alone and uncertain. The only one not telling me what to do was Elsa, who lay on the kitchen floor, chin on paws, dark eyes tracking my every move.

I got up and fetched her leash from a hook by the back door. "Okay, big girl, let's get some exercise."

There was nothing else I could do. Nothing except wait and see what Dr. Banks found.

Elsa didn't want to go far, and no wonder. I'd tested the sunbaked pavement before we started out to be sure it wouldn't burn her feet, but the heat bore down on us whenever we left the shelter of oaks and jacarandas that lined our streets. My dog was panting, and I was working up a sweat by the time we got home, but our brief walk had done nothing to quell my itchy restlessness.

A lonely afternoon and evening stretched ahead as I glared at my useless reflection in the hallway mirror. Nick had finished filming and was between jobs, so he'd replaced me as Maddie's caregiver after school. Steven, working late, didn't need me, either. And despite the newly youthful glow to my skin, I looked frumpy and old-fashioned.

Stop feeling sorry for yourself, I told my reflection. Instead of enjoying the rejuvenation's good effects, now I was focusing on the bad ones, the uncertainty and worry. No amount of improved skin tone or revived hair color could counteract that.

"Snap out of it," I muttered as I turned away from the mirror. A lock of hair poked me in the eye, and I yanked it away, overcome by a sudden urge to get out my scissors and chop away. Like that would do any good.

Instead, I phoned my usual hair salon and finally caught a break— Becca, my favorite stylist, was working that afternoon and even had an opening in less than an hour. Things were looking up.

"Don't let vanity cloud your common sense," Steven had warned me. Even Maura had accused me of giving appearance priority over everything else. Was I really that superficial? Did I think a silly haircut would solve my problems this time? Maybe not, but it sure might cheer me up.

* * *

Becca, like a lot of others who hadn't seen me in a few weeks, did a double take when I walked in. She didn't ask questions, but curiosity was written all over her face. Becca was in her early forties, and she had two teenage daughters—which kept her on her toes and in touch with the latest fashions and hairstyles. She'd been cutting my hair for so long that once upon a time she'd been able to pluck out the gray, but we'd given up on that long ago.

Now she inspected my roots and clicked her tongue. "If you've been stepping out on me, they did a great job. This looks natural."

"It is," I replied.

"And how did you manage this miracle?"

I gave Becca an abbreviated version of the mutation explanation, and she accepted it without much discussion. That was one of the many things I liked about her, plus the fact that I knew she wouldn't gossip. Becca had more secrets inside her head than any other ten people.

"So," she said, lifting a lock of my once-again auburn hair, "what are we thinking here? Want to switch things up a bit?"

When I first came to Becca, I'd worn my hair in longish wavy layers, just grazing my shoulders, which I could pull into a ponytail when it got messy. As I climbed the corporate ladder at Gardner, we'd transitioned to a chin-length page boy and kept it that way, but now it appeared lumpy and dowdy.

"Let's do it," I said. "Work your magic."

She did. I doubted I'd be able to replicate the look, although Becca assured me the style would practically fall into line on its own: shorter than the page boy, feathered at the sides and lifted at the crown. The new hairdo took even more years off my face, and I studied myself in the mirror, pleased with the result. *Hello, superficiality.* I refused to let that thought ruin my enjoyment.

"You're a genius," I told Becca, and she grinned.

I left her a heftier tip than usual and strutted into the still-warm afternoon, ready to take on the world again. The thought of Wayward Vine floated in. What would Jordy think of my new look? I hesitated for a moment before backing out of the parking space, then decided that would have been the ultimate act of foolishness.

I drove home to Elsa, feeling very virtuous. And glamourous.

* * *

Steven came in a little after nine, appearing worn out and discouraged. He dropped his briefcase and heaved a sigh. Then he looked at me. Twice.

"Hello, Stranger," he said as he kissed me. "Where'd you put my wife?"

Since he'd seemingly gotten over our earlier disagreement, I pushed the memory aside and kissed him back, longer and deeper than my usual greeting. "I sent her on vacation."

His arms closed around me, pulling me close. "Let's hope she's having fun."

"Not as much as we're about to have," I said. "Right here in the kitchen."

Steven stared at me as I peeled off my t-shirt and jeans, and his expression shifted from eager curiosity to something close to fear.

"What?" I said as I went to work on his shirt buttons.

"It's… unnerving."

"Unnerving how?"

"Your appetites, Diane. Frankly, I'm not sure I can keep up with them."

What the hell? Our fragile truce shattered.

"My *appetites?*"

"You've become a different person."

My desire for him evaporated in a puff of anger.

"I should think that would turn you on, Steven. It certainly did at one time."

Flooded with angry humiliation, I grabbed my clothes and stomped upstairs.

With nothing better to do and no outlet for my hurt feelings, I washed my face and studied my reflection in the bathroom mirror. Yes, I looked good with the new haircut, the smoother skin, but what use was it if I disgusted my husband?

Steven tapped on the half-open door as I was scrubbing my teeth.

"Diane, I'm sorry. But I'm confused by this whole thing, and I don't know how to act sometimes. I don't know how to *react* to you."

I spat a mouthful of toothpaste. "The way you always have."

He eased into the room. "That's what I'm struggling with. You've changed, and I haven't. And I'm beginning to wonder how long until you're dissatisfied with being married to an old man."

His confession dissolved my anger. Steven's shirt was half-unbuttoned, his chest firm as a younger man's, but even there the hair was graying. Was he an "old man?" No more than I was an old woman, but neither of us was young anymore, and I suddenly ached for our stupid, youthful innocence.

I put down my toothbrush and hugged him tight.

"You're not an old man, darling. And I will always love you. That hasn't changed, and it never will."

I meant my words at that moment, but deep down I wasn't completely sure I could keep that promise.

Chapter Fifteen
High Drama

The day before my appointment with Dr. Banks, his nurse Lucy Gervais phoned me.

"Dr. Banks won't be able to keep your appointment tomorrow."

Well, that's just great! Steven had moved two meetings around so he could come with me.

I took a breath before I replied. "That's disappointing. When *can* he see me?"

A heavy sigh on the other end of the line. "I don't know, Mrs. Devlin. Dr. Banks has become ill."

"Oh." The memory of his gaunt, shadowed face came back to me. "I hope it's not serious."

"I'm afraid it is." Her voice trembled. "He's had a stroke."

"Oh, no! Is he going to be all right?"

Out of old habit, I grabbed a notepad and pen to jot down what she told me.

"We don't know yet. We can only hope he'll recover—it's too soon to tell. But I know he'd want me to check on you and offer to get you an appointment with one of his associates."

"Dr. Willis?"

A long silence followed my question. How much did Lucy know?

She had to have access to Dr. Banks's file notes, so probably a lot. And she'd been in the office the day Dr. Willis stormed out, so maybe she knew what that was all about, too.

I pushed the pen tip into the soft white paper.

"I doubt that," Lucy said, drawing out the words like she was being careful of her choices. "But there are other doctors involved, and I can reach out to one of them."

I shuddered at the idea of starting over with another doctor. More tests, more questions, more examining me like I was some kind of lab specimen. *Damn it, Dr. Banks, couldn't you have picked a better time?*

Wait a minute—what was wrong with me? It wasn't like he did it on purpose. The man probably had a family—a wife, kids, maybe grandkids. No doubt they were frantic with worry about him, and here I was focusing only on what this meant for me. Since when did "me" become the most important word in my vocabulary?

Since this mutation kicked in, that's when. Since I found that hardly anyone understood what was happening—or had the faintest idea what *would* happen. Since I realized that I'm the only one watching out for *me*.

No, that was wrong. Steven was watching out for me, too. Steven —I needed to let him know tomorrow's appointment had been canceled. Maybe he could salvage his own calendar now.

I'd been doodling on the notepad while I talked with Lucy Gervais, and the tangled squiggles and swirls had come together in the shape of a tornado vortex, which pretty much captured what I was experiencing.

Could one of his "associates" explain to me what might happen if I let the rejuvenation continue? Somehow, I doubted it. We'd be back at the starting gate with no assurances I wouldn't keep getting younger and younger. It was fun so far, but not if I ended up even younger than Maddie. And what if some new physical calamity ambushed me, something worse than the migraines or the bone and muscle pain? Banks and Willis were on the verge of figuring all that out.

Dr. Willis—maybe I could reach out to him. Maybe he would get on board again, since he and Steven and I agreed that patents and marketing were not our top priorities. Maybe he could help me sort through the confusion, help me figure out the risks of letting the rejuvenation continue, at least a little while longer. Maybe he could help me convince Steven—and myself—that it was safe, or even discover a way to stop it, if I had to.

Lucy was still on the phone with me; I could hear her breathing and realized I hadn't responded to her offer of getting one of Dr. Banks's colleagues involved.

"That won't be necessary, Lucy, but thank you. Please let me know how Dr. Banks is doing. I hope he recovers."

After we disconnected, I shuffled through the folder Dr. Willis had given me and finally found his business card. I'd try reaching him, I decided, before I told Steven what had happened. That way I might have something positive to share.

I tapped out Willis's number, and the woman who answered peppered me with questions in a harsh, officious voice—my birthdate, my name, my phone number. I heard the click of computer keys as I responded. After a silence so long I thought we'd been disconnected, she said, "You're not a patient of Dr. Willis's."

I fought the urge to fire back, "I could have told you that."

Instead, I snapped off the tip of the pencil I was holding. "No, but he's been consulting with Dr. Banks about my case, and I need to talk with him as soon as possible."

"Dr. Willis is at a conference in Boston. He won't be back until next week."

"Next week! Is there a way I can talk with him before then? I just learned that Dr. Banks is seriously ill, and Dr. Willis is the only one who can help with my... condition. Can I call his cell phone?"

Another round of silence before she said, "He's the keynote speaker today, and I doubt he'll answer his phone. Give me your name and number, and I'll leave him a message that you called."

That was all I could get out of her, so I left my contact information and sat staring at the phone like it could explain what was happening. When the thing rang a minute later, I almost jumped out of my chair.

Maura's name popped up on the screen.

"Hi," she said, sounding a little winded. "Whatcha doing?"

Oh nothing, just staring into space and puzzling over my next move.

I filled her in on Dr. Banks's stroke and Dr. Willis's disappearing act.

She whistled softly into the phone. "Good grief, Di. Now what?"

"I don't know. Maybe Willis will call back. If he doesn't…"

"If he doesn't, you call your own doctor, okay? It sounds like those two jokers don't know what they're doing anyway." She sent a ladylike snort over the phone. "But you're okay, right? No more scary stuff going on?"

I didn't want to lie, but this was not the time to describe more of the "scary stuff." I chose to not answer her directly.

"This whole thing is so complicated. I know it's too good to be true, and I should be trying to find a way to stop it, like everybody wants me to do, but Maura—I feel so good most of the time. And I can't help thinking, maybe Dr. Banks's stroke is a kind of sign, to leave things alone and just let it happen."

"Diane. This is me, your friend. And I need to remind you that denial is not a river in Egypt. There's been some bad stuff happening to you, I saw that for myself. And I bet there's more that you haven't told me because you don't want to think about it."

Oh, dear God, she knew me so well.

"Well, maybe a couple of—"

"I thought so! You don't know what else might be going on, and you sure as hell don't know if you'll keep getting younger and younger and…"

"Why does everybody keep saying that? Maybe it will stop on its own, and I'll be fine, still me, only better."

"And maybe I'll sprout wings and fly to France."

"Ha."

"Honestly, hon, I'm happy for you, for the good part. But the other stuff worries me. And Steven. As it would anyone who cares about you."

"I know. And I'm grateful, even if I don't always act like it. But you didn't call to hear me whine. What's up?"

"Oh, yeah. Well maybe this isn't such a good time for it… but you could probably use a distraction anyway. This is last-minute, and I know it sounds crazy, but a few days ago Robert called and invited me to the Taper tonight with another couple, old friends of his. Now one of them has the flu, and we have these extra tickets, and I was hoping you and Steven would come with. The play's supposed to be a winner, and—"

She was talking so fast that at first, I thought I'd mis-heard her.

"Wait. Slow down. Robert? Paris Robert?"

"I said it sounds crazy. I was gonna tell you about him calling, but… I could hear *that* tone of voice, and I didn't want a lecture."

"I see. It's okay for you to lecture me about my life, but it doesn't work the other way?"

"Di, please. Let me finish. He sounded so mournful when he called, said he missed me, he realized he'd been an asshole, but he'd been afraid he was doing a lousy job of showing Paris to me so he got all uptight and took it out on me. He wants a chance to make it right."

"And you bought it?"

"I did. Di, let's face it—at my age, the field is narrow, and he's handsome and rich and sexy. I know I'm being stupid, but it was so good between us until Paris."

"What happened to Neil?"

"Ah, Neil. He's really sweet, and I like him a lot—but he's so *young*. I don't mean just in years, but in the way he sees things. We don't like the same books, the same music, the same movies. Besides, he works nights so much of the time. And I got tired of getting double takes when we went out together; I was always waiting for someone to ask about me and my son."

"Since when do you care about what other people think?"

"Since I turned sixty and started seeing my mom's face in the mirror, Di. Something you used to complain about. Anyway, please come with us. The play sounds interesting… and I could use the moral support. And your take on whether there's any hope for Robert. I'm counting on you to be honest with me."

I'd seen a review of the Taper play in the *Times*—it did sound good, about a widow trying to pull her life back together when she meets and starts dating a widower whose wife died of the same thing her husband did. Despite the grim premise, the reviewer claimed that the play had its funny moments along with the drama.

"I'd love to do that," I told Maura.

"But?"

"But nothing. I'd love to. Let me call Steven and make sure he doesn't have a late meeting tonight."

Steven hated spur-of-the moment get-togethers, but at that point I didn't care. I really did need something to divert me from the worry and confusion about Dr. Banks, and about where I could—or even if I should—get help, or at least some good counsel, about my body turning back the clock. And I was dying to meet Robert and see what kind of mind game he might be playing on my best friend.

I phoned Steven and first told him about Dr. Banks.

"Damn," he said. "Now what?"

I filled him in on my plan to reach Dr. Willis and my hope he might be willing to step in.

"I hope so," Steven said. "Because if you have another episode like last week—"

"If he doesn't get in touch, I'll call Dr. Dennis, okay? I promise."

"Fair enough. I'll hold you to that."

"I know you will. Meanwhile, Maura invited us to the theater tonight with her friend Robert. The play sounds good. I know it's last-minute, but can you go?"

Steven had an irritating habit of saying "yes" to something he really didn't want to do, and then his reluctance showed up in sneaky ways. I braced myself.

After an eon of silence, he asked, "Who's this Robert? What's the play about?"

Steven didn't know about Maura's history with Robert; since he'd never warmed to my girlfriend's many charms, I rarely shared her romantic misadventures with him.

"He's an old friend of hers," I replied and then tried to describe the play from the little I knew. I heard myself rambling and stopped.

"If you don't want to go, just say so, Steven. I'll ask Jeff—or I'll go on my own."

"I didn't say I didn't want to, Diane. Give me a minute to adjust, will you? It's been hectic around here today, and this is the last thing I expected to have to think about."

I heard papers shuffling in the background and then a put-upon murmur.

"Sure," he said finally. "Why not? I can get out of here by six. It might do us both some good, take our minds off... things."

* * *

The minute we met up in front of the theater, Maura commented on my new hairstyle—which, as Becca promised, had practically fallen into shape on its own.

"You look *gorgeous*, Di."

"Thanks. I should've done this ages ago. That Becca knows what she's doing."

"And you gave her lots to work with, pal."

As we entered the lobby, Robert threw one admiring glance my way and turned his attention back to Maura, but that instant of appreciation sent an electric current through my whole body.

Robert must have had some connections at the Mark Taper Forum because our seats were second-row center—not that there's a bad seat in the place. The play started out sad, and sparks flew when the two principals met and began sharing stories of their loved ones' illnesses and deaths, but it *did* have its funny moments, too. I didn't recognize either actor, but Maura whispered she'd seen the woman in a TV miniseries earlier in the year. Both performers did a great job, pulling drama and humor and empathy from their lines effortlessly. Steven didn't appear as engaged as I was, but he didn't doze off and start to snore either.

As for me, I was completely absorbed in the play, and unlike other times when a wave of drowsiness threatened the minute the lights dimmed, I had never felt more alive.

Afterward, Robert invited us for a nightcap at an elegant-looking bar across the street. I was all for that because I hadn't had much of a chance to talk with him at intermission and wanted to see what kind of guy he *really* was. And when he mentioned they had terrific light appetizers he got my vote. There'd been no time for dinner before the play because Steven got held up last-minute, so he and I had shared a quick snack of cheese and crackers. It kept my stomach from growling during the play, but hunger pangs were arising.

Steven gave me a thin smile. "We can't stay long, though. I have to get up at the crack of dawn."

I loved him for making that effort, but once we sat down at a glossy black lacquered table, his contrary side surfaced.

I suggested that Robert order the appetizers, since he seemed familiar with the place. However, Steven insisted on studying the menu first; then he wrinkled his nose.

"No octopus," he said.

Maura chuckled. "How about some chicken strips and fries then, Steven?"

He glared at her.

Robert may have felt he was hanging out with peasants, but he ordered fried mozzarella sticks and shrimp satay—both winners in my book.

The drinks arrived first, but the food wasn't far behind, and it *was* tasty. Maura and I clinked glasses and complimented Robert's choices. Even my husband seemed satisfied, although he didn't say much until Robert began praising the actors' performances.

Steven interrupted him. "It's not so hard. All they have to do is remember the words the playwright gave them."

"And deliver them with emotion and nuance," Maura protested.

Steven actually snorted. "Nuance. Please."

"Acting's not that easy," Robert said, his tone mild. "I tried it in college—I sucked."

Robert looked much like Maura had described him—tall and fit, with chiseled cheekbones, a tiny cleft in his chin, and blue eyes that truly sparkled. He clasped Maura's hand on the tabletop and gazed at her with obvious affection. So, maybe Paris *had* been an aberration; maybe he wasn't a villain after all. For Maura's sake, I hoped so.

"How about you, Steve?" Robert asked. "You ever give acting a try?"

I winced, because Steven usually bristled at being called "Steve."

My husband only smirked. "Not me. I'm not much for pretending."

"But when you're trying a case," I reminded him, "that's kind of a performance, isn't it?"

He patted the back of my hand the way he did with Maddie when she made a silly childish statement. "The stakes are a little higher, my dear."

I chose to ignore the condescending gesture and instead made a toast. "To the theater." We clinked glasses again and sipped. Maura and I had both chosen the house Pinot Noir, and its smooth fruity taste lingered on my tongue. I twirled my glass and admired the rich red color of the wine.

Maura seemed supremely content as she leaned against Robert. When had I ever seen that happy a smile on her face? *Good for you, Maura. Glad you gave him another chance.*

Steven, however, drummed his fingertips on the shiny black table-top. He'd been sipping his whiskey without enthusiasm, I noticed, and was probably more than ready to leave.

Maura had noticed Steven's obvious boredom, too, because she lifted her chin and asked, "So Steven—how's that juicy lawsuit coming along?"

The *Los Angeles Times* had run a brief story about Steven's copy-right infringement case. A photographer was suing a local artist for unfair use of a photo she'd taken, one that had won awards and received lots of press coverage. The artist had parodied the image, and when his painting appeared in a group show at the Museum of Contemporary Art, the photographer saw it and went ballistic. She had enough money to hire Steven's firm, and a reporter for the *Times* picked up the story. Steven cringed at seeing his name in the newspa-per, and when Maura read about it, she'd teased him about being a celebrity.

Steven cocked his head as if framing a reply to Maura's question. *Here we go*, I thought—*another dull, meandering story.*

"Don't bother asking," I said. "He won't give you any dirty details. He's a slave to confidentiality."

"Would you want *your* deepest secrets aired in front of strangers?" he retorted.

I shouldn't have snickered, but I did. "Besides, he mostly handles the boring part."

Maura tried to intervene. "Diane—"

I was on a roll, however. "You know, writing briefs full of complicated language that only another lawyer can understand."

"Is that what you think I do?" Steven asked.

Even the hurt on his face didn't deflect me, however. Fueled by wine, the urge to belittle him overtook me, baffling and mean, when the only thing he'd done was to mildly patronize me. Oh, and act like he was doing me some big favor by going for a drink with my friends. That was what really annoyed me, I realized. I wanted to get even, but I'd gone too far.

I glanced across the table. Maura and Robert were now sitting upright, and a worried frown had replaced Maura's relaxed smile.

Robert lifted his martini and took a healthy sip. "I've only needed a lawyer once," he said. "But you're right about the convoluted language! I needed someone to translate the contract when I bought my house."

He really was all right, I decided. He'd managed to shift the conversation without disparaging anyone.

Warm with gratitude, I asked, "And where is your house?"

He set his drink down. "Hancock Park."

Steven whistled softly. "Nice area."

We'd considered Hancock Park for our first home, too, but decided it was beyond our means even then. A historic and mostly affluent neighborhood just far enough from downtown Los Angeles, with a lot of mansions from the early twentieth century, it boasted its share of celebrity residents.

"It's turned into a real money pit, though," Robert added quickly. "You know the routine: replacing the plumbing, the roof, the windows. Updating the kitchen. Repainting." He held out his hands, palms up. "I'd have done better to knock it down and rebuild, but the city wouldn't let me. Besides, I like it having some history." He turned those blue eyes on me. "I understand you have a real estate background, Diane. I don't have to tell you about market value. Can you think of anything else I should do?"

"With the house? No—sounds like you've got it covered. Kitchen updates are a big factor in resale value. So are bathrooms."

Robert laughed. "Yeah, the bathroom is pretty pathetic, and there's just the one. But it does have a fabulous shower—you should see it! Somebody had it retiled, just gorgeous. Why they didn't go all in and do the rest, I'll never know."

Hmmm, I'd like to see that shower. I'd like to see that shower with you in it.

Good grief! Where did that come from? *Get a grip on yourself, Diane.*

I took a deep breath to steady my pulse. "You might consider adding a second bath. That's a big selling point. But are you planning to sell?"

"Not right away. But I keep my options open. If the right buyer came along… I hear stories about people knocking on doors, with briefcases full of cash. I should be so lucky."

He looked right at me, the way he had at Maura, as if we were the only two people in the world. As if he *wanted* me. And "sexy" didn't begin to describe him—those eyes, that mouth. Maura had said that sex with him was fantastic, and I believed her. I visualized Robert and me in that shower, naked, flesh wet with the spray and desire, him pressing me against the tile, his hands exploring, touching places Steven had never found. I was getting turned on just thinking about it, and from the way Robert looked at me, I imagined he was, too. *I bet he wouldn't complain about my "appetites." What a find, Maura.*

I went to clasp Maura's hand, but somehow, I grabbed Robert's instead. His flesh was warm and soft, and he didn't pull away, as if a connection flowed between us in those few heartbeats of touching him.

It took all my will power to release him, and I avoided looking at Maura, afraid of what I'd see. Robert let his hand rest on the table, inches from Maura's.

We shifted the conversation to current events, seizing harmless topics like the way the Los Angeles Dodgers were playing, and did they have a shot at the World Series. A cautious cordiality hovered over our words.

I bit back an impulse to interrupt Steven when he began one of his rambling baseball stories—he knew a fellow who'd served as a Major League team's substance abuse counselor a couple of decades earlier. Sometimes he'd fumble for a word, and I wanted to jump in and supply it, but I didn't.

I did notice Maura's eyes on me now and then as I drank my wine and let the three of them talk for the most part.

Our glasses and plates empty, we stood to leave, and Steven thanked them heartily for a pleasant evening. However, when I suggested we do it again sometime soon, no one whipped out their calendar.

* * *

On the way home, I leaned back in the plush leather seat, feeling mellow and privileged.

"Thank you for tonight, Steven," I said. "I had a good time. I hope you did, too."

He kept his eyes on the road and didn't reply.

"Maura's friend seems nice."

Steven shifted in his seat. "Clearly you thought so."

Uh oh. "What does that mean?"

"And for the record, no, I did not have a good time, Diane." His hand banged the steering wheel. "I'm tired and I have to go to work early and write my boring briefs, and I did not enjoy watching you and Robert flirt like a couple of teenagers."

Ouch. I sat upright. "We were not flirting! Where did you get that silly idea?"

He still didn't look at me. "Never mind. I just want to go home and get some sleep so I can go back to my *boring* job in the morning. Someone has to pay the bills."

Double ouch. He might as well have slapped me. I felt tears gathering in my eyes and couldn't tell which emotion came through strongest: indignation or remorse.

We finished the trip in silence, and when we got home, I called out to Elsa to put a buffer between us. Normally she met us at the door from the garage, tail wagging with delight at having her pack reunited. But Elsa didn't come when I called her.

I found her on the service porch, tail between her legs and head lowered, and when I saw the puddle on the floor, I knew why.

"Elsa? What happened, girl?"

She whined and put her head down.

"What's going on?" Steven asked as he came up behind us.

I pointed to the puddle. "She hasn't done that since she was a puppy. And I took her out to pee before we left."

I crouched and put my arms around her, murmuring "It's okay, baby. We all have accidents. You're not in trouble."

She whimpered a little and then licked my face. Steven joined us on the floor and ran his hand along her back in long, soothing strokes. "That's my girl. Poor Elsa. I should have put in that dog door we talked about."

We had discussed it and decided against it because our neighborhood hosted all kinds of other creatures like skunks and possums that could use it as well.

"This weekend I'll check into the kind that only opens if she's wearing a transmitter," Steven said. "I thought about it and then forgot."

I squeezed his hand. "We've both had more than enough on our minds. It's okay. The floor's only vinyl. If you'll take her outside, I'll mop up the floor."

He rose and dusted his slacks. "It was probably just a one-time thing. But at her age, maybe she's having trouble controlling her bladder."

"We'll watch for it," I said, and crossed my fingers. "I hate it that she's getting old."

He hugged me. "Wish we could give her whatever you've got."

"Wouldn't that be nice? Give it to Elsa—and to you. So we could be young forever."

"Except…"

He didn't have to finish the sentence. We both knew what he would have said.

Except what about the kids? And Maddie? And an endless list of family and friends. We couldn't enjoy eternal youth if they weren't along for the ride. Besides, nobody knew how far back in time our bodies would go. Or if at some point they'd stop rejuvenating and start aging again. Really fast, to catch up.

Yes, I hated Elsa getting older, and I hated being at the center of a medical mystery. But at least Steven and I were on the same team again. I took slight comfort in that as I got out the mop and floor cleaner.

Chapter Sixteen
Nightmare

The smile on Dr. Dennis's face dissolved as soon as she saw me. "Good grief, Diane. You look even—"

"Younger. Yeah, I know."

She blinked, recovered her professional demeanor, clicked some keys on her computer, and squinted at the monitor. "According to Dr. St. Onge, you were talking to a specialist at Wallace Taylor."

"Right. Dr. Banks. Lewis Banks."

"I've heard of him." She rubbed her chin. "He hasn't sent me a report on his findings, though. I assume you asked him to?"

"I did. But he hasn't been very forthcoming."

As I told her what I'd learned since our last meeting—the mutation, the patent, and Dr. Banks's stroke—the incongruity of the situation overwhelmed me. There I was, sitting on her exam table, in a space so familiar to me, so *normal*, describing the way my life had become anything but normal.

Fear and confusion spilled over into my words, and I'm sure I sounded incoherent, probably stupid, because as I talked, I realized how deep into denial I'd fallen, how I'd ignored the flashing red warning signs because I wanted to feel younger and younger, to be freed from an aging body and all its failings. Yesterday, however, a triple-whammy had ambushed me, and I couldn't pretend any longer that I had nothing to fear from this rejuvenation.

* * *

I'd been alone except for Elsa when the aura came on. Crushing pain followed, although this time my vision didn't black out. Instead, my stomach cramped up in a wave of nausea. I barely made it to the bathroom in time to throw up, and every heave sent a fresh wave of agony into my throbbing temples. I slumped to the floor. Elsa sidled up, licked my face, and must have decided I wasn't playing; she whined softly and flopped down beside me. I stroked her back and tried to reassure her that I was okay, but I didn't fool either of us, because as the pain in my head receded, the long muscles in both legs contracted so sharply I screamed. Elsa stood, ears perked, ready to defend me from this new, invisible enemy. I leaned forward and tried to massage the tension out of those rock-hard muscles, every movement triggering a fresh reminder that the migraine hadn't completely released its grip on my head. All I needed was a new wave of agony in my bones, and I was absurdly grateful to be spared that much.

As soon as I could function, I phoned Dr. Dennis's office, and I must have sounded pretty whacked-out and pathetic, because the receptionist gave me a next-day appointment.

* * *

When I got to the end of my story, Dr. Dennis's neutral demeanor vanished.

"What have the specialists said about all this?" she asked.

"I told Dr. Willis about the muscle spasms, but he said they needed more information before he could figure it out. I was going to tell Dr. Banks about the rest of it, but then there was that big scene with Dr. Willis. I thought I'd get another chance with Banks, we had an appointment set up, but then…"

Dr. Dennis stroked the hummingbird pendant around her neck without speaking.

I went on. "...I don't think either of them gives a rat's ass about me and my problems anyway. Banks got what he wanted from me. And neither of them would discuss what might happen to me if I keep getting younger."

Her eyes widened. "That worries me, too. They have no theories?"

I shook my head. "Not as far as I know. And even if they did, I doubt they'd have told me. I think Banks wants to watch and see what happens—or he did, until the stroke."

I described my own research and my theory that CRISPR might be a way to stop the rejuvenation. At that point, I was ready to do whatever it took.

"But Banks didn't want to talk about CRISPR—said it wasn't an option in my case."

Dr. Dennis had been taking notes on the computer as I spoke. She stopped typing and turned to face me. "I've read about CRISPR. It has fascinating potential, but the guidelines for using it are strict. And it's not foolproof—it could cause changes in other genes, unintended consequences that might not show up until much later. Dr. Banks was right to be cautious."

"But he's *patented* the mutation, so he must have been going to use it for *something*! Can he just do that? Isn't that some kind of ethical conflict of interest?"

Dr. Dennis hesitated. "It's actually not that uncommon. You probably signed a release giving him the right to do it."

"I did, but I never dreamed this would happen! And now Banks has what he wants, and I'm nothing more than some kind of scientific experiment."

The furrows on Dr. Dennis's forehead deepened. "You're describing very unprofessional behavior. It's hard to believe someone as respected as Dr. Banks would treat a patient with that kind of heartless disregard."

"I'll probably never know, given the stroke and all. But if Dr. Willis would call me back, maybe he'd help me, especially now. I had more trust in him from the start."

"Perhaps. There should certainly be some options, since they've apparently extracted your mutation for study in the lab. I suppose, in theory, they could destroy *your* altered gene now—maybe with chemo-therapy."

"Like cancer?"

"Don't let the word scare you. I'm only speculating. This whole thing is way above my pay grade."

"I know—sorry. But I didn't know where else to go. I'm scared."

Dr. Dennis straightened her spine. "I know. You were right to come in. I wish I could promise that you don't need to be frightened, but I can't. All I can do is try to help get you some answers. First let's see if I can at least figure out what's causing all this pain."

She did some reflex tests, shined a piercing light into my eyes, ran her strong fingers up and down my neck, and asked me a ton of questions about my diet and exercise routine.

"I'm even more certain the migraines are coming from a hormone surge," she said. "The rejuvenation has kicked your estrogen into overdrive."

"That's what I think, too," I said. "I've been accused of acting like a teenager. And sometimes, I feel like one."

Dr. Dennis smiled. "How's your libido?"

I was probably blushing as I described my attraction to Maura's boyfriend, and Luke the librarian, and even my own son-in-law. When I described the humiliating scene with Steven, and how he'd complained about my "appetites," I was grateful she didn't laugh.

"Your hormones are definitely reviving," she said. "Let's run some other tests and see if we can confirm that."

"Do I need an MRI?"

She leaned forward. "Not unless you're eager to be stuck inside a tunnel with loud clanging all around you."

"Sorry," I said, "I just remember hearing about people with headaches having an MRI."

"Actually, they're not all that helpful to diagnose most headaches. At this stage I'd say no. Now, this bone pain: did you ever get 'growing pains' when you were a kid? Not everyone believes in them, but I had them myself, and I remember they hurt. Where did your bones seem to hurt?"

I showed her, and she palpated both legs.

"It only happened once?" she asked.

"So far."

"I don't detect anything, but I didn't expect to. I suppose, as your body rejuvenates, some of the bone you've lost in adulthood could be regenerating, too. Another less likely possibility, and I don't want to alarm you, but if it happens again, I'll want to rule out osteosarcoma."

"Bone cancer?"

She reached over and touched my shoulder. "It's treatable, Diane, and it doesn't sound like what's going on with you. But I want to go over all the possibilities. This is new ground for me, too; I've never had a patient with such a drastic genetic mutation."

"Lucky you."

"The muscle spasms could be related to something similar. Maybe your muscles are growing, and it's causing contractions. I honestly don't know. Let's start with some blood work, and then see where to go next."

I sighed. "More needles."

"I know. But to look at you, all I see is a fit, healthy woman—in her prime." She tapped my chest. "We need to find out what's going on inside."

"Okay. Meanwhile, is there any way you can find out what's happening with Dr. Banks? And maybe get Dr. Willis to phone you? He might respond to a fellow doctor."

"I can try."

I gave her Willis's contact information, and she ordered a prescription for a medication that might fend off more migraines. Then she showed me some exercises for the muscle spasms and recommended I keep tonic water on hand and told me it quelled her own episodes with a few sips.

* * *

That night when Steven came home, I kissed him hello and decided to get things out in the open. "I saw Dr. Dennis today."

He'd started to scan the mail which sat in a pile on the breakfast table, but my greeting grabbed his attention. Guilt gnawed at me: I hadn't even let the poor man change out of his suit and tie or pour himself a drink, but I wanted to get my confession over with.

He'd witnessed the bone pain, but he didn't know about anything else, and he was appalled that I hadn't told him before I took my worries to Dr. Dennis.

"I'm frightened for you, Diane," he said as he wrapped his arms around me. "Something is very wrong."

His embrace soothed my worries, even though I'd just added to his. I wasn't alone in this. His end-of-day stubble grazed my cheek as I inhaled what I thought of as his office scent: a mixture of paper, ink, and, inexplicably, leather. Behind us the oven cycled on, roasting our dinner of chicken and potatoes.

"I'm scared too," I told him. "But at least now Dr. Dennis is investigating whatever's going on."

He rubbed the back of his neck. "Those other two jokers… I can't believe how irresponsible they are."

"Maybe I'm wrong about Dr. Banks, but there's no way to find out right now. I did ask Dr. Dennis to try and reach Willis, though. I got a feeling during that last meeting that he had a theory about stopping this reverse aging, but he freaked out and left before I had a chance to ask him about it."

"If he does know something, then damn him for withholding it."

"He might not even know about Dr. Banks's stroke. I'm betting on Dr. Dennis at this point. Her I trust."

Steven kissed my forehead. "I'm losing faith in all doctors at this point."

I tugged at his necktie. "Don't. Now go change out of your work clothes while I fix you a drink. And maybe while dinner is cooking…"

I wiggled my eyebrows suggestively, but Steven didn't take the hint. Not that I expected him to, but I hadn't stopped hoping.

While he was changing, I poured two fingers of Crown Royal in a glass and dropped in an ice cube. Just the way he liked it. I thought I'd take it to him in the bedroom and make one more try at getting him in a romantic mood.

In the hallway, something made me pause and quiet my approach, and I was glad I did, because I caught sight of him in front of our mirrored closet doors; I was at an angle where he couldn't see me, fortunately, because my proud husband was standing in his briefs, sucking in his stomach, pulling up his shoulders, and lifting his chin—clearly trying to erase the effects of gravity and time. Seeing him like that nearly broke my heart.

I turned and tiptoed back to the kitchen, where I noisily busied myself with meal preparations.

* * *

We kept dinner conversation to other topics, like our kids. Jeff's negotiations with the television network had stalled, which he claimed was fairly common, but I was disappointed for him. Steven said he hoped Jeff might now find time to work on the adult novel he always wanted to write, and we had fun speculating about how many family secrets might be aired if that happened. Afterward, Steven helped me clean up and then tackled some work projects while I took Elsa for a stroll. He was still at his desk when we got back, so I washed my face and brushed my teeth, then read myself to sleep before Steven came to bed.

* * *

How did I get back in Dr. Dennis's exam room? She's holding a thick folder —my chart. I recognize it, but it's supposed to all be on the computer now. She pulls out a piece of paper. Her voice is so soft, I can barely hear her, my ears feel plugged, and she's talking fast.

"If you don't take your meds, you'll never recover," she says in a stern, angry way.

Why is she mad at me?

"I do take them," I protest.

"All of them? Are you sure? What did you forget?"

She looks at her watch; it's huge on her wrist, and I can see the hands flying around the dial, speeding up time.

"It's too late," she wails. "You forgot!"

I try to run away, but the exam room door won't open. I turn to ask for help, and Dr. Dennis is gone, but her accusation echoes as the walls dissolve, and I'm by the ocean, the waves lapping the shore. I let the water wash over my feet, and it's warm, not cold the way it should be, the way it always is.

There are snakes in the water, I realize, as one slithers close to my feet. I turn and try to run, to scream, but I can't. My voice is frozen, my feet are stuck in the wet sand, and the snakes swarm over my paralyzed feet.

Steven's there—where did he come from? It's Steven, but not Steven, it's someone else. I know him but can't place him—who is he? His skin begins to dissolve, and he melts into the sand, shreds of his skin sizzling over the snakes.

Again I hear Dr. Dennis, her voice stern and accusing. "You forgot your meds!"

* * *

I woke myself up yelling, "I forgot!" At least I thought I was yelling, and my heart thudded loud enough to wake the dead—but I hadn't disturbed my sleeping husband, apparently. As I forced air into my lungs, wisps of the dream rippled through my consciousness. Elsa stirred from her bed as I shuddered. The tendons in my neck burned, and my jaw ached.

"My meds!" I whispered as I yanked the covers aside.

I was halfway to the bathroom before I woke up enough to realize there were no medications I'd forgotten. I pulled open the mirrored door on the medicine cabinet, to be certain. The night light revealed only eye drops, antacids, Tylenol, and toothpaste. I hadn't even gotten around to picking up the prescription Dr. Dennis had ordered. Was that what I was supposed to have taken? I closed the cabinet and pressed my forehead to the smooth, cool glass.

Elsa had followed me to the bathroom and nudged my leg with her wet nose. I dropped to my knees and embraced her.

"What the hell was that all about?" I asked her. What medicine had I forgotten to take? Did it represent something else, something important I'd forgotten to do, or something I needed to do? What did it all mean, and what was up with the ocean, and the snakes?

Elsa had no answer, but her presence soothed me. My pulse slowed as I stroked her furry ears and let her lick my face, until finally I felt calm enough to try and get back to sleep.

Part of me yearned to wake Steven, to bask in his calm reassurance and get his take on what the dream meant. It had felt so real, and the panic was definitely real. It was as if my whole life depended on taking that medicine. What had I forgotten?

Elsa settled back on her bed beneath the window as I slipped under the covers and finally drifted to sleep again. When I woke the next morning, I felt none the worse for my nightmare. I yawned and stretched and enjoyed the sensation of my muscles coming awake. Nothing hurt as I got out of bed. I felt great, energized, ready to take on the day. How much longer could I enjoy this rejuvenation? The reality of its price tag hovered, along with fragments of the dream, but in the soft morning sunlight none of it seemed to matter as much.

Chapter Seventeen
Confessions

Memories of the nightmare haunted me in the days afterward, as I went about my routine chores and tried not to worry about what Dr. Dennis would—or wouldn't—find when the lab results came in, or what she might learn from Dr. Willis. Since Nick was still unemployed, I didn't have the distraction of caring for Maddie, and in all honesty, I'd begun to enjoy the freedom to do what I wanted, when I wanted. I even enjoyed housework; the vacuum didn't weigh me down as I hefted it along the stair treads, and I could stretch without a single twinge in my back as I dusted the top bookcase shelves.

Elsa was more clingy than usual, following me from room to room while I cleaned, always underfoot. I started calling her "Velcro Dog," but she didn't mind.

Steven phoned Wednesday afternoon to tell me that a last-minute client meeting had come up and would run through dinnertime. Since I had a free evening, I was about to call Maura and propose a night out, but the phone rang again. To my surprise, it was Nancy this time.

"Hi," she began, and something in her voice set off my mental alarm bells, especially when she asked if I was busy. She usually assumed that I wasn't.

"Not really," I said, expecting that something had come up with Maddie, and they needed Grandma's help.

"I'm leaving work now," she said. "Can I come over?"

"Of course. Is something wrong?"

"Sort of. But I don't want to talk about it over the phone. Don't worry, Maddie's fine. She and Nick are going horseback riding after school. It's something else. Something serious—that's why I want to talk to you."

* * *

Curiosity blossoming, I put on a pot of decaf coffee. Nancy and I almost never had alone time anymore, and although I was concerned about the reason for her visit, I looked forward to seeing her.

We'd been so close when she was a baby, my firstborn little miracle. By the time Jeff came along two years later, however, Nancy and Steven had bonded, and he had begun to spoil her past the point of reason. When Steven and I fought back then, which wasn't often, it usually involved how he let her have her way on *everything*. Nancy resented Jeff from the moment he came home from the hospital, and growing up, the two of them bickered constantly. Some of it was normal, I knew, but sometimes it went beyond that into vicious quarrels that made me feel like a referee at a boxing match. I tried to emphasize how lucky they were to be siblings—as only children, Steven and I both felt the lack of a close blood relative after our parents died.

* * *

Nancy arrived holding the strap on her handbag in a death grip; there were shadows under her eyes and a taut set to her mouth. Elsa greeted her with tail-wagging frenzy, and Nancy stopped to pet the dog, burying her face in Elsa's soft fur. Then she hugged me so tight I could barely breathe.

"How are you doing, Mom? You look great."

"I'm fine. But how about you? I was going to offer coffee, but maybe you'd rather have something stronger."

She hesitated, as if making a choice was too much for her.

"Sit down, darling. I'll pour us some chardonnay. It's almost happy hour anyway."

She didn't argue but took her old spot at the kitchen table, and Elsa settled at her feet.

"So," I began after we clinked glasses, "what's going on? I can see you're upset."

"I am," she began, and paused to take a drink of wine. "Nick's having an affair. Or he was anyway."

That was the last thing in the world I expected, although maybe I shouldn't have been surprised. Nick was a handsome guy, surrounded on the set by temptation every way he turned.

"When? Where?" I asked. "Are you sure?"

She traced a squiggly line in the condensation on her glass. "It was while he was on that shoot up north. I thought there was something weird the weekend Maddie and I went up to see him—there was this one actress who was awfully interested in him, and a couple of times they huddled together, like they were going over a scene, but the way she kept looking at him, so *worshipful,* and touching his arm... I don't know. And he didn't mind one bit, even with Maddie and me there. And I caught her glaring at me a couple of times, too. I teased Nick about it, and he got all uptight, said she was just a kid who wanted to succeed and was using him to learn the ropes. I could tell he was flattered by the attention. I've seen that before, especially the young actresses, they get a crush on him. Sometimes he'd joke about it. This time, though, he never once joked."

"But that doesn't mean—"

"No, but I started to wonder. And then when he came home on weekends, he was so preoccupied."

She went on to describe a pattern of behavior that was burned in my own memory, even after all these years. Unexplained absences, hushed phone calls that ended when Nancy came in the room, a vague distractedness. *Oh, dear God—history repeats itself, doesn't it?*

"Then when the shoot ended and he came home, he didn't act all that eager to go back to work," she went on. "I don't think he even bugged his agent to find something. He seemed to enjoy just hanging out with Maddie, but then he'd have some kind of meeting, and at first I thought maybe it was about a new role, but when he got back, he was... different. Like his mind was somewhere else. And he didn't... he never wanted to make love—that's not Nick."

She blushed, and I reached over and clasped her hand.

"He started tackling some repair jobs around the house, stuff he'd let go for ages. Almost like he was trying to compensate for something."

"So you confronted him?"

She nodded. "You guessed it—I did. Last night. Mom, I was so scared. Scared he'd lie to me, scared he'd confess."

"And?" I knew what was coming.

"He admitted it, but he claims it's over. Said it was a big mistake, and he knew that right away, but there he was, far away, and this *woman* was throwing herself at him. And he's only human, right? *Only*? Like that makes it okay."

"The lamest excuse ever," I agreed. "He told you it's over—with the actress?"

"He did. He wants us to try and put it behind us, but I don't think I can."

She started to cry, and so did I. Her tears were a knife in my heart, and I wanted to grab Nick Ross with my newfound strength and shake him until his perfect white teeth fell out. *How dare you do this to my daughter?* I didn't have to imagine what she was experiencing; I knew firsthand.

I rose and fetched the wine bottle from the fridge, topped off both our glasses, then bent and kissed her cheek.

"I am so sorry, darling. So sorry."

She clutched my arm for a minute before she let me go.

"I have to divorce him, Mom. How can I be with him after something like that? But Maddie—this will devastate her. And how can I afford to live on my own? Nick brings in more money than you'd think, but I don't know how much of it I could count on in the divorce. And raising Maddie on my own… Mom, I'm *really* going to need your help now. More than ever."

And there it was. My immediate reaction--O*h no! Just when I'm starting to enjoy life again*—appalled me. This was my *family!* My own flesh and blood, in terrible pain.

But I couldn't let go of the dread of being tied down as Maddie's caretaker. I'd had a taste of freedom, and I liked it.

I sat down across from Nancy. "Before you make a rash decision, let's talk about it. You honestly don't believe you can forgive Nick? Not if he truly has ended the affair?"

"How could I? How could anyone? How could *you?* Not that you'd ever have to confront something this awful. Daddy would *never* cheat on you!"

There's no excuse for what I did next, although maybe I should have done it long before. Nancy had always—always—idealized her father, comparing every boy she dated to Steven, and every one of them fell short, until Nick. I suspected that even then, she held up a mental yardstick, and Nick would never match her notion of Steven as the Perfect Man.

"Don't be too sure," I said as I took a hefty swig of wine.

Nancy swiped the tears from her face, and I ached for her. Her cheeks were stained with blotches and mascara, her hazel eyes rimmed in red. I knew the searing pain of betrayal, and I had a horrible secret to share, but I also had one that might redeem this selfish act. Maybe, I thought, I still had something to teach my daughter.

I took another sip of wine and began.

"There's something you need to know about your father. I'm not saying this to destroy your image of what a fine man he is, but he is *not* perfect. And he strayed, too, in his day."

Nancy's eyebrows came together, and her mouth hung open, like she was trying to grasp a foreign language. "You're kidding me, right?"

I shook my head. "I know this will shock you, but it's not fair to Nick that you compare him to a myth."

The kitchen was silent except for the sound of Elsa breathing. Her fur grazed my ankle, and I leaned over to stroke her side.

Nancy was clearly trying to process what I'd said. "Mom, what are you saying? *Daddy* had an affair?"

I groped for the right way to explain as the refrigerator's compressor kicked on, filling the void with a low whine as I decided to begin at the beginning.

"It was very long ago. You and your brother were still children. And I was so caught up in being a mother—it was all I thought about. Your father was still making a name for himself at the firm, working long hours. We lived in separate worlds."

I paused for a sip of wine, and Nancy leaned forward.

"I get it," she said. "You two lost touch with each other."

"Yes. We did. And there was this woman at the office…"

Nancy's body tensed, and the knuckles of her hand holding the wine glass turned white. "I don't like where this is going."

"I'm sure you don't," I said. "It's an old familiar story, isn't it? Only that time it was *my* story."

"Daddy fell for her?"

"He did. Big time. At least at the start."

As I talked, the old outrage and hurt flooded me with a bitterness I'd never been able to totally put to rest. Steven's affair had happened decades before, but sometimes the pain was as sharp as yesterday. We'd been married seven years—Nancy was five, Jeff three, and I was constantly frazzled, trying to keep up with them. I felt as desirable as the Goodyear Blimp. In fairness to Steven, the bright young intern had practically seduced him. In fairness to me, that was a feeble excuse. I never met the girl, and it didn't last long, but those days had a nightmare quality: I'd phone the office at a time when he should have been there, and he wasn't. No Susie Chen to cover for him then, just a lot of unexplained absences. And when he did come home, there was something different about him, a sort of distractedness. If I hadn't been so busy with the kids, I probably would have noticed it sooner.

"How did you find out?" Nancy asked.

Her anguished expression tore at my heart, and I had to force the words out, but I made myself go on.

"The same way you did—I suspected. I confronted him. And I was every bit as terrified as you were. But it got him to confess."

Nancy gulped her wine. "What happened?"

I bit my lip and tried to let go of the anger. Tried, but didn't entirely succeed. "He ended it. I think he was ready to anyway, and realizing that I knew what was going on gave him the courage he needed."

My fear was that Steven would say, "Yes, I'm in love with her, and I'm leaving you." Instead he started to cry—and Steven almost never cried. Maybe he'd been hoping I'd call him out; maybe he was relieved. He apologized, broke it off, and told me the intern had taken a job at another law firm, so he wouldn't see her again. I believed him, and I never had reason to suspect him of being unfaithful again in all the years that followed.

"I can't believe it," Nancy said. "Daddy?"

"I know," I said. "It seems impossible. But it happened. You need to realize that your father and I were different people then. Younger, and probably stupider."

"What did you do?"

Because I loved Steven ferociously, because he was the father of our children, I forgave him. But I was never able to forget, or to completely banish the hurt of betrayal. The pain diminished over time, but every now and then, although I didn't want to, I'd imagine him with *her*, and it filled me with rage and sorrow and some other emotion I couldn't name.

However, I wasn't about to tell Nancy that.

"I forgave him because you and Jeff were so young, and I didn't want you to grow up without a father. I loved Steven very much—and still do. He was so distraught, and he swore he'd never make a mistake like that again. And as far as I know, he never did."

"As far as you know?"

"Darling, I'd stake my life on it. Really."

"I never had a clue about all that."

"Of course you didn't. You were a child."

She drained her glass. "You never told Jeff either?"

"Certainly not. And I wouldn't be telling you now, except to help you understand that I know what you're going through, and to show you that it's possible to get over something like this, even though it's a huge bump in your marriage."

"But you just let it go? Mom, that's… staggering."

I rose and opened the fridge. "I'm going to fix us a little something to eat," I told her as I took out a slab of pepper jack cheese and an apple. "That wine has gone right to my head, and I bet to yours too."

"It has," she agreed. "But I don't mind. It helps numb the pain."

While Nancy wiped her tear-stained face and blew her nose, I pulled a box of wheat crackers from the pantry and poured some on a plate, sliced the apple and cheese and brought our snack to the table. Nancy dove in like she was starving, and the poor girl probably was. I remember my own experience, how my appetite deserted me until everything was out in the open with Steven. Then I was ravenous, as if I could drown my angst in food. I refilled our wine glasses and left the bottle on the table; we might need the rest of it, I thought.

"You need to take a long look at your marriage," I told her between bites of apple. "Right now, you're angry, and you're hurt—you have every right to be. But ask yourself honestly—do you still love Nick?"

"Sure I do! Next to Maddie, he's been my whole world."

"Then you need to figure out if you love him enough to put this behind you. To forgive him."

"I'm not sure I can—if I can do what you did—just let it go."

"I know you're not—the hurt is too fresh. You need to take some time and really think about this—about what's best for you. And for Maddie."

"Maddie," Nancy whispered. "Yes. I have to consider her. And I know she'd say—'Don't make a big deal out of it. Get over yourself.'"

"She might surprise you. She loves *both* her parents."

"Yes. And she'd want them to stay together." Nancy chewed thoughtfully on a slice of cheese. "How did you do it, Mom?"

"It wasn't easy, and it didn't happen overnight. In fact, there are times to this day when I think about it and get upset all over again, only not as much, and not for long. It got easier over the years to put it behind me. Your father's a good man, and I do love him, in spite of that one mistake. That one big mistake."

"I can't imagine Daddy doing that."

"But he did. Men stray. It happens. More often than you might think."

"I can't simply pretend it didn't happen. Right now I feel so betrayed."

"That's natural. It will take time, and a lot of effort on your part— and Nick's. You can't wave a magic wand and erase what happened."

"I want to, though. And I want to hurt him, as much as he hurt me."

"That's only natural." I gripped her hand. "You're going to be all right, Nancy. No matter what."

"I wish I believed that."

"You will," I promised her. "You're a strong woman."

That earned a smile from her. "I wonder where I got that."

We munched our makeshift meal for a few minutes and chatted about other subjects, like Maddie's latest academic achievements and how she loved her art lessons. When Nancy mentioned an upcoming ballet recital, I considered using it as a chance to see if there'd been any more "incidents" with the girl in her class, or any other. Suddenly, I thought of something else.

"So, you suspected Nick's affair ever since you went to Monterey?" I asked as I washed an apple slice down with wine.

She frowned. "Yes. I kept trying to tell myself it was nuts, but when he came home weekends and acted so odd, I started to put two and two together."

"Do you think Maddie sensed it, too?"

"I doubt it. I certainly didn't say anything to her."

"But do you think Maddie may have picked up on the shift in your attitude?"

Her chin went up. "Why would you think that?"

I didn't want to point out the obvious. Always the clever girl, however, Nancy followed my train of thought.

"I see where you're going, Mom, and you're wrong. Don't you know me better than that? I've been very careful not to let Maddie think anything's going on. She worships Nick, and she's been so happy to have him back home. I'd never do anything to burst her bubble."

"I'm sure you tried to hide your feelings… but you know that sometimes we convey meanings without being aware of it. And Maddie's very perceptive. I can't help but wonder if—"

"You can stop wondering, Mom! God! I can't believe you're bringing this up now, of all times! Maddie's fine, she has no idea anything's wrong, and even if she did, she'd come to me so we could talk about it."

"I'm sure she would. But if she *did* sense you and Nick are having trouble, she might be afraid to come out and ask."

"Did she say something to you?" Nancy demanded.

"No," I said.

"Well, there. If she was afraid to ask me, surely she'd have gone to you."

"You're right. I'm sorry—it was just a random thought. Sometimes children feel a general tension, maybe even unconsciously, and it can come out in ways they're not even aware of."

We didn't talk much more as we finished eating. I think both of us were afraid to. Nancy helped me clear the table afterward and then picked up her purse.

In a tense little voice I knew all too well, she said, "I should get home before they do. Thanks for letting me talk this out, Mom."

I didn't want her to leave like that. She'd come to me for help and instead I'd upset her even more. And I might have let my own selfish wants get in the way of offering her the help she really needed. Maybe, in her situation, divorcing Nick would be the right answer.

I hugged her as tight as she'd held me earlier. "I'm so sorry you're going through this. I wish I could make it better. But I can't. Just know that whatever happens, your father and I are there for you and Maddie. Always."

The furrows on her forehead softened. "Thanks, Mom. I may be a terrible parent, but—"

"You're not a terrible parent! I didn't bring that up to make you feel worse!"

"Right. Just like you told me about... about Daddy. To make me feel better?"

"I did it so you'd know it's possible to survive something like this."

"Right," she said again. The word oozed cynicism.

I kissed her goodbye, and I was the one feeling like a terrible parent.

* * *

Nancy phoned me the next day after work. I couldn't tell for sure over the telephone, but I thought she was still annoyed with me.

"I'm thinking it over, this thing with Nick" she told me. "I'm taking your advice and not making any decisions right away. I told him he's on serious probation until I can figure out whether or not I can forgive him. Meanwhile, if I catch him so much as looking at another woman, I'll file for divorce so fast his head will spin. And he knows it."

"What did he say to that?"

"Mostly he's really grateful I might—*might*—give him a second chance."

"He should be grateful," I said.

I heard her loud sigh, and I hurt for her. "It won't be easy," she said.

"Most worthwhile things come with a price, Nancy. I've learned that if nothing else."

"You're right, Mom. As usual."

Sarcasm came through loud and clear.

"And in all this commotion," she continued, "I almost forgot about our pool party."

"Good grief—so did I. Are you up to doing it?"

"If I don't, Maddie will know something's wrong, and I can't put it off. This may be our last warm weekend 'til next year."

Nancy had invited Steven and me, and our son Jeff, to a pool party that Saturday afternoon. I usually loved these family get-togethers, and I knew Maddie did as well.

"Your father's looking forward to seeing you and Maddie." I winced as soon as the words came out, because I was probably adding a load of guilt onto Nancy.

"Oh Jeez—have you told Daddy about Nick and me?" she asked.

"Not yet. But if you want me to, I will. I need to pick the right moment, though."

"I guess you should."

I could visualize her gnawing her lip.

"He already doesn't like Nick," she continued. "This might make it worse."

"I doubt that," I replied.

* * *

After Nancy's call, I started a shopping list, including the ingredients for Maddie's favorite peanut butter cookies. However, I was not looking forward to the party with as much anticipation as I had been. I knew there would be tension in the air between Nancy and Nick. Would I be able to control my own animosity? Despite my urging Nancy to think about giving him another chance, I seethed over what he'd done to my daughter. How dare he?

And when I told Steven...

It was certainly going to be an interesting afternoon.

Chapter Eighteen
Temptation Calls

"Diane? It's Robert—Robert Drake."

While I sifted through my mental list of contacts, the voice on the phone continued, "Maura's friend? We met last week at the theater."

Nancy's marital drama had chased most other thoughts from my mind, and I'd almost forgotten about the evening with Maura and Robert. Honestly, I kind of wanted to forget, since I'd embarrassed myself and hurt Steven that night.

"Yes—hi, Robert." I said. "I had such a good time. Thank you again for inviting us."

I didn't know what else to say. Would it have been rude to ask why he was calling?

"I hope I haven't caught you at a bad time, because I have a favor to ask."

My purse hung from my shoulder, and I'd been reaching for my car key when the call came in. I wanted to get my grocery shopping done early.

"What's the favor?"

I heard a deep chuckle on his end. "You're very direct, Diane. I like that. This is a little awkward, but I need a woman's help, and since you and Maura are good friends, I thought... well, it's like this. I know I missed Maura's birthday last month—we weren't seeing each other then. And I'd like to get her something special, to make up for it."

"That's very thoughtful, Robert," I said. "I could make a couple of suggestions."

"Actually, I have a gift in mind. I saw some lovely earrings at DiMarco's."

Wow. Only the most expensive jewelry store in town. Robert *did* want to make up for being late with his gift.

"Sounds like a wonderful idea."

"Would you take a look at them? You know her taste better than I do."

I hesitated. DiMarco's was halfway across town, but I had nothing on my schedule until dinnertime. I hadn't yet told Steven about Nancy and Nick, but time was running out before the pool party. I planned to fix a special meal to put Steven in a good, relaxed mood before I broke the news.

"I suppose I could run by this morning," I said.

"Wonderful! Could you meet me there in an hour or so?"

"I was actually on my way to the grocery store, but I could meet you right after."

"The grocery store." A soft laugh. "Somehow the idea of you as the busy little housewife just doesn't fit with my image of you."

Was that a compliment? I didn't reply.

"How about this? We meet at DiMarco's at eleven, and after you've given me your verdict, I'll take you to lunch to show my appreciation."

"Not necessary," I said, although the idea did appeal to me.

"I insist. Besides, we didn't have much of a chance to get to know one another the other night."

Since I wanted a distraction from what I feared would be a big scene with Steven, I agreed to meet Robert and then hurried off to the supermarket, feeling nothing like a "busy little housewife." I usually didn't bother with makeup just for the market, so after I put the groceries away, I quickly applied eyeliner and mascara and changed out of my jeans and t-shirt into a pair of dark dress slacks and a pink sweater. After all, DiMarco's was a pretty swanky place.

* * *

Robert was emerging from an adorable blue two-seater Audi when I pulled into the jewelry store's parking lot. He smiled and waved and looked so casually elegant in dark blue jeans and a red polo shirt that I was glad I'd dressed up a bit. He clasped my hand and thanked me again for this little errand.

I pulled my hand away. "Not a problem. Anything for Maura."

He cocked his head. "You're a good friend to her."

Was he being ironic? It kind of felt that way.

The salesman at DiMarco's greeted him by name, and Robert put his arm around my waist when he introduced me as a "friend of the lady I'm buying those little baubles for." The man bowed his head as he took a box from the display case.

Oh, dear God, I thought when I saw the earrings: slender white gold hoops set with tiny diamonds—tiny, sparkly, perfect diamonds, at least to my untrained eye. They were exquisite. I wanted them. *Maura, you are damned lucky.*

"They're beautiful," I said to Robert and the salesman. "Maura would love them."

Robert picked up one of the earrings and held it beside my face. "Let's see how they'll look."

His hand grazed my cheek and lingered.

I let myself enjoy the sensation of his skin against mine for a few seconds before I stepped back. "My coloring is way different than Maura's."

The salesman was studying the display case instead of watching us.

Robert chuckled and returned the earring to its velvet box.

He motioned to the salesclerk. "Wrap them up, will you?"

The man bowed his head again, ever so slightly, and smiled. "Excellent choice, Mr. Drake. The lady will love them."

Robert took out his wallet—a slim, expensive-looking one. "At that price, she'd better."

"Robert," I said, "that's a very extravagant gift. I know Maura would be happy with something less... costly."

The clerk wet his lips. "If you're having second thoughts, I can show you some others that are priced more moderately."

Robert waved the suggestion away and handed the man his credit card. "No. I like these."

How casually he spent that kind of money—as if it were nothing. Steven's earnings were probably comparable to Robert's, but he'd never blow three thousand dollars on a set of earrings for me—not voluntarily. If I'd asked, he'd have done it, but not without some throat-clearing, and it was something I'd never consider anyway.

"It will be just a few minutes while we wrap them," the salesman said as he accepted Robert's credit card.

Robert pointed to the box. "Is there a price tag in there?"

The clerk appeared offended. "No. Our fine jewelry never—"

"Naturally," Robert said. "I just wondered."

Did he want Maura to see the price? I remembered her telling me about their Paris trip, and how he made sure she saw how much everything cost. *I guess people really don't change all that much.* None of my business, I decided.

While the earrings were being wrapped, Robert leaned against the glass display case and studied its contents. Then he nudged me. "See anything you like, Diane?"

I waved my hand over the display case. "I don't see anything I *don't* like."

"Steve doesn't take you jewelry shopping?"

"No, that's not his thing." I held up my left hand to show him my wedding ring. "Except for this. He picked it out himself."

Robert took my hand and studied the ring. His flesh was warm and soft as he ran his finger over the ring's surface. "Very classy. Steve has good taste."

He gazed at me so intensely that I think I blushed. There was something unreadable in those vivid blue eyes. I shivered.

The salesman approached, and I withdrew my hand and moved away.

"Here we are," the salesman said as he handed Robert a small silver bag with the DeMarco crest printed on it. "I know the lady will be delighted."

I half-expected Robert to say, "At that price, she'd better," again, but he only grinned and thanked the man for his help.

As we walked to our cars, Robert asked, "Where shall we go for lunch? You have a favorite place?"

Autumn sunlight, soft and golden, slanted across his face, and the air held a musky whiff of fallen leaves, a reminder of passing time and changing seasons. Over the last few years, autumn had brought a sense of urgency, of my time on earth running out.

We'd reached my car, and I clicked the remote to unlock it, then turned to him. "That's really not necessary, Robert. I was happy to help."

He moved so near to me that I could smell his after-shave—something as tempting as an ocean breeze. Even up close, he looked pretty good. How old was he, anyway? I thought of Steven, and how the sunlight had revealed patches of scalp through his thinning hair. Robert's dark-brown hair was still thick and shiny.

I had trouble breathing. My God, he was handsome. And he seemed as attracted to me as I was to him. How long had it been since a handsome man flirted with me? *Really* flirted?

What is wrong with you? He's Maura's! But oh, how good it felt to be desirable again. To be filled with that power, to attract a man. To have him seek me out, to see those admiring glances, the yearning in his eyes. I hadn't realized how much I'd missed feeling that alluring.

"I insist," Robert said. "Tell you what—there's a charming little Italian place around the corner. We can stroll over there, have some pasta and maybe a glass of wine? I'd like to know you better, Diane. You *are* Maura's best friend."

The way he said it, it made sense to let him take my arm and guide me toward the restaurant. Behind us, I heard my car chirp as the door re-locked itself, since I hadn't opened it. The sound was vaguely reproachful, or maybe I only imagined it.

* * *

The restaurant was small and not crowded, and the host here too greeted Robert by name. He seated us by a window, at a table set a bit away from the others, and Robert ordered wine for both of us after asking my preference ("red or white?"). The place smelled deliciously of simmering tomatoes and oregano, with a touch of garlic, and the menu was elegantly simple.

"Since you obviously are a regular, what do you recommend?" I asked Robert, and then let him order for both of us.

And although I tried feverishly to avoid comparing him to Steven, I couldn't help it. No pondering the menu, no muttering or changing his mind two or three times.

The wine came quickly, a delightful Pinot Grigio, crisp and cool. We clinked our long-stemmed crystal glasses as Robert said, "Here's to Maura. Happy belated birthday." I inhaled the wine's scent and took a sip, let it roll around in my mouth, then swallowed and closed my eyes for a second. When I opened them, Robert was staring at me.

"You like it?"

"Who wouldn't?" I replied.

"I thought you might."

The bread came next, and the salads Robert had chosen, and it was all delicious, including the *penne arrabiata* that followed.

After a couple of exploratory bites, Robert put down his fork and asked, "So how did you and Maura become such good friends?"

"College," I replied before taking another sip of that heavenly wine.

"Really?" His eyebrows went up. "You're the same age?"

I nodded. "I'm a year older. Maura skipped a grade in elementary school—she's that smart."

"You're kidding! Oh, not about Maura, I know how sharp she is. I just thought that… good Lord, Diane. You look so much *younger.*" He bit his lower lip. "Is that a bad thing to say?"

"No, it's not." I wasn't about to go into the whole mutation thing with someone I barely knew, so I tried to gloss over it. "But it's all smoke and mirrors, really. And a little makeup."

Robert shook his head.

I tried to shift the conversation. "And you? How did you and Maura meet?"

"She staged a client recognition event for my firm—a harbor

cruise. And you know Maura, she had to be there to make sure every-thing ran smoothly."

I laughed. "That sounds like her."

"Yes, it does. Anyway, we got to talking at the bar, and what can I say? Sparks flew. I asked her out. And… the rest is history."

"She seems very happy," I said.

"I hope so. I'm very fond of her."

Soothing sounds enveloped us: the gentle clink of silverware, the low murmur of conversations. I relaxed for the first time in ages, relieved not to be worrying about Nancy, Nick, and Maddie.

The waiter approached with an inquiring look, and Robert ordered more wine for us. He winked at me. "I should have ordered a bottle."

"And two straws. It's delicious, but I really shouldn't. I'm driving."

"I'll walk you around until you sober up," he said, and somehow he made "walk you around" sound suggestive, almost dirty.

He smiled and continued. "Tell me more about yourself, Diane. I see you as the most content woman I've ever met."

"Really? I suppose I am, although I didn't think life would lead me where I ended up."

Something in his manner, his obvious focus on me—or maybe it was the wine and the penne—made it easy for me to talk, to tell my life story. I tried to skim over the boring parts and confided something I rarely told anyone, especially a stranger—how I'd envisioned a career in journalism but found the job market too competitive.

"I can't imagine a beautiful woman like you having trouble getting hired, anywhere."

I felt like his eyes were devouring me. *I used to be beautiful.* But that, I reminded myself, had been ages ago.

"You're too kind, sir. So, you always flatter your lunch dates like this?"

I realized I'd tilted my head like some old-fashioned coquette.

"Only the ones who merit it."

I fought down an urge to grab his hand, to thank him for making me feel attractive again. Instead I leaned forward and sipped my water. The wine had really scattered my thoughts and inhibitions.

"Too bad you weren't the hiring editor, Robert. I might have tried to be more persuasive in my interview."

He grinned. "Oh, really? How so?"

I lifted my chin. "Oh, I think you have an idea of what I mean."

Another head-tilt. *Good Lord, Diane, get a grip on yourself.*

I took another drink of water. "Anyway, then I kind of drifted into real estate. Answered an ad in the paper for an office manager. And, I liked it well enough to pursue getting my license."

"And I bet you sold a lot of houses, now didn't you?"

I drew my index finger over the pattern in the tablecloth. "I had a decent track record. But those long hours and the weekend work began to get to me. And then I met Steven, and…"

"And the rest is history," Robert finished for me.

I suddenly felt diminished by the choices I'd made. Robert probably thought my life was boring.

"I'm not sorry how it turned out," I assured him. "It's just that I hadn't expected it to go that way. You know, settled down, raising kids, happily married."

"And are you? Happily married?"

I considered my answer for a few seconds. "Most of the time, yes, I am."

"And the rest of the time?"

"I don't think any two people get along one hundred percent."

Robert laughed, deep and loud. Then he toyed with his wine glass and stared at me again, with those penetrating eyes.

"If you ever want to move past happily married, Diane—forgive me, this is wildly inappropriate, but I'd be first in line. Seriously."

"Now *you're* being direct."

"It's the only way to get what you want. To ask. It's surprising how many people say yes."

"I suppose that's true. Well, thank you, Robert. I'm flattered. But no thank you."

My face may have been flaming red by then. And I really did want to say yes, because he was so handsome, so charming, so full of social grace. My whole body quivered with longing. I might never get another chance like this. I yearned to find out what Robert Drake would be like as a lover, and I already knew he'd be good. *Where's the harm? Who will ever know?*

I would know, that's who.

I looked away and tried to steady my thundering heartbeat. Robert watched me without saying anything. Did he have any notion of the war going on inside my head while the angel and the devil fought it out? Would he even care?

"Robert, I'd never betray a friend like Maura in the first place."

"Maura doesn't own me! We've only dated a few times."

"Enough time for you to buy her those earrings."

"That? Oh, you silly girl. That was just a pretext. To get to see you again."

"Again, I'm flattered, but—"

"Doesn't it bother you, Diane—to be married to a dried-up old man? Don't you ever want to experience passion again?"

"You're presuming I don't with Steven."

"Am I wrong?"

I couldn't answer.

We were finished with our penne by then, and I'd drunk a second glass of wine, but I knew I had to get out of there before I said, or did, something stupid. I wiped my mouth and smiled at him.

"This has been a lovely meal, Robert. Thank you. And now I need to be going."

His hand closed over my wrist, and the touch inflamed me. I wanted to seize his hand, to let him take me home with him, or anywhere, to let him undress me and kiss me like I'd never been kissed before, to make love to me with all the passion I'd been yearning for. I wanted to find out what that would be like, and I knew I could have him—all I had to do was give him a sign.

The waiter arrived with the check, and Robert tossed some bills on the table. "Keep the change," he said.

I stood and dusted my slacks. Could Robert hear my thundering heartbeat?

"Are you all right to drive?" Robert asked.

I nodded, but I must have seemed uncertain.

"I'll walk you to your car," he said, "and see for myself."

The walk was endless, and with every step I fought the over-whelming urge to turn to him, wrap my arms around him, and let him have his way with me. The scene played out in my head, and my whole body throbbed with longing. He could take me right there in the parking lot, in the back seat of my car, anywhere he wanted. I was ready for him, and he had to know it.

We were almost to my car when an old, ugly memory surged up, a reminder of how betrayed I'd felt over Steven's affair, as if the ground under my feet had given way, and I'd fallen in a sharp dark chasm of hurt. Then I remembered the anguish on Nancy's face when she told me her husband had been with another woman. There are no words to describe the depth of that pain. I would not inflict it on Steven, or on Maura, and I was pretty sure that both of them would find out, one way or another.

I clicked the remote to unlock my car, and this time I vowed to open the door before I could change my mind. I reached for the handle and then turned around.

"Robert, you've a very attractive man, and I'd be lying if I said I'm not tempted, but—"

His lips were on mine, soft and warm and delicious. He pressed me against the car. "Come home with me, Diane. No one will know. No one will care."

Oh God, how I wanted to say yes, even knowing how wrong it was, even despite my stern warnings to myself. I wanted to let Robert Drake carry me off to an afternoon of spectacular lovemaking, and it would only be that once, but I'd have the memory of it to treasure the rest of my life. It would feel *so good.*

I hadn't meant to, but I kissed him back, I parted my lips as his tongue gently flicked over them, I pulled him closer to me. I couldn't breathe. I couldn't think. I could only *want.*

The car door chirped again, and it was like a scream of distress.

I pushed Robert away.

"I can't," I said. "I've never been unfaithful to my husband, and I won't start now."

His eyes narrowed, and he leaned back, studying me. "You'll be sorry."

I pressed the remote one last time. "You're probably right," I said. "But it won't be the first time I've been sorry for something."

He stroked my hair and then, unexpectedly, he kissed my cheek. "My bad luck to meet up with the last ethical woman in Los Angeles."

"And probably the only one immune to your considerable charms."

He chuckled and stepped away from me as I opened the car door.

I smiled at him one last time. "Thank you for everything, Robert. I really am flattered. But please—Maura's a great woman. Be good to her."

He sent me a lopsided smirk and waved before he walked away.

Chapter Nineteen
Less Than Perfect

Elsa welcomed me home with her usual enthusiasm, although I thought I saw accusation in her dark eyes—my own guilty conscience, probably. I put down my purse, hugged the dog and leaned against the kitchen counter, bracing my hands on the cool, calm tile while I carried on an argument with myself.

I didn't do anything!

You almost did.

Almost doesn't count!

Yeah, but you wanted to, didn't you?

Who wouldn't, with someone that handsome coming on to me?

You shouldn't have gone to lunch in the first place. You should have known better.

And in some cultures, something like this is considered normal and human. France, for example.

I smiled; the irony wasn't lost on me.

And so it went, as I took my second shower of the day and started dinner preparations. As I peeled potatoes and carrots and browned the roast, I tried to put the scene with Robert out of my mind and focus on the conversation I planned to have with my husband about our daughter. I didn't entirely succeed, however. While I chopped an onion, I started to cry, and it wasn't the onion's fault.

* * *

Steven came in looking glum, dumped his briefcase in the office, and poured himself a drink.

"Tough day?" I asked as I kissed him hello.

"Vic DeWitt announced his retirement."

And there went all my plans for how the evening would go.

"Oh, no. I'm so sorry."

Victor had mentored Steven as a new hire, and Steven worshipped the man. He got along fine with the other two partners, although he and I agreed that Teddy Royce was a lightweight who bought his way into the partnership, and Albert Jernigan had the personality of a dead mackerel.

Steven sank into his usual chair at the kitchen table and rubbed his face. I'd hardly ever seen him so sad.

"With his illness and all, I suppose it's not a huge surprise, though. Right?"

I was trying to make it better, to slide past it so we could talk about Nancy, but Steven wasn't ready to let go.

"To me it is. Once he finishes chemotherapy, I assumed he'd come back to work full time. But he's decided that when treatment's over he's going to spend more time with Alice and the rest of his family, maybe sail his boat around the world."

I opened the oven door and checked the roast. Our dinner, at least, was going according to plan.

"He's entitled to do that, isn't he? Besides, he's been MIA a lot this year. It's time he made it official."

Steven scowled at me. "The man has cancer, Diane. But despite that, he's been working from home as much as he's able, and he's tried to keep up his share of the load."

His tone of voice shattered my good intentions to try and put him in a relaxed mood before I told him about Nancy's marital crisis.

"Well, excuse me! From where I stand, you've been shouldering a big part of that load. At least I thought that's what all those extra nights and weekends at work were for."

He took a hefty pull on his Crown Royal. "What's that supposed to mean?"

"Nothing! Except you told me that unlawful discharge suit you took over from him was what burned up so many hours this summer. Or did I misunderstand?"

He walked away without responding, and I followed him to the bedroom where he was yanking off his tie.

Elsa had been dozing on her bed, but with both of us in the room she struggled upright and wagged her tail. I rubbed her ears and ran my hand along her back.

"Hey," I said, "You must be devastated about Victor. I'm so sorry."

His reflection glared at me from the mirror on the back of the closet door. "Are you? Since when do you care how I feel?"

"What are you talking about? Of course I care how you feel!"

Had he somehow sensed my near-miss with Robert? Not possible, I thought—unless someone saw us and said something to Steven. Unlikely, but I hadn't been paying attention to the few people around us. *And nothing happened! Oh sure—nothing except you kissing Robert like an oversexed teenager.*

"Not lately, Diane. You're so caught up in your own little world that you—"

Elsa slunk out of the room, but I couldn't have cooled the hostility we were radiating, not if my life depended on it.

"*My* little world? Excuse me—I thought it was *your* world, too. I thought you were as concerned as I am about this... this rejuvenation and what it might mean. But I'm not blind to other things going on with *our* family—things you've been too busy to notice."

Now, that was a low blow; after all, I'd only known for two days. But I was so mad at him by then that I didn't care.

Steven pulled off his shirt and hurled it in the laundry hamper. "Such as?"

I took a deep breath. "I'll tell you if you promise to calm down and not make a big deal of it. At least not yet."

The angry lines on his forehead deepened. "I can't promise anything until I know what you're talking about."

"Fine. It's about our daughter—your little princess."

He folded his arms and leaned again the wall. "Go on."

I told him, as succinctly as I could, given my annoyance with him, about Nick's affair and how Nancy was considering divorce. I watched his expression morph from anger to shock and then—or maybe I imagined this—a trace of shame. *Good. I'm not the only one feeling guilty now. Familiar story, Steven, isn't it?*

He clenched his fists when I finished. "That son of a bitch. I'd like to knock some sense into him. Or throw him in the trash where he belongs."

"Don't you dare! This isn't your fight, or mine," I said. "They're trying to work through it, and either of us getting involved will only make things worse. You have to promise me you'll behave tomorrow."

"Tomorrow? What's happening tomorrow?"

"Nancy's pool party. Don't tell me you forgot!"

Steven pursed his lips. "I most certainly did not forget. But shouldn't we cancel? In light of the situation?"

"We can't. Maddie would be heartbroken."

He rubbed his chin. "I suppose you're right."

"You know I'm right! And our only job tomorrow is to be there and act like nothing's wrong. It won't be easy, but we have to. Can you do that?"

Steven pressed his lips together, like he was biting back a nasty retort, but he must have lost the fight. "I for one am capable of putting my own feelings aside for the sake of the family. Can *you?*"

The question was so ridiculous I didn't bother to answer. I turned and went back downstairs to put our meal together. *Yes, Steven, I'm getting pretty damned good at putting my feelings aside for the sake of the family. You have no idea how good.*

We ate in a silence so tense I could barely swallow. Elsa didn't want her dinner, either, and she darted out the back door when I opened it.

Steven came up to me as I was loading the dishwasher. "Anyway," he said in a matter-of-fact voice, "the firm is throwing a retirement party for Vic. You don't have to go, but I do. They've asked me to say a few words, God knows why."

"Well of course they would! You're a wonderful speaker." The compliment slid out easily, because it was true, and I was relieved to have something kind to say to Steven. He *had* always been the go-to guy for speeches and toasts at company functions, and he was good at it. His reputation for delivering killer openings and closings at trial was untouchable.

He shrugged off the praise, however. "I don't know about that, but it will be sincere at least."

I touched his arm. "You'll do great. You always do. And certainly I want to go. I like Victor, too."

"The other partners and I are going in tomorrow to start work on the transition. No hike for us, I'm afraid."

Our hikes had become less regular anyway, and I suspected Steven's excuses were just that—ways to avoid seeing me outpace him on the climb. Sometimes I forgot to slow down until I was far ahead of him on the steeper part, because it was easier to follow my own momentum. But I honestly tried not to make him feel bad about falling behind.

"That's all right. There'll be other Saturdays. Just be home in time for Nancy's party."

He pointed a finger at me. "Don't lecture me, Diane. I'll be there. And yes, I'll behave. Even though I want to throttle that husband of hers."

Had he totally missed the irony of the situation? Or was he deliberately not recognizing it? I didn't know what I wanted from him—maybe a small acknowledgment that he had caused the same kind of grief for me that Nick was causing for Nancy. He didn't give it to me, however, and I began to wonder if he'd totally forgotten about his own affair with the intern. How could he? The possibility made me feel like a model of virtue. I'd been tempted, too, but I hadn't given in. I had, however, come mighty close.

* * *

I woke the next morning with a sensation that something was wrong, but as I stretched my strong, supple muscles, I pushed the notion away. Steven was already up and showering. As I got out of bed, I caught sight of my reflection in the mirror. Robert Drake had called me beautiful, but at that moment I thought I looked more guilty than beautiful. *Stop thinking about him!* I touched my toes, stretched my back and flexed my arm muscles. No aches or pains. *If only I could stay this way...*

After a quiet breakfast, with no mention of anything we'd discussed the evening before, Steven left for work. I took Elsa for a short walk and then baked Maddie's peanut butter cookies. Elsa tried to help, but once the kitchen heated up, I put her outside. The day was mild, and she settled on the patio in a shaft of sunlight that gilded her tawny fur. In that light, the white of her muzzle stood out, reminding me—as if I needed it—that she was getting old. Too soon. Far too soon.

While the cookies cooled, I went shopping. My one-piece bathing suit was getting saggy, and I hoped I could pick up a new one on sale; fall merchandise had mostly displaced summer gear. I considered asking Maura to come along, but I only had a couple of hours. With Maura, two hours wouldn't have been enough.

I struck gold at Indulgence, a small boutique on Honolulu Blvd. in Montrose, one of my favorite places when I needed something special. Beatrice, the genial, raven-haired store manager, always greeted me by name and remembered my preferences, which made it a pleasure to spend money there. When I explained what I wanted, she led me to the rack of bathing suits, all on sale. I fingered a shiny black one-piece, and Beatrice gently slapped my hand away.

"Honey, don't you go hiding that figure in something so drab!" She slid several suits aside and produced a nifty two-piece printed with palm trees against a band of crimson sunset. "Humor me," Beatrice said.

I tried it on, and it was stunning. It fit perfectly, as if it had been made for me.

I pirouetted in front of the full-length mirror. "It's beautiful!"

Beatrice adjusted the top's straps. "*You're* beautiful! And you must let me in on what you've been doing to get a body like that. New diet?"

I laughed. "Exercise mostly."

That was at least half true. With my renewed energy I'd been flooring it at the gym.

"It's worked miracles. If I wasn't so lazy..."

I patted her arm. "You look fine."

That wasn't quite true, but she smiled at the compliment anyway.

* * *

Laughter and the sound of splashing greeted us at Nancy's as we walked up the driveway and opened the gate into the backyard, which had been professionally landscaped by a fellow who was a fan of Nick's and had given them a good deal on the plants and hardscape. Clusters of scarlet carnations and white hydrangeas, intermingled with multi-colored ranunculus, nestled in raised planters surrounding the lawn and the fenced-off swimming pool, while sweet peas and red roses scented the air. Two slender palm trees waved their fronds from the far corners of the yard, and the pool sparkled a luminous turquoise in the afternoon light. A Southern California paradise.

Nick, Maddie and Jeff were already in the pool. Maddie sent up a spray of water as she waved to us.

"Grandma! Grandpa! Come in with us!"

Steven needed no urging. He loved to swim, especially in an immaculate pool like Nancy's. He'd worn his swim trunks under a t-shirt and baggy shorts, which he all but ripped off poolside.

"Remember what we talked about," I murmured to him.

He glared at me. "I'm not an imbecile, Diane."

My annoyance with him revived. I'd been about to make a funny comment like "Nice legs, Sailor," to try and forge a truce, but my good intentions dissolved. He'd left his shirt and shorts in an untidy heap on the pool deck, fueling my aggravation. I set down the tray of cookies, picked up his clothes, and made a show of folding them neatly and draping them over one of the lawn chairs.

Then I peeled off my sundress, suddenly conscious of the revealing two-piece I had on underneath. My discomfort turned to mild delight when I heard a chorus of wolf whistles from Jeff and Nick, however.

I looked toward Steven to see his reaction.

"Really, Diane?" He thrust out his lower lip.

"Is that all you can say?" I demanded as I gave his belly a soft poke. "More crunches," I added.

Steven ignored me and dove into the pool, surfacing with a sea-monster roar as he grabbed Maddie. She squealed and wrapped her arms around his neck.

"You're finally here," Nancy said from behind me.

I turned toward her, my anger at Steven coloring my reaction. "You sound disappointed."

"No," she replied, and turned back toward the house.

I picked up the cookies and followed her.

Nancy kept her back to me as she began rinsing a mountain of corn ears, rubbing the silk with so much focus that I had to raise my voice to ask how I could help. She startled at that, and an ear of corn tumbled to the floor.

I bent to retrieve it. "Sorry."

I handed the corn to her. She wrinkled her nose and tossed it in the wastebasket, which I would never have done.

"New swimsuit?" she asked. "I don't think I've seen it before."

"Yes," I said, "it is. Do you like it?"

Nancy turned back to the corn. "It's pretty."

After a brief silence, she asked, "Did you tell Daddy about Nick?"

"I did. He's furious, naturally. But I warned him to be on his good behavior, for Maddie's sake if nothing else."

"And what about you?"

"I'm angry, too. What mother wouldn't be? But if you're asking if *I'll* behave—sure I will. How could you think otherwise?"

She didn't respond as she cleaned the silk from another ear of corn.

I reminded myself to be kind. The scene with Robert haunted me and probably colored my interpretation of her words.

"Your father has a lot on his mind beside your marital troubles. One of the partners is retiring, and Steven has been taking up his slack. Far more than he should be."

She glanced at me over her shoulder. "Daddy works too hard. When are you going to persuade him to slow down?"

That's all you're worried about? I pulled a bottle of chardonnay from the fridge and poured myself a very full glass without asking. "When hell freezes over. He loves his work too much. Besides, he'd drive me crazy if he was home all the time."

Nancy shut off the water and glared at me. "That's a terrible thing to say."

She was right, but instead of an apology, what I said was, "Maybe, but it's true. I can just imagine him prowling the house, peeking out at the neighbors, asking me what they're up to."

"Daddy's not like that!"

"He would be if he didn't have work to distract him. He'd start some home improvement project and then realize he was in over his head and leave it unfinished."

"When did he ever do that?" she demanded.

"Remember the garage door?"

Three years ago, Steven had decided to replace the side door on our garage because it had warped so badly that both sunlight and rain seeped in. He'd ordered a new door and removed the old one before he discovered that hanging a door was far more complex than he'd anticipated. We lived with a plastic curtain over the opening for three weeks before he gave in and hired a professional to do the work.

"That's the only time," Nancy said with a little sniff. "He did plenty of other projects just fine."

True, and I tried to suppress my inner bitch.

"He needs his work," I said. "It's part of his identity. You of all people should understand that."

She picked up another ear of corn and focused on it for a minute, then dropped it in the sink and turned to me.

"Mom, more and more you're not acting like *you*. I know you enjoy getting younger, but you don't have to be so mean to everyone."

"Who am I being mean to?"

She didn't respond to that. Instead she shivered. "It's weird—you look like my sister, not my mom."

I sipped—no, I gulped—my wine. "That scares you?"

Nancy wiped a strand of hair from her forehead. "It worries me. You're the only one who's *not* worried about you."

"That's not true—I'm worried," I replied after another drink of chardonnay. "But I'm also enjoying parts of it. Anyone would."

She shot me a glare that said she didn't agree. "Have the doctors come up with any new information?"

I'd told her about Dr. Banks the other night, but with all the raw emotion running wild, she'd probably forgotten.

"Nope. Like I told you, the lead doctor had a stroke, and he won't be explaining much of anything for a while, poor guy."

"I can't believe he doesn't have someone working with him to take over the research though. That's not very responsible."

"He didn't expect to have a stroke, Nancy."

I didn't mean to snap, and she hadn't said anything that I hadn't thought myself, but I didn't like talking about the uncertainty I faced.

Nancy flinched at the "what's it to you, anyway?" undercurrent in my voice.

I tried to change the subject. "How's Maddie's horseback riding?"

She wrinkled her nose. "Oh, she's over the moon about it, and Nick is egging her on, encouraging her to go faster, to try jumping, all that stuff that gives me heart failure. But so far, she's done fine, and it's terrific they can spend some time together. He's missed out on so much of her growing up."

"And he's done nothing to make you suspect that he—"

She rolled her eyes. "No, Mom, he hasn't. And, naturally, Maddie is so much happier with her father around. To spend all her after-school time with family."

Her words hurt. Hadn't I been enough family for Maddie? I clutched my wineglass so tightly the stem almost snapped.

I started to form a curt response, but Nancy kept going. "I'm trying to keep up the happy family illusion, for Maddie's sake. And I need to stay civil anyhow. If we do break up, I'll need his financial help. Whether or not he's working, at least he has residuals coming in. Meanwhile I'm cutting back on expenses."

I resisted an impulse to point out the pile of sirloin steaks I'd seen in the fridge could easily have been switched for ground beef if she really wanted to cut back.

I reached for an apron in the pantry, but Nancy stopped me. "Go swim," she said. "Help Maddie keep the boys in line."

Fair enough. I drained my glass—not that there was much left—and set it on the counter.

Jeff, Maddie, Nick, and Steven were horsing around as I eased into the water, which was the perfect cross between warm and cool. The tang of chlorine filled my nostrils. The pool, shallow enough to stand at both ends, invited me in.

Jeff swam over and splashed water at me. "Hey, Moms. You feeling as good as you look?"

When I'd explained to Jeff what was happening to me, he didn't act as alarmed as Nancy—he even told me he thought there was a good story in there somewhere. But he did begin calling more frequently: "Just checking up on you, Moms," he'd say. "Don't want you going all wild on us now that you look like a supermodel."

I kissed his cheek. "I'm fine. Never better."

He seemed reassured. "Care for a friendly volleyball game?"

"Yeah, Diane," Nick called out from a few feet away, "You and me against the three of them?"

He was holding a ball about the same size as a regulation volley-ball, but it was bright red, and before I could answer he tossed it to me and pointed to two pool floats that lay opposite each other on the deck.

"Those mark the net," Nick said. He sounded so earnest I almost laughed. Was this silly game the only thing that concerned him?

"You can serve, Moms," Jeff called out, grabbing Maddie's hand and side-stroking to the other end of the pool. "Come on, Dad. Let's whup 'em."

"Good luck, suckers," I yelled as I raised the ball, stood on tiptoe and gave it a good whack.

"Whoa!" Jeff yelled. The ball hit the water in front of him with a mighty splash.

Steven seized the ball and launched it toward me, and I lobbed it into the air again. This time Jeff was ready and volleyed it back toward

Nick, whose palms connected with a loud slap, and back it went, toward Maddie this time. The water was almost to her shoulders, but she made a valiant leap, and down she and the ball went into the water.

Jeff helped her up and served the ball toward me, and when I returned it, I honestly didn't smack it that hard, but it flew up and over the imaginary net, almost bonking Steven in the head before it landed on the deck behind him. He shot me an annoyed glare, as if he thought I was deliberately trying to hit him.

"Come on, Steven," I called out. "Look alive!"

"Awesome, Grandma," Maddie squealed. "You've been practicing, huh?"

"Yeah, Grandma," echoed Jeff. "Awesome!"

Jeff served again, and this time Nick returned it. Then Steven slammed the ball at Nick. I may have been the only one aware of the rage behind that volley, and Nick barely reacted in time but sent it back to Jeff. *Careful, Steven—you promised.* I was too far away to remind him, though.

We volleyed back and forth until Maddie got a shot at returning the ball. It headed toward me, and I meant to fumble it for her sake, but somehow my right hand connected, and back it went toward Steven. He lunged for it but missed.

I noticed his chest heaving and tried to call a time-out, but they all ignored me. I did try to restrain my volleys, but I couldn't. Maybe I was more buzzed from the wine than I realized. I gave in to the pleasure of shooting the ball across the "net." My muscles uncoiled with each serve and volley, and I felt the same childish enthusiasm Maddie displayed. *Hey, this is fun!* My shoulder didn't catch or throb; my ligaments and cartilage glided in perfect synchrony. I didn't need wine to make me happy when I owned this pure, painless energy.

Steven's grimace told me he didn't share my delight, despite Maddie's gleeful shrieks. The game took on the tone of a grudge match. Jeff's competitive side surfaced, and Steven matched it with obvious determination to seize victory from Nick and me. He lunged and grunted like a deranged walrus. By then I was slamming the ball at him with way more force than necessary. Where did that anger come from? And why? Was it the recent reminder of how he'd cheated on me all those years ago? Was I mad at him for getting older? For not being as attractive as Robert Drake? For not desiring me the way he used to? I *wanted* to hurt him, and I felt as ashamed of that urge as I did over kissing Robert.

Jeff gave in first, and I think he did it for Maddie's sake because she wasn't getting much of a chance to play. Or maybe he was worried about his father, who had obviously over-exerted himself.

"Enough," Jeff said, clutching his chest in what I hoped was pretend distress. "You're too good for me, Moms. Maybe you should turn pro."

"Awww," Maddie whined. "I was just getting into it."

I swam over to her. "Give the grownups a rest, precious, and maybe we'll be good for another game. Meanwhile, let's see your back stroke."

She grinned and glided backward through the pool, moving swift and graceful like a sleek seal. A wave of pride washed over me. Pride and gratitude that this perfect little being was part of my bloodline. Maddie was the only family member who hadn't reacted to my getting younger. She seemed to accept it. From time to time I wondered if she did have concerns, but I didn't probe. Had Nancy told her anything? I doubted it.

* * *

Nick knew his way around a grill; the steaks were done perfectly, a pink medium-well, tender enough to slice easily. And perhaps he was an even better actor than I thought, or else he didn't understand how much trouble he was in—not only with Nancy, but also with Steven and me. I'd worked all afternoon at concealing my outrage. Except for a few times in the pool, Steven had too, or maybe he was also a good actor.

"Hey, Nance—you finally learned how to cook corn," Jeff said, gnawing away at a second golden cob, dripping with butter.

Nancy stuck her tongue out at him, and for an instant the years fell away and we were back in our first little house, with the two of them squabbling at the dinner table.

"Now, now," I said to Nancy, tilting my head toward Maddie. "Role model."

Nancy shrugged and bit into her steak, shooting one last glower at her brother. Ironic that her hateful glance was directed at Jeff, not Nick.

"We should do this more often," said Jeff.

"Oh sure," Nancy replied. "Like we have so much free time."

Jeff wagged his finger at her. "Scarcity mentality, Nance."

Nancy put down her fork with a clang. "Not all of us are rich enough to hire help, you know—Mr. Big Shot with his TV deal."

"You two, cut it out," I told them. "Act like grownups."

Steven cleared his throat. "So, the network came through after all? It's a go?"

"I think so," Jeff said. "I'll believe it when the check clears. I was waiting until I knew one hundred percent before I said anything."

Jeff's feeble excuse was no match for the hurt on Steven's face, and I felt equally excluded. *He could have said something, even if he wasn't sure.*

"I suppose that's wise," Steven replied; he looked down at his plate.

I knew that posture, that "pretend I don't give a damn" set of his shoulders.

"Well," I said, "I'm a bit angry you didn't tell us. Big news like that —and your sister knew? We could have brought champagne."

"Which is exactly what I didn't want, Moms. This thing is still wobbly—it could go south any time, and I didn't want you and Dad to get all excited and then be disappointed."

"I'm not a child, Jeffrey," Steven said. "I can deal with some disappointment."

"Yes," I said. "And you've handed out your share."

In the silence that followed, Nick murmured, "Ouch."

Nancy did shoot him a stormy look then. She stood and began clearing the table, even though Steven and Maddie still had food on their plates.

When I got up to help, Nancy motioned me to sit. "I can handle it."

"I know you can, but—"

Jeff rose and put a hand on my shoulder. "Let me make myself useful. You entertain the kid."

Maddie had watched the little family drama wide-eyed, and the anxious expression on her face melted my own annoyance with everyone else at the table.

"Maddie," I said, "tell me about horseback riding. What are you learning?"

Maddie glanced at her father as if asking permission. Since when did Nick control what she said? This "carefree" dinner party had produced even more irritants than I expected.

Nick handed Maddie his cell phone. "Why don't you show Grandma and Grandpa your video? Meanwhile I'll pour us grownups some after dinner drinks. Brandy, you two?"

Steven and I nodded.

Maddie's delight lifted my sagging spirits as she tapped the phone's screen and scrolled through several icons until she found what she wanted.

As she handed me the phone, I started to remove my glasses so I could see better. Then I realized I wasn't wearing them. When had that happened? When had I begun to see clearly without help?

On the cell phone's screen, Maddie sat astride a beautiful bay horse that looked as big as a house. She bounced easily on its back as the horse cantered around the ring. My heart fluttered when the huge animal flew over a hurdle, but Video Maddie seemed utterly at ease. Then she pulled back on the reins and the horse slowed and stopped. Video Maddie grinned and waved at the camera.

"That's Raleigh," my precious granddaughter announced, pride ringing in her voice. "He's my favorite."

"He's beautiful, Maddie," I told her. "And so are you."

Steven squinted at the phone's screen. "Is that safe? Jumping like that?"

"It is if you know what you're doing, Grandpa."

Steven scratched his chin. "And you clearly do, sweetheart. You like riding, don't you?"

"I love it! Someday maybe I can have my own horse, Daddy said. Maybe we can move to the country, on a ranch like Gramps's, and I can have a horse and a dog."

Nick's father, Ed Ross, owned and worked a sheep ranch in Wyoming. Maddie had only visited the ranch once, when she was six, but it had gripped her imagination ever since.

Nick came back with the brandy. "Big dreams, little girl," he said, ruffling her hair.

Nancy and Jeff still hadn't returned, so I got up and went to see if I could help.

As I entered the kitchen, I heard Nancy speaking to Jeff. "I don't care if she gets mad." Her voice was raised over the flow of water from the kitchen faucet and Jeff faced her with his arms crossed. "There's something bothering him, I can see it. And she doesn't even *care.*"

"Come off it, Sis. Dad can take care of himself."

"Sure, that's just like you. Take her side. Make excuses. Well, it's *wrong*, and the way she—"

"The way she what?" I demanded, since I was certain they were talking about me.

Nancy's chin went up, the picture of defiance I remembered from her childhood. "The way you've been acting, like you're enjoying what's happening to you, and that's all that matters."

Jeff put his hand on her arm. "Nance, you're not being fair."

Nancy pulled away. "*She's* the one not being fair. It's not fair to Daddy. Not fair to us."

"To you? How is this unfair to you?" I demanded.

Jeff looked like he wanted to melt into the floor.

"It's not fair for Maddie to have a grandmother who's acting like a teenager. Who looks twenty years younger than she ought to. Why are you going along with this? So you can dress like a college girl? You don't care about what Jeff and Daddy and I will do when—"

Jeff put his hand over her mouth. "Stop it, Nance. Just stop."

Nancy slapped his hand away.

I had a momentary flashback to when the two of them were children, fighting over a toy both wanted. Only now they were fighting over me.

"You kids cut it out! We *are* all adults, even if we don't act like it. And I'm sorry I'm causing all this distress, I truly am. But I didn't ask for this to happen, and there's nothing I can do about it, not yet. So how about letting me enjoy the good parts for a while? Do you know how long it's been since I woke up without my back hurting? Since I had the energy to climb a flight of stairs without having to stop for breath? Don't begrudge me that. Please."

"We don't," Jeff said. "We're just scared of what this means for you long-term."

"So am I," I replied. "So is your father. And we're doing all we can to find out. But the one person who has the answers can't communicate. There's another doctor who *may* be able to help, but I haven't been able to talk to him. I don't know how to reach him."

"Doesn't he belong to a medical board or something?" asked Jeff.

"He mostly teaches; I don't think he treats many patients."

"Where does he teach?" Nancy asked. "You could track him down that way."

"That's genius, Nance," Jeff said. "Find out when he's teaching and confront him!"

"That *is* smart, Nancy," I replied. "I'll check into that Monday."

"Sic 'em, Moms."

Jeff's earnestness dissolved the tension among us.

All three of us stepped back from the anger that had threatened to consume us.

"I'm sorry for what I said before, Mom," Nancy told me. "When I get scared, I get snippy. It's how I cope."

I hugged her tight. "Don't I know that better than anyone, darling? Now let's go have some brandy with Nick and your father."

* * *

Nick had taken the drinks outside and given Maddie the OK to go watch TV—one of his older movies was playing.

"G-rated Western," he explained with a smirk.

We sank into cushioned white wicker chairs, although Nancy claimed the seat between Steven and me, not next to Nick. No one offered up a toast as we sipped brandy in silence. Tension crackled in the soft evening air.

Nick lit a cigarette, and I felt a momentary longing for one myself. I'd quit smoking when I was pregnant with Nancy, but that urge still lurked somewhere in my subconscious. Instead I took a sip of brandy; it burned on the way down, enough to pull my thoughts away from nicotine.

Nancy gave Nick another annoyed glance as the smoke drifted toward her. She waved it away, and he got the message. After one more puff he put it out in the planter beside him.

Nancy frowned at him.

I didn't dare look at Steven. Two marriages on rocky ground— would either of them survive? My irritation with Steven hadn't ebbed over the evening, and Nancy defending him made me even angrier.

Nick wiped his mustache—which he'd let fill in once filming ended—and studied the sky, which was turning crimson and orange to the west. "This is why we live here, folks."

"Amen to that," Jeff agreed. "Another day in Paradise."

I caught Steven suppressing a yawn. Despite my earlier aggravation, I could sympathize; his workday had begun early, and had to have been stressful, preparing for Vic DeWitt's official departure. I drained my glass, stretched, and faked my own yawn.

"This has been delightful," I said, "but I think I've had too much fun. I'm exhausted. Will you kids excuse us?"

Nancy rose quickly. "Sure. It was nice of you to come. Maddie loves you both so much." She turned toward the house and the open patio doors. "Maddie! Grandma and Grandpa are leaving. Come say goodbye."

Maddie didn't come running the way she usually did, so I went in the house to tell her we were leaving. Her bedroom door was ajar, so I pushed my way in.

"Maddie, darling, your grandfather and I have—"

She was curled up on the bed, face buried in a pillow, and when she turned to me, her red, tear-streaked face alarmed me.

"Maddie! What's wrong?"

I sank onto the bed, and she clung to me like a drowning victim.

"Mommy and Daddy are getting a divorce! Like Emily's parents! I heard them talking last night, and... oh, Grandma, it will be awful! Emily's parents fight over her all the time. She thinks it's all her fault. It's not my fault, is it? I love them both. I don't want them to get a divorce."

I stroked her hair with one hand and wiped her cheeks with the other. "Oh, darling, I don't think that will happen. And none of this is your fault! Sometimes parents have disagreements about things you're not old enough to understand, but they would never—never ever—blame you for anything that goes wrong between them. I can't promise you they won't get a divorce, but whatever happens, they will always love you, more than anyone."

"Emily has to stay with her dad every other weekend," Maddie said between sobs. "And he has a girlfriend, and she's mean to Em."

"That's terrible! But don't worry. Neither your mother nor father would ever let that happen to you!"

"Don't they love each other anymore, Grandma?"

"Of course they do! And I know they're trying to work through this."

"But Emily—"

I hadn't heard Steven approach, but there he was in the room with us, and he must have overheard some of our conversation because he eased down on the bed next to me and kissed Maddie's damp, blotchy cheek.

"You are not Emily," he said gently. "And you have a secret weapon Emily doesn't have. Did you know that?"

Maddie turned her trusting blue gaze on him. "I do?"

"You bet you do! You have Grandma and Grandpa! And that means that no matter what happens, you will be safe, and you will be loved. I can't promise much else, but I can promise you that."

Maddie let go of me and grabbed hold of Steven, and I felt tears gather in my own eyes. How did he know the exact right thing to say? It didn't matter; he had eased Maddie's misery, and that was all I cared about. Maybe there was hope for all of us yet.

Maddie came back outside with us, and if the others noticed her tear-reddened eyes, they didn't say anything. I kissed Nancy goodbye and whispered that I was going to call her later. She gave me a puzzled look but didn't say anything.

My little blonde beauty stood between her parents and waved goodbye to us, and the sight of them was so deceptively perfect that I almost started to cry again. But I managed to keep myself under control. For once.

Chapter Twenty
Showdown

I phoned Nancy from the car on our way home.

"I realize you can't promise Maddie something that won't happen," I said, "but the child is devastated by the idea you and Nick are divorcing. You need to talk to her about it."

"And here I thought we'd been so good at concealing it from her," Nancy muttered.

"Children don't miss much. And the sooner you and Nick resolve this, the better it will be for Maddie."

"Don't try and push her into the wrong decision," Steven said.

I shushed him. "You just drive," I said.

He glared at me but turned his focus back on the road.

"I know that," Nancy replied. "What I don't know is whether I can snap my fingers and pretend this never happened."

"No, darling, you can't do that," I told her.

"Can't do what?" Steven demanded.

I pointed out the windshield and motioned him to focus on driving. "Can't pretend it didn't happen," I told him. "Now stop eaves-dropping."

We were home by then, so I disconnected after making Nancy promise that she and Nick would have a good long talk with Maddie and do their best to convince her that she would be fine, no matter what happened between them. I wasn't sure they'd succeed, but I had to let them try. It was out of my hands.

* * *

Monday afternoon, I was doing laundry when it hit me—a wave of searing pain like nothing I'd ever felt before. "Like my bones are on fire" was how I'd described it before, but that had only been in my legs. This time every bone in my body, from my skull to my toes, was burning.

I screamed and grabbed for the side of the laundry sink to break my fall as I crashed to the floor. From a distance, I heard Elsa's nails scrabble across the kitchen floor, then a thump, but I was in the grip of the worst agony I'd ever known and couldn't look to see what happened.

I don't know how long I lay there, gasping, before the pain released me, inch by inch. I gritted my teeth and hauled myself upright when I heard Elsa whining in the kitchen.

She lay on the floor, back legs splayed, but she lifted her head and licked my hand when I knelt beside her.

"What happened, baby? Did you fall?"

I forgot about everything else as I worked my hands around her body, helped her stand, and explored her legs. Nothing felt broken, but her shoulders were hunched, and she acted dazed.

"Can you walk, Elsa? Let's see."

I patted my leg and took a few steps back. She followed, moving more slowly than usual but not limping.

"You were running to rescue me, weren't you, Elsa?"

She wagged her tail.

"Good girl!"

I led her into the living room, and by then she was walking normally. She settled on her bed in the corner, where she'd probably been napping when she heard me scream. Then she'd run to see what was wrong and lost traction on the vinyl floor.

I stroked her back, grateful no permanent damage had been done. Such a good dog.

Traces of the bone pain lingered now that I turned my attention from Elsa, but it was bearable. Cautiously, I flexed my fingers and stretched my legs, and the movement didn't arouse a sleeping demon. But I knew it was there, waiting, and I didn't want to meet it a third time because I was fairly sure I wouldn't be able walk away again.

* * *

Dr. Dennis phoned later that afternoon. "All your blood tests are normal, Diane—and no cancer markers showed up."

She went over the details—an abbreviated version of the explanations I'd gotten from Drs. Banks and Willis. Nothing I didn't already know, or at least expect.

Boiling with exasperation, I described the burning pain I'd felt in my bones, which was only a bad memory by then.

"Do you want to come in and have me check it out?" she asked. "I can squeeze you in."

"What good would that do?" I heard the aggravation in my voice and winced.

"Probably none," she said mildly, "But I want to you to know I'm there for you. I'm on your side."

"I know. I didn't mean to bite your head off, but I'm scared. What other part of me is going to go haywire next?"

"I understand. That's a reasonable concern, and I wish I could help." I heard papers shuffling in the background as she continued. "I did speak with Dr. St. Onge, and he contacted Dr. Banks's office. He got some somber news—Dr. Banks's prognosis is not good. He isn't expected to regain consciousness any time soon, if ever. The stroke was massive, and devastating."

"So, there's no hope of finding out what he was going to tell me."

"I'm afraid not. But Charles—Dr. St. Onge—tried to find out if Dr. Banks was working with any colleagues on your case. No one in his office had any information, except they knew he and Dr. Willis had been collaborating on an age disruption study, but they had a major falling-out a short time ago."

"I knew about that," I said, and my aggravation returned. "You doctors and your secrets! I am so damned tired of the runaround."

She didn't speak for a moment, and immediately I regretted my outburst. This wasn't her fault, and I shouldn't have lumped her in with Banks and Willis. I was scared and confused, but that was no excuse for taking it out on her.

"Diane," she said at last, "I really am trying to help you. I tried to reach Dr. Willis, but he has one tough gatekeeper. At first, she wouldn't even tell me if he's in town, but I finally got her to confirm that he is. He is also a 'very busy man'—she must have said that five times. She claimed his teaching schedule is so heavy this term that he's not making any appointments except with students."

"Did you believe her?"

"I don't know. This whole thing is completely outside my experience. I asked Charles if he knew of any other specialists we could bring in, but he said in light of your diagnosis, Dr. Willis is probably our best bet. I did leave an urgent message with his office that I need to speak with him about your case, so let's cross our fingers that his conscience forces him to call me back."

Ashamed of the way I'd yelled at her, I tried to make up for it. "You really have gone above and beyond, Dr. Dennis. I know I don't sound like it, but I'm grateful. Honest. I just want someone to tell me, is this thing going to get worse? Is there a way to stop it? Do I have to give back what I've gained from the rejuvenation to keep from having more scary things happen?"

"I understand, Diane. I would feel the same way, and I am so frustrated I can't get answers for you. When—if—Dr. Willis returns my call, I'll let you know immediately, and we'll take it from there."

I thanked her again before I hung up. Dr. Dennis might be frustrated, but that was nothing compared what I felt. No answers, only more questions, and no one to answer them. If only I could talk to Dr. Willis. He was my only hope.

I decided to act on Nancy's brainstorm.

I booted up the computer, found Wallace Taylor University's

website, clicked on "Faculty," and entered Willis's name in the search box. The listing for Peter Y. Willis, M.D. detailed his impressive academic credentials. Then I went to the link for "Class Schedules." It took a little digging, but I found his name shown for five different classes, including one held Tuesday and Thursday mornings: Advanced Human Genomic Analysis Methods. Good grief, could they have added a few more syllables?

I printed the class listing and mapped out the best route to the university. My phone rang as I was planning what I'd say to Dr. Willis if I was able to find and confront him.

"What's up, Moms?"

Jeff's cheerful voice jolted me back to the present.

I explained what I'd been doing and that, thanks to his sister's suggestion, I had a lead on Dr. Willis and was going to try and catch him after class the next day.

"Fabulous. I'm going with you."

"That's sweet, but you really don't need to."

"I know I don't *need* to, Moms. I *want* to. Nance and I talked it over after you guys left, and we decided to get more involved in this thing. These doctors are letting our mom down, and we don't like it. So, no arguments. What time do I pick you up?"

* * *

I wore a businesslike gray flannel blazer and black gabardine trousers. Full-on make-up. And my stilettos. Maybe they didn't quite go with gray flannel, but they were comfortable *and* empowering.

Jeff grinned as he kissed me hello and opened the passenger door of his shiny black BMW. "You look ready to rock 'n' roll."

"You look pretty spiffy yourself," I replied. "And very professional."

He did—a soft suede jacket over a pale blue shirt, and navy-blue corduroy trousers.

I'd decided not to tell Steven about our exploit until we'd had a chance to talk with Dr. Willis. He might have insisted on coming along, and I didn't want father and son jockeying for dominance if a confrontation took place. The guilt I felt over keeping my plan from

Steven was balanced by the pleasure of some alone time with Jeff, despite the reason for our mission.

* * *

As Jeff eased us onto the southbound freeway, I recapped my plan to surprise Dr. Willis as his class was letting out just before noon. I didn't find his name on another class until two, so I'd have time to try and get him to discuss his ideas for disabling the mutation.

"The thing is," I confessed as Jeff shifted gears and moved to the fast lane, "I'm still conflicted. I *like* being younger." I hadn't told him about yesterday's bone pain; actually, since it left no traces, I'd almost forgotten about it. Almost.

"Who wouldn't? Heck, Moms, there are mornings when I'd give my right arm to jump out of bed with the energy I had in my twenties. We don't appreciate things like that at the time, do we?"

I checked the map on my phone; we had several miles to go until the transition to the eastbound freeway. "We sure don't, son."

There was little else to say on that subject, so I switched topics. "Have you heard anything else from the network?"

Jeff exhaled noisily, which I took as a sign of disgust. "Yeah, they want me to guarantee another five books before they'll agree to start production. Five books!"

"Is that a problem? You wrote the others so easily—from my perspective anyway."

"Yeah, well, the first three *were* easy, and fun, but these last two, Moms, they were a grind. I had them in my contract with the publisher, so I had to do 'em, but I'm running out of ideas. There's only so much an imaginary dog can do, you know."

"And if you don't agree?"

He took one hand off the steering wheel and ran it through his hair. "Then I guess I lose out on a shitload of money."

I patted his hand when he put it back on the wheel. "We're both facing some hard choices, aren't we?"

"We sure are—but yours are more critical than mine."

I tugged a lock of hair off my forehead. "Still… what will you do if you retire Defender Dog?"

That got a laugh out of him. "I've always wanted to write a *real* book—a grown-up novel. And I finally have the concept I want. I've even played around with a rough outline."

"That's wonderful! Can I confess something to you?"

He nodded. "Please do."

"I always felt you were… well, not exactly wasting your talent, but that you had more in you, something…"

I broke off because I didn't know how to phrase it.

"Something *relevant*?" Jeff finished for me.

"Defender Dog *is* relevant to children who love those books! No, but something… challenging."

He snorted softly. "Yeah, this will be challenging, all right. And poverty-inducing."

"You know your father and I could help you out."

Jeff flicked the turn signal and began transitioning to the eastbound freeway without my prompting. "Ah, Moms, that's sweet. No, seriously, I'll have royalties coming in for the rest of my life, probably —it just won't be as much as the network would pay. Lucky for me I inherited the frugality gene from you and Dad. And there's a chance the network will settle for one or two more books. That I could manage."

"I wish I could tell you what to do, Jeff."

He glanced at me briefly and smiled. "Maybe you have, Moms."

The Wallace Taylor School of Medicine wasn't located at the main downtown campus; it sat on its own out in East Los Angeles. Traffic in L.A. hasn't been light since the 1950s, but this location was comparatively easy to reach. We found visitor parking, located a campus map, and got to the classroom where Willis was lecturing a few minutes before the doors opened and students filed out, talking or texting on their phones.

As the procession thinned, we edged our way inside. Dr. Willis was leaning against a wooden lectern, listening to a pretty young woman with jet black hair and multiple earrings. He laughed at something she said, and then she noticed our approach. She gave me a "what the hell do *you* want?" glare, which morphed into a smile when she saw the handsome young man at my side. Willis's gaze followed hers, and he straightened, all wary attention.

He turned back to the young woman. "It sounds like you've given it some thought, Natalie. Why don't you draft a proposal, and we'll talk next week?"

With one final stink-eye in my direction, Natalie flounced off.

Visibly uneasy, Dr. Willis held out his hand, and I shook it.

"Diane. This is a surprise."

"I'm sure. But you're a hard man to reach, and I have questions only you can answer."

He studied me for a minute. "Yes. I can see even more rejuvenation."

I introduced Jeff and explained the reason for ambushing him. It turned out he'd only just learned about Dr. Banks's stroke the day before.

"I did get your message, and your physician's, and I intended to call both of you back, but I need to do some research first. I checked on Lewis this morning, and it's not good."

"I know. I had to have my own doctor find that out."

"I am sorry." He grimaced. "Tell me what you want from me."

"You're our only hope at this point, doc," Jeff said, putting a protective arm around me. "You're the only one who might know how to fix this mutation."

Dr. Willis pulled out his phone and studied it a moment. "I was going to grab some lunch. There's a Starbucks nearby—let's go over there and talk."

He led the way out of the building and across campus, none of us speaking as we walked. The autumn sunshine that had accompanied Jeff and me earlier was gone, replaced by high thin clouds that hinted at winter's chill. I pulled my blazer closed and buttoned it.

Starbucks was crowded and noisy, but we got lucky and snagged a corner table. I held it while the men ordered. Dr. Willis picked up a sandwich along with his coffee, and Jeff got lattes for both of us. He'd offered to get food, but I wasn't hungry.

I took the lid off my latte to let some of the heat escape. Willis skipped that step and took a drink from the covered cup.

"Are you feeling well?" he asked.

"Most of the time. I haven't had this much energy in years."

He smiled. "And you *look* well. You must enjoy the experience."

It wasn't a question, but I treated it like one. "Not entirely, Dr. Willis."

I described the migraines, muscle spasms and yesterday's excruciating bone pain.

"I have to believe the rejuvenation is causing them."

Jeff was appalled by my description. "Moms, why didn't you *tell* me?"

I patted his hand. "Because there was nothing you could do."

I glanced from Jeff to Dr. Willis. "And, I confess, I've worked hard at convincing myself they were just flukes and wouldn't happen again. Until yesterday."

Dr. Willis put down his sandwich. "Very disturbing. And I agree that they're connected. I can give you medical explanations, which I'm sure your own doctor has already done. And they may well get worse. No one has studied reverse aging in this way, as far as I know."

I waited until he took another bite before I decided to go all in. "My personality is changing, too. And I don't always like the person I'm becoming."

Both Jeff and Dr. Willis looked at me with almost identical curiosity.

Dr. Willis swallowed. "How so?"

I didn't want to explain, in front of my son, how I'd caught myself romance-novel fantasizing about younger men like my son-in-law Nick and Luke the librarian. Not to mention flirting with the bookstore clerk or almost letting Robert Drake seduce me.

"I'm acting very selfishly," I replied, and with a nervous glance at my son, I continued, "I've been having inappropriate *urges*." I felt a blush rise in my cheeks and quickly went on. "I've been rude to people, including my husband, and that's not how I want to be. It's not how my family sees—or saw—me."

Jeff put his hand on my arm. "You're not that bad, Moms."

"You saw how I treated your father at Nancy's barbecue," I pointed out. In retrospect, had it really been that bad? Yes, it had. For me anyway.

Behind wire-rimmed glasses, Willis's gray eyes widened. "You're not behaving like the polite, mature adult people are accustomed to seeing?"

"Exactly. I mean, barging in on *you* like this—is this something a polite, mature adult would do?"

He looked away. "Perhaps. If she were desperate."

I sipped my latte and wiped the milk foam from my upper lip. "I *am* desperate—for information. Desperate to know how far this... *rejuvenation* will go, and whether I can, and should, stop it."

"There's another aspect we need to discuss," Dr. Willis began slowly, like he was forming his thoughts as he spoke. "Dr. Banks touched on this, and although I disagreed with him, it needs to be considered. Especially now." He picked up his sandwich and then set it down without taking a bite. "You've been given a rare and precious gift, Diane. It could possibly be the secret to eternal life—or at the very least, long-lasting youth. I'm sure you realize that."

No one had put it that directly before, and the notion made my head spin.

"Lewis Banks wanted to share that gift with all mankind," Willis continued.

"He did suggest that" I said, "although I honestly suspected he wanted it more for himself."

"That's possible—but I know Lewis, and I'm positive he saw the bigger picture."

Which I evidently had not. Now that I did... "But he didn't really care about my own situation. Not as much as he did about getting credit for finding the Fountain of Youth."

"You're being harsh."

"I am—what did I tell you? I'm not the polite little woman you first met. I'm harsh, and critical, and impatient. Impatient for answers and *action* before I run out of time and end up a babbling infant like Dr. Banks will be if he ever even wakes up."

I clamped a hand over my mouth as I heard my own words.

Willis leaned forward. "I understand, Diane. It's terrifying to contemplate."

"That's just great! But what good is your 'understanding' if it doesn't help get this thing out of me?"

For a moment we stared at each other without speaking.

Jeff broke the silence. "Dr. Willis, you're the scientist. You must have been researching this mutation. Please—if you have any ideas of how to stop it, now's the time to speak up."

I added, "My personal physician, Dr. Dennis—the one who's trying to reach you..." At this Willis scrunched up his shoulders, but I kept going. "...I hate to even bring this up, she thought maybe chemotherapy would work."

Jeff grabbed my hand and squeezed. "Moms, you didn't tell me that. Chemotherapy—that's ugly. Drastic."

Willis swallowed a bite of his sandwich and took a sip of coffee. "It *is* drastic. And it probably isn't the answer. However, only this week I learned of a new experimental procedure that's been successful with some cancer patients, and I immediately thought of your situation. I intend to contact the researchers conducting the study, but I simply haven't had the time with my course load this term. I promise I'll reach out to them this week—tomorrow at the latest. But keep in mind, even if this procedure were to work, there are risks. Serious risks."

"Such as?" asked Jeff.

Dr. Willis bit his lip and then continued. "What we don't know, among other things, is whether the aging process may accelerate once the mutation is removed. And there is that larger issue to consider. Can we—*should* we—replicate the mutation? Lewis has applied for a patent, and I'm sure that if he doesn't recover, one of his colleagues will complete the process. It will take a long time, but they'll get their patent—I'm positive of that."

"Who are these colleagues?" I demanded. "They're like ghosts—no one will tell me about them."

Dr. Willis put his forearms on the table. "They're very real, I assure you. But the entire process surrounding the patent is, understandably, guarded very closely."

Jeff mimicked Willis's pose. "Because there's a lot of money involved, right?"

"There is," Willis agreed. "But there's more than money at stake. If another scientist learned what we—what Lewis—was doing, they might…"

He hesitated, and Jeff leaped in. "They might try to hijack the project? Beat him to the punch?"

Willis frowned. "It's not unheard of."

"And if he, or someone else, does get the patent—what then?" I asked. "Bottle it and market it?"

"It could happen," Dr. Willis said. "But that's a long way in the future. There will need to be tests, animal and human trials, applications for approval to use it commercially."

Jeff sat back and folded his arms across his chest. "But if they do get permission, then who decides who gets it and who doesn't? Will it be like any other drug, with some insurance companies paying for it and some not?"

"Don't think I haven't considered questions like that myself. It's one of the reasons I was concerned when Lewis brought up the idea. And there are other possible consequences. For example: what if people stop aging and dying?"

That conjured nightmare visions of gridlocked roads and over-flowing housing tracts. Crime, filth, and air pollution destroying an already compromised environment.

"On the other hand," Willis continued, "think of the benefit to humanity. No more age-related illness—diabetes, heart disease. Cancer. Quite possibly eradicated. Or significantly reduced."

"It would change our world," I said, as the implications sank in.

"Yes, it would. Lewis and I discussed all this at great lengths, and he was determined to proceed. But I wanted him to take time, consult with others, study the possible outcomes. Then decide. He didn't want to wait."

"Obviously," I said. "He needed the mutation himself, and he probably knew *he* was running out of time."

Willis scowled. "That's a remote possibility."

Not as remote as you want to believe, I thought.

"As you can see, there is no clear-cut answer," Dr. Willis said.

"Who gets to decide then?" Jeff asked.

"Excellent question. One thing I know is that it won't be me."

"Or me," I said. "But who?"

Willis's eyebrows formed an almost solid line. "I tried to contact Lewis yesterday. I was hoping to convince him of the need for further study before going forward. But then…"

"You found out about the stroke. Which, if he'd given himself the mutation, might not have happened."

"You're assuming that he didn't," said Willis.

"Of course," I replied. "Because if he had—"

"Diane, we don't know enough about this to be sure. I do know that he sequenced the mutation in your HSCs and that he found the key to activating SIRT3. It's possible he inserted the mutation into his own DNA, and the stress of it triggered the stroke."

"You think he did that?"

"I honestly don't know. That's the problem. Nobody, not even Lewis Banks, can know for sure. It has never been done before, to the best of my knowledge. It's a bit like landing on the moon: we can speculate, plan, and prepare, but when you're going where no one has gone, unexpected events—catastrophes even—can occur."

Jeff drained his coffee. "So, what happens next, Dr. Willis?"

Willis swallowed a last bite of sandwich. "We wait and see if Lewis wakes up."

"That could take forever," I protested. "I don't have forever."

Jeff spoke up. "Can't someone at least test him and see if he does have the mutation?"

Willis sighed. "I suppose that could be done. But it wouldn't have the kind of answers Diane needs."

"It might," Jeff replied for me. "If his using it gave him a stroke, then maybe it's not such a miracle cure after all. My mother's mutation occurred naturally—sort of—instead of being added to her DNA."

Dr. Willis finished his coffee, removed the lid, and dropped the sandwich wrapper inside, then replaced the lid.

"This is something that will have to be considered," he said. "I've left messages for some of Lewis's colleagues to see if they'll share his research notes. That will tell us some of what we need to know. Meanwhile, Diane, if you've truly decided to try and stop the rejuvenation, I will get more aggressive in investigating the experimental procedure I mentioned."

"Can't you at least tell me what this procedure is?" I asked.

"It's complicated, as you might imagine, but it involves harnessing the power of your own immune cells to seek and destroy the mutation. It's theoretically possible."

"Theoretically," echoed Jeff.

"Yes, but highly likely."

Hope bloomed, and then faded as he continued.

"However, if we succeed, the rejuvenation will stop. Completely. And as I warned you, we don't know what the subsequent effects will be, whether you'll resume aging, stay as you are, or grow older rapidly. The miracle—and that's what it is, you know—will be gone, and you can't get it back."

"Irrevocable," I whispered.

"Irrevocable," he repeated.

He looked down at his phone. "I need to get back. My bioethics class starts in twenty minutes."

Jeff stood and picked up our empty cups. "Bioethics, huh?"

Willis chuckled. "Ironic, no?"

We parted in front of the lecture hall, and Willis promised to call me the minute he had any news from the research team or from Dr. Banks's colleagues. Meanwhile, I had some decisions to make.

As we walked back to Jeff's car, I didn't know whether to laugh or cry. I was sure we'd found our answer, and now it would be up to me. I suddenly felt dizzy and took Jeff's arm for support, so thankful he'd been with me to hear the discussion. He might be able to explain it more calmly than I to Steven, and to Nancy. I fastened my seat belt and leaned my head back as one word kept echoing in my brain. *Irrevocable.*

Chapter Twenty-One
Sacrifice

"This is crazy," Jeff said as he backed out of his parking space. "It's like we fell into a sci-fi movie."

"Except it's not fiction."

"What he said—stuff I never thought of. Using it to cure disease, man, that's wild!"

"Wild," I agreed, although "irrevocable" kept fighting for my attention.

"And this hush-hush thing with the patent, just so they can market your mutation. *Your* mutation. You know that's where it's all headed. The way Willis is stalling, I think he knows more than he's telling us. Maybe he wants in on the money they'll make. He wants to be sure the patent goes through and they have enough of whatever the hell it is they got from you to sell it to Big Pharma."

"Big Pharma? Jeff, you're talking like this is some kind of conspiracy."

"Are you so sure it isn't? Moms, we have to tell Dad about this. He can put a stop to it."

"No, son, he can't."

I explained about the release I'd signed—against Steven's advice.

"Are you sure? I mean, Dad's really good, Moms. If anybody can find a way to derail their scheme, Dad can."

I wasn't about to tell Jeff about the trouble his father had in grasping the scientific data unless I spoon-fed it to him.

"I'm afraid this is beyond even your father's expertise."

Jeff shook his head. "I sure don't like where this is headed. You've got some serious decisions to make about your own health, but at the same time Willis was trying to saddle you with responsibility for the fate of the world."

"Not really. What they do with the mutation once they patent it is out of my hands. It's on the University's conscience. And I do believe Dr. Willis wants to help me. I have to trust *someone* to get me through this."

"But he doesn't seem so sure about what he's doing, or about the outcome. Like if he *can* kill your mutation, what if you start getting older again, really fast? There'd be no way to stop it."

"Don't think I'm not worried about that. But the alternative isn't attractive either, Jeff. I may keep get younger and younger—younger than you, even. Younger than Maddie."

He didn't have a response to that.

"I do need to talk to your father," I said. "But I want to clarify things in my own mind first. If I can."

"Dad could help."

"I know. And he will."

"I hate the way these jokers are—"

"Look out!" I yelled as another car cut in front of us abruptly, without a signal. Jeff hit the brakes and blasted his horn. The other driver kept going like nothing had happened.

I relaxed my death grip on the armrest. "Let's not talk about it anymore for now, Jeff. Let me think things through and then I'll discuss it with your dad."

"And me."

"And you. And Nancy."

Despite the near miss scare, my brain was racing through the discussion with Dr. Willis, processing the information so quickly I needed a quiet place to let the puzzle pieces click into place. Concentrating on absorbing the latest information, at first I didn't notice the tiny dark zig-zag in the center of my field of vision, but it didn't take long for the jagged pattern to unfurl. *Oh, please, not here, not with Jeff.* That morning, preoccupied with getting dressed and planning my approach to Dr. Willis, I'd forgotten to take the medicine Dr. Dennis prescribed to forestall migraines, so I closed my eyes and watched the saw-toothed crescent, rimmed with scalding light, enlarge until it filled the space behind my eyelids. Further thinking was out of the question, so I focused on breathing, not getting sick, and masking my misery from Jeff. He didn't need one more thing to worry about.

Some of the anti-migraine medication must have still been in my system, because the aura gradually softened; no pain, no nausea this time. If Jeff wondered why I was so quiet, he didn't probe. He probably had enough thoughts of his own to ponder.

He dropped me off and promised not to tell Steven or Nancy what we'd learned until I was ready. I thanked him for going with me, kissed him goodbye, and—grateful I didn't wobble as I walked—I went inside, gulped a glass of water and changed into jeans and a sweater. Then I brewed a cup of strong coffee and sliced an apple and some cheddar cheese. I wasn't hungry, but my brain needed food. By then the aura's pattern had faded so I could concentrate again.

I'd been faced with tough decisions all my life, but nothing as life-changing as this. To continue growing younger, enjoy this strong new body, this quick new brain—or to destroy the miracle that had brought it about? To leave the mutation alone and risk more painful side effects, more migraine auras, probably accompanied by pain and nausea? Or end up looking more like my granddaughter than my daughter, or my husband? To get ruder and more impatient, especially with Steven, to let my awakening hormones propel me into more than a harmless fantasy? On the other hand, to stop it and confront the possibility of catching up to my chronological age, with all the withering? To grow even *older* than I'd been before the whole thing started?

Meanwhile, the doctors at Wallace Taylor were busy getting ready to package my mutation—*my mutation*—for sale to the highest bidder. I could only hope they would follow responsible protocol, do those tests Dr. Willis described, find out if Dr. Banks *had* given himself the mutation and if that had triggered his stroke. Those choices, however, were out of my hands, and I was thankful for that. And maybe those doctors in their lab coats would use it wisely, to prevent and even cure age-related diseases. I might read about it in the paper some day and think, *that's because of me.*

Elsa's nose nudged my elbow and I gave her a small bite of cheese. My sweet Elsa. I stroked her head and rubbed her ears the way she liked.

"I wish you could talk, girl. Maybe you could tell me what to do. I need somebody who's not in the middle of all this."

I thought then of Maura, who always gave me the best possible clear-headed advice. I pictured her face, but shame and guilt washed over me. We hadn't talked since our night out at the theater, and I'd avoided calling her especially after that scene with Robert. I hadn't figured out whether I should tell her about it. Another impossible choice for me to make. She deserved to know how easily he would betray her, but she'd been so *happy* with him. Did I really want to ruin that? And, I admit, I didn't want her to know how close I came to betraying her too.

It was odd, though, that she hadn't called me either. We usually talked a couple of times a week, even after things got hot and heavy with her and Robert.

Well, this was as good a time as any to get in touch. Maybe talking with her would help me make both decisions—whether to tell her what a rat Robert was (and what a lousy friend I was) and whether to push for whatever "cure" Dr. Willis was checking into.

"Hey," I said when she answered the phone, "where've you been?"

"Why?"

Her voice had an unfamiliar edge to it.

"Everything okay? I haven't heard from you in ages, and—"

"I don't have anything to say to you, Diane."

Oh, shit. She knows. Robert told her already. I should have been prepared for that possibility, but I wasn't.

Silence crackled between us. I broke it first.

"Maura—what does that mean?"

The whisper of a laugh.

"As if you don't know!"

Suddenly, I wished I had a drink in my hand—and I wasn't thinking of coffee. I needed liquid courage for sure. I bit my lip while I tried to figure out what to say next so I could find out how bad the damage was.

"Come on," I said, "let it out. What's going on?"

"Really? You spend a whole night flirting with Robert and have no idea how that made me feel?"

A whole night? I took a sip of my cold, rancid coffee and figured out she wasn't talking about last Friday. Huge relief!

"You mean after the theater? Maura, I wasn't flirting, honest."

"What would you call it then? Afterward he asked me if all my friends were so 'forward.' And the way you kept *looking* at him. Like you hadn't eaten in a month, and he was a nice big juicy steak."

Had I really done that? I remembered grabbing his hand by mistake, and thinking what a great guy he was, but flirting? Had that given him the idea he could seduce me as easily as snapping his fingers?

"Listen, I'm really sorry if you thought that—if Robert thought that. Swear to God I didn't mean to flirt with him. It was late, I was tired, the wine went to my head, and if I got a little careless, I apologize."

"You were more than a little careless, Di. You have not been yourself since this rejuvenation thing started. You're acting crazy, being selfish, acting like nothing and no one matters but you. You throw yourself at *my* boyfriend, with your husband sitting right there, and then you deny it. I suppose you're blaming it on whatever this thing is that's happening to you. But that doesn't work. You need to grow up—again—and start taking responsibility."

The unfairness of her words infuriated me. She might as well have slapped me. She had no idea of how *responsible* I'd been, resisting Robert's come-on in the parking lot. No idea at all what I'd sacrificed for her sake.

At least that was what I was feeling when I fired back at her, although it's a damned poor excuse.

"Is that right? Well, I've got news for you, Maura, I have been pretty fucking responsible, and if you'd come down off your high horse you might see for yourself that this guy you're with isn't so pure and noble. *He* came after *me*, when you weren't around, and I practically had to pepper-spray him to get away."

"You're lying."

"Am I? Did he just give you a special late birthday present? Did he?"

She didn't speak for a minute, and I cringed. This had spiraled out of control, and I didn't know how to stop it.

"How did you know about the earrings?" she said in a quiet, hurt voice.

"Because he phoned and pretended he needed help picking them out. I fell for it, and afterward he tried to seduce me. But I shut him down, Maura, because of *you*. Because he's yours, and I'd never betray you like that."

Is that right? You were ready to, though. Admit it.

"You're lying," she said again.

"Ask him, Maura. See for yourself."

"I will," she said slowly. "But I don't understand. Why would you tell me something like that? Why would you want to wreck what I have with him? Are you so miserable you can't stand for anyone else to be happy?"

I stood up and started pacing. Elsa lay in the corner, and she lifted her head, ears perked. She knew something was wrong. Something big. And she was right. My friendship with Maura was unraveling, and I didn't know what to say to stop it.

"You're wrong, Maura. I didn't say it to hurt you."

Oh really?

"I felt that you needed to know. He'll betray you again, and again. He's that kind of man. I didn't want you to go on believing in someone who's not really there."

"Why not? Where's the harm?"

She was crying then; I heard her sobs, and I wished more than anything that I could transport myself through the phone and hug her. Why had I caused her so much sorrow?

"The old Diane would have understood," Maura went on. "I miss her—I miss my real friend. You're mean now, and more selfish than I ever imagined."

I let out the breath I didn't even know I was holding, and that was all it took to snap that thread tying us together.

"I'm sorry you feel that way, Maura. Maybe someday you'll understand."

I disconnected the call.

And that was the last time I ever spoke to Maura Salcedo.

Chapter Twenty-Two
More Angels and Devils

I spent the next two days under the heaviest blanket of dread I'd ever known. I'd lost my best friend, and at a time I needed her most. But there was no going back; I'd trashed our friendship beyond repair. Maura's words haunted me. "You have not been yourself since this rejuvenation thing started. You're acting crazy, being selfish, acting like nothing and no one matters but you."

She was right. And the rejuvenation, no matter how wonderful it was in many ways, had cost me Maura's friendship, for the stupidest of reasons. *Had* I led Robert on, let him think I wanted him? Let him assume I was his for the taking? And then I'd lashed out at Maura, and even if I'd told her the truth, it was a hurtful truth, and I hadn't even tried to sugarcoat it.

Anguish over losing Maura almost drowned out the other big concern: what to do with the information Dr. Willis had shared with me. Why hadn't I told Steven about it? The longer I waited, the angrier he'd be that I'd kept it from him. Steven would try to influence my decision, though, and he was an awesome persuader. He did it for a living, after all.

Besides, he always insisted on diving into the science parts, even when he had trouble understanding them until I explained several times. It exhausted and frightened me to realize his lightning-quick brain was no match for the convoluted scrambling of DNA sequencing and SIRT3 activation.

By Thursday, however, I couldn't keep it from him any longer.

He came home early for once—he'd been buried in the work of taking over Victor DeWitt's caseload—so we took Elsa out for a stroll together. The tension between us had eased since Nancy's barbecue, and I hated to reawaken it, but I had to let him in on the latest development.

"I have a confession to make," I began, after we'd walked halfway around the block.

"Do tell."

"I tracked down Dr. Willis and met with him."

Steven stopped and turned to me. "When?" His voice was mild, but I detected an accusatory undertone.

I ignored it. "Tuesday. I was going to tell you then, but... No, there's no excuse. I don't know why I—"

"What did he say?"

I tugged gently on Elsa's leash and started walking while I poured out the story, skimming over Jeff's role and ending with the "irrevocable" comment.

"But that's great! He knows a way to stop the process."

Here we go. I knew this was going too easily.

I didn't respond.

"You do want to stop it, don't you?"

Elsa lifted her head, almost like she, too, was asking the question, but I didn't answer.

Steven quit walking and took hold of my arm. Worry lines creased his forehead.

"Diane, it's dangerous to let it continue. No one knows what the outcome will be. No one knows what sort of risks you're facing."

I pulled away from him as turmoil swirled inside me. It was such a lovely afternoon, a bracing hint of autumn in the air, our faces dappled by gentle sunlight through tree leaves. Why did conflict have to come and rear its ugly head?

I drew my shoulders back. "And what about the risks if this experiment works? Or didn't you hear that part of what I just said?"

Elsa pulled her ears together and winkled her forehead. That dog had more expressions than some humans. Poor girl. She wasn't used to us quarreling, and this *was* escalating into a quarrel, despite my resolve to keep it civil.

"I heard you," said Steven. "He doesn't know what will happen if it works. I understand that. But I have a damned good idea of what will happen if we don't try. This *thing*, Diane. It's like a cancer. It's eating away at your personality."

I started walking again but made myself slow my pace for Elsa's benefit. "Oh really?" My words could have sliced through glass. "It's not that you resent the way I get out of bed in the morning without every muscle aching?"

"That's ridiculous."

"Is it? You grumble every day about how much your back hurts, or your shoulder. No, Steven, what's ridiculous is that you believe I should give up this wonderful gift and feel as bad as you do!"

He didn't answer until we got to our street and turned toward home. "If your physical strength was all that's been changing, I wouldn't believe so strongly in the need to stop. But there *is* more, and I think you're aware of that, even if you won't admit it."

He sounded like Maura. Since when had they ever agreed on anything?

In the back yard, I unleashed Elsa and watched her slurp water from her bowl. Steven stood a few feet away, and I didn't want to look at him.

"I'm *aware* that I'm not acting like my old self, and I'm also *aware* that you're threatened by having a younger wife," I said over my shoulder as I stomped into the house.

* * *

We scarcely spoke the rest of the evening. By the next morning, we were able to hold a civil conversation, as long as we stuck to neutral topics, like his speech at Victor DeWitt's retirement party that night. I kept my voice cordial as I assured him that the speech would go fine and that I'd had his Tom Ford suit cleaned and pressed. So, I wasn't such a screw-up as a wife, now was I?

I resolved to be kinder to Steven. He and Maura were wrong, and I intended to prove it.

* * *

That evening, more friction arose when Steven couldn't find his favorite cufflinks. We were running late, so I joined the search, but not without venting my annoyance, despite my good intentions.

"Why can't you pay attention to what you're doing? Why can't you put things back where they belong? I spend half my life helping you look for things you've lost."

"That is a gross exaggeration, Diane. You're a fine one to talk about not paying attention."

I ignored the jibe. "Can't you wear another pair?"

"I could, but Vic gave me those cufflinks when I made partner."

With a put-upon sigh, I upended the polished walnut box where Steven kept his accessories. There was his high school class ring, my father's pocket watch, a silver-and-gold rope bracelet Jeff had given him more or less as a joke, and two pair of cufflinks, one sterling silver and onyx, one with a compass design. But not the stainless-steel rectangles with a tiny diamond in the center of each.

Where might he have put them?

Following a hunch, I went into the bathroom and opened the drawer where he kept his shaving gear and other toiletries. There, toward the back, behind a travel-size can of deodorant, sat the missing cufflinks.

Triumphant, I held them out to Steven.

He squinted at them. "How did they get there?"

"Like I said, you never pay attention to where you put things. You just throw them around and expect me to find them when you want them again."

He inserted them into his shirt cuffs. "Perhaps I did set them on the counter and intended to put them away, but you came along and brushed them into the drawer because *you* were preoccupied with how wonderful you feel these days. How youthful. Unlike your useless old husband."

"You're welcome," I said in reply.

I was going to ask him to zip up my dress but decided to wrestle with it myself. Then I slipped into my red stilettos, and, like magic, they reassured me that I wasn't frumpy old Diane anymore.

Without pausing to compliment me on my appearance, as he usually did before a dress-up event, Steven grabbed his wallet and car keys. "Let's go."

So we began the evening crackling with hostility.

* * *

Steven reluctantly surrendered his Lexus to the valet at the swanky Sur La Plage Hotel in Santa Monica. I'd never been inside, and I refused to let my irritation with Steven dilute the pleasure of taking it all in, especially a panoramic view of the Pacific Ocean and the coast-line all the way north to Malibu. The décor was beach-town elegant, lots of fake-weathered white wood and bright blue upholstery, a mammoth Bird of Paradise arrangement on a marble pedestal in the lobby.

I took Steven's arm as we entered the ballroom, and he must have overcome his own resentment because he rested his hand on mine briefly before we went to greet Victor.

A reformed smoker and unreformed drinker, Victor DeWitt had always been on the slender side, his skin mottled and wrinkled from years aboard his beloved sailboat, which was docked not far away. "Slender," however, was a mild description that night. His cheekbones stuck out so far that they cast shadows on the lower part of his face, and shaking hands with him was like touching a skeleton. I'd tried to prepare myself ahead of time not to be shocked when I saw him, and I hoped I'd succeeded.

Victor, however, didn't mask his surprise at my appearance—we hadn't seen each other for several months. His eyes widened as he caressed my hand.

"Diane, I'd forgotten how stunning you are. It's wonderful to see you again. It's been far too long."

Alice DeWitt glided up beside her husband and air-kissed my cheek. "You do look lovely tonight," she said with a knowing smile.

Alice had had plenty of work done on her own face—she never tried to keep it secret—and her expression told me she assumed I'd done the same. I said nothing to correct her belief, but I couldn't help comparing her taut forehead and unnaturally full lips with my own non-surgical rejuvenation.

"So kind of you and Steven to be here," Victor said. His dark eyes twinkled. "I hope he won't be airing any dark secrets from my past tonight."

I laughed. "I can't imagine you having dark secrets, Victor. No, what could he possibly say but good things about you? I know he's going to miss you terribly. Everyone will."

Victor's chin trembled slightly as he waved an age-spotted hand around the room. "I will miss most of them, too. But I've put the firm first for far too long." He took Alice's hand and patted it. "It's time to enjoy my lovely wife's company and play with my grandchildren."

"You've certainly earned that," I said.

The conversation was edging toward uncomfortable. Clearly, Victor didn't want to discuss other reasons for his sudden decision to retire, and I sure didn't want to probe.

Steven exchanged a few pleasantries with Alice and Victor, then steered me away toward the bar.

"My God, Steven, he looks ghastly! The poor man."

"Believe it or not, it's an improvement over a couple of months ago. I sure hope he beats this thing."

Cancer. Something the doctors and scientists patenting my mutation might be able to defeat. I shivered.

Without asking, Steven ordered a glass of chardonnay for me and then his usual whiskey, but he didn't even take an exploratory sip when it came. *He's nervous about his speech*, I thought, and then another worry hit me: the trouble he'd been having lately understanding and remembering things. *My God, I hope he doesn't blow it! He never uses notes—what if he blanks out?*

We mingled with the rest of the guests and greeted Steven's colleagues, most of whom I'd known for decades. Their names came to me effortlessly—my memory was working overtime—and I confess that I enjoyed the envious glances from some of the wives.

Steven introduced me to two new associates—both women—and their companions. One brought her husband, and one was with another woman, whom she introduced as her wife.

My, my, I thought, *the firm is finally getting progressive.*

All four of the newcomers were young and shiny, and a year ago I'd have envied them their youth and vigor. Now, not so much. The one with the husband, Yvonne, was dark-haired and dainty, with a gentle grip when we shook hands, which her husband more than made up for, crushing my fingers in a big solid paw. I squeezed back, however, and was gratified to see a flicker of surprise in his confident grin. The other young attorney, Juliet, was willowy and elegant, and her wife Susan, a tawny-skinned beauty with dark hair in long thin braids, explained that she worked for an animal rescue group. When I told her how Steven had rescued Elsa, she hugged him.

"Jules told me I'd like you," she said with a flash of white teeth.

* * *

We had assigned seats at the linen-draped tables, but fortunately whoever planned the event didn't try splitting up couples. I'd always found it mildly uncomfortable to sit with strangers, and many of the attorneys and their spouses *were* strangers, people I saw only once or twice a year and who probably couldn't have told you my name if their lives depended on it. Juliet and Susan were also seated at our table, across from us. I knew the other two couples slightly and remembered that one of them had just returned from a riverboat cruise in Eastern Europe. They seemed pleasantly surprised at my questions about the cities they'd toured, and it kept the conversational ball rolling through the salad course. Steven was quiet, and I knew he was mentally rehearsing his speech. It would sound spontaneous, and only he and I knew the hours of preparation that went into making it appear that way. *He'll do fine.* I crossed my fingers.

The entrée was surprisingly tasty for banquet food—we'd been given three options, and I'd chosen salmon, which was perfectly cooked and tender; the rice pilaf had a lively seasoning with a nice hint of dill. The servers kept the wine flowing so that a mellow contentment embraced us all.

As the servers cleared the table, I made a quick trip to the ladies' room, not only out of necessity but also curiosity. The anteroom, painted a complexion-flattering shade of pink, had four skirted tables in front of light-framed mirrors. The plush carpet and chrome door-handles exuded elegance, but my pleasure in the ambiance was shattered as I approached the louvered door into the main bathroom. I heard voices from inside.

"I want her surgeon's name," said a voice I didn't recognize.

"That Steven is a fox," replied someone else. "No wonder she had to get herself fixed up. She was getting dumpy. You know she's older than him."

I coughed loudly and shoved the door open, imagining myself icily correcting the speaker's grammar along with their false assumptions.

Two women stood at the sinks, drying their hands with cloth towels which they tossed in a wicker basket on the floor between them. I recognized them as Mavis Royce, the wife of one of the partners, and Rosemary Vance, whose husband Dennis was in the running to replace Victor DeWitt, according to Steven.

Neither of them appeared the least bit guilty about their catty comments but gave me warm smiles as fake as the color of their hair.

"Love the shoes," Mavis said.

"Thanks," I replied before I went into a stall. They weren't worth the trouble of making a scene.

* * *

After dessert—a chocolate lava cake with enough carbs to put everyone in a coma, Teddy Royce rose and shambled to the lectern. I always thought the third founding partner was something of a twit, with a gaudy laugh and a distracted manner. Steven never criticized him overtly, but over the years I inferred that it was money rather than talent that got Teddy's name on the firm's letterhead. He'd clearly had his share of liquor; both his rusty hair and his black tie were askew. He was soft and paunchy, and his white shirt was in danger of coming untucked. None of this bothered Teddy, but a glance at Mavis made me wince. If looks could kill, Teddy would have fallen dead on the spot.

Teddy tapped the microphone, producing an annoying *thwonk* that hurt my ears, but it got our attention.

"Guess this thing is working," he muttered. Then he seemed to realize all eyes were fixed on him and clicked his tongue noisily into the mike. "Good evening, friends. I, uh, trust you enjoyed your meals."

Mild applause followed. Why, I wondered, hadn't Albert Jernigan done the honors? I'd rarely spoken with Jernigan; the man didn't invite conversation. Still, I imagined he'd have done a better job of introducing Steven. Or maybe he felt it was beneath him. He sat, fingers steepled, at a table far to the right of the lectern, a sour expression on his craggy face.

"Um, I'm glad you all could be here to, uh, mark this momentous occasion," Teddy continued. "It is… it's, uh, both a joyous and a sad time for me, and I'm sure for many of you." He paused as if collecting his thoughts. "Vic DeWitt has been our rock—our anchor—for more years than I can count…"

Even if you were sober, you probably couldn't count, I thought, but then I felt ashamed for my unkind thoughts. Teddy had always been courteous to me, if overly familiar. I tuned him out, however, because it was more entertaining to surreptitiously study the others at our table. From Juliet's expression, I deduced that she shared my opinion of Teddy's oratory skills.

As Steven shifted position next to me, I pulled my attention back to Teddy, who'd begun to slur his words a bit.

"Um, but enough from me," Teddy was saying. "Somehow, we were, uh, able to coax one of our best—um, not one of, but our very best speaker, to say a few things about Victor. He needs no introduction, but I'll… I'll give you one anyway: Steven—don't-call-me-Steve —Devlin. Ladies and gentlemen, Steven Devlin."

Applause rippled through the room as Steven rose and walked confidently to the lectern, exuding poise. I had never seen him in court, but I could imagine how he held judge and jury spellbound during his summation. *That's my husband up there, and doesn't he look great?*

He shook Teddy's hand, then took his elbow and gently guided him away from the lectern. With a smile, Steven removed his glasses and surveyed the room. After a moment's pause, he said, "Here's something many of you here tonight probably don't know. Back in the day when I came aboard, the firm's process for pairing new associates with mentors was a little simpler than it is today. We didn't feed the partners' and associates' data into the computer and then let an algorithm pair us up."

The clatter of silverware died down as he continued, "No, nothing so elaborate and analytic." He paused and smiled again. "They put the associates' names in a hat and then the partners drew."

Surprised laughter made the rounds. Susan leaned across the table and asked, "Is this true?"

I shrugged. "Could be."

Steven didn't wait for more reactions. "How fortunate," he continued, "how blessed was I that Victor DeWitt plucked my name out of the hat."

I glanced at Victor—whose face was flushed. Behind his thick glasses, I thought I saw tears.

"I couldn't have had a better teacher and friend than Vic, and if I'm the least bit successful as a trial lawyer today, it's because he showed me how it was done."

Appreciative applause stopped him for a minute, but he held up his hand and continued speaking, recounting Victor's many skills and successes. And as I watched my husband hold the audience enthralled, hot shame flooded over me. Steven was a good, caring man—the best kind of husband. And I'd been treating him so badly, doubting and criticizing and generally being a bitch.

If this was part of the rejuvenation, I didn't want it. I loved Steven fiercely. I always had, but somehow that love had been subverted by this newfound youthfulness, and I hadn't given much thought to its effect on him. He'd held my hand when I got scared of the process, he'd tried to understand the science behind it all, and in return I snarled at him and devalued him.

The siren call of youth fought back, and I truly did feel as if I had an angel on one shoulder and a devil on the other. Sitting in that elegant ballroom in my finest clothes, the warm glow of wine still with me, I might not have looked like the centerpiece in a life-or-death battle, but looks sure as hell can deceive.

"But enough praise," Steven concluded. "Victor's modesty must be having a melt-down about now. I'll stop extolling his virtues and let the man himself say a few words."

He stepped back from the lectern and extended his left arm to summon Victor, who appeared even frailer as he approached the front of the room.

Steven held out his hand, but instead of a handshake, Victor wrapped his arms around Steven and hugged him the way a kid hugs a teddy bear. Steven clapped him on the shoulder and made his way back to our table. I squeezed his thigh when he sat.

"Well done, my love," I whispered.

Victor's voice trembled as he thanked everyone in the room— "especially Steven Devlin for those embarrassingly kind words"—and reminisced briefly about his long career at Jernigan, DeWitt, Royce and Devlin.

Steven was a tough act to follow, but Victor's talk was sincere and nostalgic, and he got a standing ovation at the end.

* * *

"You were magnificent," I told Steven on the way home.

He dismissed the compliment. "I wouldn't go that far," he said, "but I think I gave Vic a decent send-off."

"More than decent." I twisted in my seat to face him. "You reminded everyone of what is great about Victor. That's a marvelous achievement."

He grabbed my hand and kissed the back of it, never taking his eyes off the road. "I'm glad you approve."

* * *

Elsa greeted us with her usual exuberance when we got home, and all was right with the world. After taking her out for one last visit to the grass, I brought her back inside. Steven had already changed into pajamas and was propped up in bed, reading a Michael Connelly mystery.

Casually I sat next to him and asked him to unzip me, and he ran his hand down my bare back.

"Mmmm," I murmured and turned around to kiss him. He kissed me back with unexpected enthusiasm and then gently peeled off the top of my dress. By then I'd unbuttoned his pajamas, and we eagerly finished undressing each other before he pulled me into bed with him. Maybe it was the afterglow of the applause he'd received that night, or maybe not, but he made love to me like he hadn't done in years. Afterward as we drifted to sleep, I reflected that I had one more thing for which to thank Victor DeWitt.

Chapter Twenty-Three
The Call That Changed My Life

When the unfamiliar number popped up on my cell phone, I almost declined it. *Damn telemarketers—can't I even finish grocery shopping without them pestering me?*

I was in the beverage aisle at the market, searching out a particular sports drink for my son-in-law—a bizarre situation in the first place—when my phone buzzed. The interruption annoyed me, but I tapped "Accept" anyway.

"Hello," I may have snarled when I took the call that changed my life.

"It's Peter Willis. I have some news for you."

And so I became one of those people I deplored, the ones with cell phones glued to their ears, blocking the aisle as they converse with an invisible presence.

"I'm at the market," I explained. "Let me find a pen and paper in my purse."

How was I to expect, and prepare for, a call from Dr. Willis on a Saturday afternoon?

"Don't worry," he replied. "I'll email you details. But I wanted to tell you right away that I've spoken with the head of the research team running the clinical study I told you about, and I do think the experimental procedure they used *might*—and I say *might*—apply to you as well."

I covered my free ear to muffle the Muzak pouring from overhead speakers, the babble of passersby and the creak of shopping cart wheels.

"Tell me," I said.

"They used it to treat a woman with advanced breast cancer who hadn't responded to conventional treatment. It's far more complicated than this, but in essence, they sequenced her DNA to analyze the mutations in her tumor, extracted some of her own immune cells, and found which ones recognized the mutations. Then they replicated those cells and infused them into the patient. The immune cells sought and destroyed the cancer. Two years later, the woman is cancer-free."

I must have looked absurd, clinging to the handle of my shopping cart, my mouth no doubt hanging open like an idiot, as I processed what he'd told me.

"That's amazing," was all I could come up with in reply.

"Yes, it is. Very encouraging. Now, you need to understand that this is not a sure thing, but it's the most promising outcome I've found. I'm sending you a summary of the protocol and some links to articles about it with more detailed information. Read them over and then call me back. This is my personal mobile number, so use it. I'll need to wade through some red tape with the university, but given the unique circumstances of your condition, I don't foresee many problems with securing approval. Assuming you want to proceed."

I remembered to thank him before I disconnected the call.

Then I picked out the electrolyte-infused water Nancy had advised me to have on hand for Nick, who'd gotten a recurring part on a situation comedy being produced locally and wanted to get in shape before production started.

* * *

When she phoned to tell me the good news about Nick, Nancy also informed me that they had entered couples counseling. And—the best part, from my viewpoint—they'd arranged some counseling for Maddie as well.

"I owe you an apology," she'd told me. "Actually, probably more than one, but I'm sorry I blew off your worry about Maddie acting out at ballet class. You were right; she had picked up on the tension between me and Nick. We're dealing with all that."

"No apologies needed, darling. I only hope you and Nick are able to work things out in Maddie's best interests."

"We are, I think. I mean, I still love him, Mom. And he loves me. And we both love Maddie. We'll do what's best for her, but I think staying together is what I want anyway." She sighed. "Besides, I've almost gotten him housebroken. Why start over?"

"That makes me happier than you can imagine," I'd told her, and it was true.

* * *

Until the moment Dr. Willis called, my head had been filled with plans for the dinner party Steven and I were hosting that night, to celebrate Nick's new role. It was "only" a supporting role, but it could last a while and would allow him to spend more time at home.

After the phone call, on autopilot, I finished my shopping, including a bottle of Crown Royal for Steven, and got in line to check out. As the whiskey rolled down the conveyor belt, the checker looked up at me.

"May I see your ID please?" he asked.

I laughed. "You're kidding, right?"

He looked sheepish. "We're supposed to ask."

The checker was probably barely twenty-one himself, and he had a funny little smirk when he added, "And I'm not supposed to try and judge ages. Looks can be deceiving, you know."

I pointed to my hair. "Do you see this on anyone under twenty-one?"

Both he and the woman bagging my groceries seemed baffled, and I realized why—no more gray. I'd forgotten.

I pulled out my driver's license and handed it to the checker. He studied it and gave it back with another sly grin.

"You fooled me, Diane," he said with a wink.

A tiny thrill coursed through me at the absurd idea I could be mistaken for someone his own age. *And I'm thinking of giving this up. Really?*

Then I noticed something else that had escaped my attention before. No one asked, "Do you need help out with your groceries, ma'am?"

It wasn't the offer that had bothered me before. It was the "ma'am." Apparently, I no longer qualified as "ma'am."

* * *

At home I unloaded the groceries in one trip before Steven joined me, and as he helped me put them away, I went over what Dr. Willis had said, paraphrasing as much as possible.

Steven almost dropped the Crown Royal. "That's incredible! They were actually able to harness her body's own immune system to kill the cancer?"

Impressed that he'd caught on so quickly, I nodded. "Dr. Willis is emailing me the details, but yes, it appears that's possible."

"Where's the email?"

"Steven, I just got home. I haven't had a chance to——"

"What are you waiting for, woman? Go see what it says. I'll take care of this."

I left him in the kitchen, puzzling over what went in the fridge and what belonged in the pantry. He'd figure it out.

I opened my laptop on the dining room table, next to the pile of research papers I'd gotten from the doctors and the Medical Library. *I'll have to move all this into Steven's office before dinner*, I realized as the laptop booted up. I opened Dr. Willis's email, scanned the summary he'd written, then downloaded and printed the three scientific papers he'd attached. I started reading, and Steven joined me, a lined yellow tablet in one hand, his rollerball pen in the other. We read without talking for a few minutes.

Steven tapped a sheet of paper with his pen. "This is fantastic. For once the science is working for us instead of against us."

I wasn't sure I agreed, but I let him have the moment. I read the final pages Dr. Willis had sent and then stood.

"I need to get dinner started."

"Diane—"

"Nothing will happen this weekend anyway, Steven. And Dr. Willis said he needs to cut through some red tape if I even decide I want to try this."

"*If?* You're not serious—here's the miracle we've been searching for, and you have doubts about trying it?"

"The miracle *you've* been searching for. The one that will un-do everything."

"Sweetheart, you don't know that it will—"

"Don't 'sweetheart' me, Steven! This is my life we're talking about. Not yours, not Dr. Willis's, not anyone else's. You don't get to decide what I want, what I'll do. Not anymore."

He started to reach out, then dropped his hand on the table.

"I don't know who you are these days, Diane. I simply don't know."

"Listen, Steven—our family is coming to dinner tonight. How often do we have a chance to be together? Can't we just put this away for tonight and enjoy their company? Can't we wait and talk about this tomorrow?"

Steven lowered his head and touched the pile of printouts. "Do I even have a choice?"

"No," I said softly. "This time you don't."

Sympathy surged through me: commanding, powerful Steven Devlin, master of the courtroom, always in charge. In all the years of our marriage, I'd seldom defied him. He was usually right, and I'd gotten used to complying. But not this time. I wouldn't be pushed into a decision this critical, this *irrevocable*. Not by him, or my children, not by Dr. Willis, not by anyone. This choice I would make on my own.

* * *

I made Steven promise not to bring up the mutation or Dr. Willis's possible intervention, but I couldn't stop Jeff or Nancy from raising the question. I realized this as I was carrying the platter of roast beef and potatoes to the table that evening. All of us except Nick and Maddie had had a pre-dinner cocktail, and the mood was cordial and relaxed. I hoped it would stay that way.

We took our usual places, a habit formed when Jeff and Nancy were children: Steven at the head of the table, me on the opposite end, closest to the kitchen, with Jeff at Steven's right and Nancy on his left. Nick sat next to Nancy, and Maddie, who used to sit in a booster seat between them, now took the place between Jeff and me. Judging from the adoring gazes Nick and Nancy sent each other, their marriage was edging toward solid ground again.

I steered the conversation toward Nick's new role, and he gladly regaled us with anecdotes about the TV show's storyline, the cast, and the crew. I loved getting his insider's take, and so did the others—even Nancy, who had to have heard Nick's stories dozens of times. The premise of the show revolved around a veterinary practice, and Nick described some of the dogs and cats that would be part of the cast.

"But no horses, Daddy?" asked Maddie. She put her fork down as she chewed her food, a touching imitation of her mother's dainty eating habits.

"No horses, baby girl—not yet anyway. But the writers don't tell me everything, so we'll have to wait and see."

The talk around the table shifted to Nancy's job, and then Steven told everyone about Victor DeWitt's retirement—the kids had known him forever and reminisced about times he and Alice had taken them sailing. We downplayed the details of Vic's cancer and put as hopeful a spin as possible on it.

Then Jeff tapped his knife on the side of his wine glass and announced, "Okay, family, I have something to tell you."

Uh oh, I thought. Surely he wasn't going to bring up our meeting with Dr. Willis—not in front of Maddie?

"The network and I have parted company. For good. I couldn't accede to their demands—doesn't that sound impressive, Dad? In other words, they wouldn't sign the deal unless I promised them five more Defender Dog books, and I can't. I honestly can't."

"Good for you!" I exclaimed.

Steven's stiff posture told me that not everyone would see it as good news. I glanced at Maddie and was surprised to see her grin broadly.

"Yeah, Uncle Jeff—good for you!" She lifted her water glass in a toast. "I was getting kinda bored with him anyway."

Nancy's fork hit her plate with a clang. "Madison!"

Jeff laughed. "I thought so, Maddie my sweet. That's why I decided to retire him. I can't have my favorite niece get bored with my books."

"I'm your only niece, Uncle Jeff."

"Still…"

Steven sipped his wine. "Do you have plans for what you'll do instead?"

"As I matter of fact," Jeff replied, "I do. I'm writing an adult novel —I told Moms about this, didn't I?"

I nodded. "You did. And I think it's a splendid idea."

"I'm taking a novel writing class with the UCLA Extension," Jeff said. "I think I know how to do it, but I can always use a little help."

"Good for you, buddy," said Nick. "I always thought you were wasting your talent with those kid books."

Maddie pretended indignation at that, but Nick blew her a kiss.

"You're beyond that, baby girl. Although I want to preview your uncle's next book before you read it. It might be too racy for you. How about it, Jeff? Any good love scenes?"

Nancy's hand covered his. "We'll read it and see."

I began to hope we could get through the evening without anyone bringing up my medical quandary. No appreciative glances from Nick, although I caught an inquiring eyebrows-raised look from Nancy. She wouldn't mention the issue in front of Maddie, however.

Jeff polished off a second slice of roast, except for a tidbit. He looked around. "Where's Elsa? I saved her a treat."

Elsa never begged at the table but always lay nearby, watching and waiting, knowing she'd get something when the meal was over. Her usual spot was empty, however.

I got up and went searching. Elsa lay on the kitchen floor, ears drooping.

"Hey, girl," I said as I approached, "you're missing the fun."

She lifted her head, and I didn't like the look of her.

"Elsa? You okay?"

She pushed herself up on her front legs, and they slipped on the vinyl flooring. She whimpered, and I knelt and stroked her back.

"You need help getting up?"

I put my arm under her belly and lifted. She stood for a minute but then her back legs gave out.

"It's okay, Elsa. I'll call the cavalry."

I stroked her head before I went to the doorway and called to Steven. He helped me work a towel under Elsa's belly to support her, and we got her up, but the minute he released the towel, down she went.

"The vet's not open this late," I muttered. "Should we take her to the emergency clinic?"

Steven squatted and rubbed Elsa's head. "What's going on, Elsa? You pull a muscle?"

Elsa whimpered again and lay her head on her paws, the picture of misery.

"What's wrong with Elsa?"

I hadn't heard Maddie enter the kitchen.

"She's not feeling good, darling," I said. "I think she hurt her back. But she'll be okay."

A minute later Jeff came in, then Nancy and Nick. We hovered around Elsa, who grew nervous under all that scrutiny.

"Listen," Steven said, "we're bothering her. Let's leave her alone to rest, shall we?"

We did, but my peaceful enjoyment of the evening was shattered, and probably everyone else's as well. Elsa was as much a family member as any of us, and I sensed that something more than a pulled muscle was going on.

After dessert, I got up to clear the table, and Nancy and Jeff rose almost simultaneously. I motioned them to sit down, but they ignored me.

In the kitchen, Elsa still lay on the floor, although she lifted her head and gave a feeble tail-wag to greet us. Jeff crouched and rubbed her ears.

"Poor baby," he murmured. "I wonder what you did to yourself."

None of us voiced the obvious—this probably was no injury; Elsa's age was catching up to her.

"I'm going to take Maddie home," Nancy said. "She's upset about Elsa. But first, Mom—have you heard anything from the doctor? Jeff told me you found him."

"Thanks to your clever suggestion, I did."

I quickly summarized what Dr. Willis had told me. Nancy and Jeff reacted almost exactly as Steven had: this was wonderful news, what was I waiting for? I soft-pedaled my reservations, explained I hadn't had a chance to study the material he'd sent, and promised to report back to both of them the minute I knew my next step.

Nancy hugged me. "You know we love you no matter what you decide, right?"

I almost started to cry.

* * *

Nancy and Nick left with Maddie, but Jeff insisted on staying.

"I'm not leaving Elsa like this," he said. "If she's not better in the morning we'll take her to the emergency vet. And I want to see the stuff Dr. Willis sent. We can go over it together tomorrow."

Elsa didn't want dinner. She lay on her side in the kitchen, looking as depressed as an animal can possibly be. I sat and stroked her until my legs went numb. When I got up, she lifted her head but made no move to follow me. Jeff and Steven got a towel under her again and took her outside to pee, then eased her into the carpeted den. She settled down, moaning softly, as if every part of her hurt. I didn't want to leave her, but bringing her upstairs was unthinkable.

I offered to make up the bed in Jeff's old room, but he wanted to sleep downstairs and keep an eye on Elsa. With my big strong son in charge, I relinquished control and went upstairs with Steven.

Except when Steven and I were traveling, that was the only time in twelve years that Elsa hadn't slept in the bedroom with us.

I slept badly, waking every few hours and worrying about her. I didn't go downstairs to check and risk disturbing her, or Jeff. A few times Steven woke, too, and put his arm around me, whispering reassurances that neither of us believed.

* * *

Sunday morning, she still couldn't walk so we took her to the emergency clinic. I was doubly grateful for Jeff's presence because he lifted her in the car as if she weighed nothing, relieving Steven of the need to play strongman and risk straining his back.

The doctor on duty at the clinic ordered an x-ray, which didn't reveal anything. "It could be arthritis," he said. "We'd need to do more testing to see."

Jeff had his arm around her as she lay on the exam room floor. "She's hurting, and she won't eat—she seems so sad."

"I'm sure she is," the doctor explained. "She's a working dog. Right now, she can't do her job, which is watching out for her people."

"What next?" I asked.

He recommended we see Elsa's regular vet the next day, since he saw no obvious injury on the x-ray. He gave us some pills to make her more comfortable in the meantime but cautioned not to over-sedate her until we knew what was going on.

* * *

We divided our time the rest of the day between hovering over Elsa and going over the material Dr. Willis had emailed. Steven spread the papers on the dining room table and began reading and scribbling notes on a yellow tablet. Jeff and I took other sections of the material and marked them up with red underlines and yellow highlighter.

"Man," Jeff remarked, "this is wild. I never knew our bodies were so complex."

"Tell me about it," Steven replied. "I had to take a crash course in biology just to understand what your mother was talking about."

"Tumor-infiltrating lymphocytes, checkpoint inhibitors," Jeff murmured. "DNA sequencing. Does this make any sense to you?"

"A little," Steven replied.

As I listened to him explain how the doctors had identified the mutation in the first place, I realized that Steven had picked up far more information than I'd given him credit for learning. Maybe my explanations hadn't been clear enough, since I was absorbing the facts myself and still processing them. Evidently he'd done some studying on his own to learn about the mystery my body had become to both of us.

Steven put down his pen. "The bottom line, as far as I can tell, is that Dr. Willis and company can use this technique to destroy the mutated cells but leave everything else alone."

Jeff yawned and stretched. "That's what I get, too."

"A miracle cure," I muttered, but I must have been the only one who felt the irony.

"That's what we want, Moms. Right?"

What should I tell them? What should I do? I had more information, but now the decision was a real one. I could stop the mutation. Did I want to? Did I really want to?

"We don't know for sure that it will work," I told them.

"It's better than sitting around doing nothing," Steven said. "And waiting to see what else happens to you. It might not all be as benign as what's gone on so far."

"And if they stop it, what then? Do I start getting older again, only faster? Nobody knows for sure. So I'll basically be a science experiment for Dr. Willis and the other doctors. That doesn't sound real good to me."

Jeff got up and stood behind me, rubbing my shoulders. "I think you need to sleep on it, Moms. Right now, you're as worried about Elsa as I am, and it's hard to think straight. Especially since you probably didn't have more than an hour's sleep last night."

My son, the grown-up. No matter what happened to me, he'd be all right. And he'd make sure Steven and Nancy were all right, too. I exhaled and felt my muscles unclench under his strong, gentle hands.

* * *

Elsa finally took a little food, and I saw that as a triumph, a sign she might get over this affliction, whatever it was. Nancy phoned in the early afternoon to check on Elsa, and I tried to be optimistic when I brought her up to date.

After Steven, Jeff, and I had read and re-read Dr. Willis's material, Jeff paid Elsa one more visit and then took off. He had a project due for his writing class in the morning and joked that he needed to change clothes because his jeans were ready to stand up and walk around on their own.

"You'll call me the minute you find out what Elsa's doc says tomorrow, right?"

I made a crisscross motion on my chest, then hugged him for about the hundredth time that day.

"Thank you, son. For everything."

He patted my back. "We'll get through this, Moms. We always do."

My son, the optimist. Oh, how I hoped he was right.

Chapter Twenty-Four
Saying Goodbye

I phoned Elsa's vet the minute they opened on Monday, and Steven stayed home from work to help me take her in.

Dr. Masood studied the x-ray the emergency vet had given us, took her temperature, listened to her heart and lungs and poked around on her back and her legs.

"She is old for a large breed," he said in his slightly-accented English. "It may be that her arthritis has worsened—but that does not usually happen so quickly."

He put down the file, squatted and took Elsa's head in his soft brown hands.

"We could do blood work to rule out infection. Although I see no signs of it, I suspect there is something happening with her spine— perhaps a tumor." He tapped the x-ray. "I see an area here that worries me."

He studied me, as if measuring how much bad news I could take, and then continued. "We could operate and see if we find anything, but at her age…"

He spread his arms, palms up. I knew what he meant. At her age, anesthesia was a risky proposition.

"And if you find something—what would we do next?" Steven asked.

I gripped his arm.

We'd been in that examining room more times than I could count over the years, and it had never changed: above the stainless steel sink, glass-fronted cabinets held bottles of medication; a model of a dog's skeleton sat on the counter next to the sink; and photos of happy, romping pets hung on each wall. The room smelled faintly of disinfectant, and—probably only in my imagination—fear, the vibes of frightened animals who had been cared for by Dr. Masood and his associates. He was a skilled doctor and diagnostician, and he'd treated our dogs forever, yet he'd never seemed to age. But that morning, I noticed a few gray hairs in his thick black mustache, and wrinkles around his dark, shiny eyes. *Time catches up with all of us,* I thought. *Well, almost all of us.*

Dr. Masood's mouth turned down. "Unfortunately, there is not a lot we can do. I have seen this happen before, in older dogs. Their legs simply stop working. You could have her fitted with a device to support her back legs, but in a dog like this, so accustomed to running and playing..."

"And protecting," I added. "She's depressed, and I think it's because she can't be our guardian angel right now."

"That is probably true," said Dr. Masood. He put his hand on my shoulder. "There is one other option."

Euthanasia. I couldn't bear to say the word.

The technician drew some blood to test, and then we took Elsa home and hoped for a miracle.

It didn't happen. We had to help her get up and walk outside to relieve herself, and afterward she lay on her bed in the living room, head on paws, panting. Steven needed to get back to work, but I had no appointments to distract me from my friend's misery. I lay next to her on the floor, rubbing her muzzle—when had it turned so white? When had her eyes gotten that milky sheen I'd seen in old dogs, but never in her? Her nose was still shiny black, her gaze focused on me, full of questions. *Why? Why is this happening?*

Dr. Masood phoned in the afternoon to tell me that the blood tests hadn't revealed anything that would cause her back legs to fail like that. Her inflammatory markers were elevated, which did indicate arthritis. The only remaining option was exploratory surgery. I thanked him and told him I'd talk it over with my family and let him know what we decided.

Then I got back on the floor and cradled her head in my lap.

"Tell me what you want, Elsa. If you want to stick around, I'll move heaven and earth if I can to save you."

She didn't answer. And she wouldn't eat. Aside from those few morsels on Sunday, she hadn't taken any food at all, and that was what decided me. Elsa had always loved her food, and her treats, and the fact that she was refusing them now gave me the answer I needed.

We called Jeff and Nancy to come and say goodbye. After a brief deliberation, Nancy decided to bring Maddie, who loved Elsa almost as much as I did. It wouldn't be right not to let them have one last time together, and Maddie was mature enough to understand what happened when an animal got old.

As I watched them gather around Elsa, who tried so hard to get up and greet them, who struggled to wag her tail and couldn't, it hit me: *This is what will happen to us all. We'll get old and frail and won't be able to do the things we love to do. We'll waste away like Elsa, unless an accident takes us out first. It will happen to all of us. Except me. Not unless I...*

In that instant, I had my own answer. Elsa's last gift to me.

Steven and I took her back to Dr. Masood late that afternoon. She lay quietly on his exam table, stoic as ever, patiently awaiting release. Steven and I stood beside her, stroking her fur and murmuring reassurance. A teardrop fell on my hand, but it came from Steven, not me. His unexpected tears almost brought on my own, but I fought them because they'd only distress Elsa. I bent close to her, and my gallant girl drew her final breath with me caressing those big furry ears. I like to think the last thing she heard was the sound of my voice, telling her how much I loved her.

* * *

The silent house echoed around us when Steven and I got home from the vet's. I was still holding Elsa's leash, and I hung it in the usual place on the service porch. I hadn't accepted the reality of it all, that she wouldn't come to greet us like always. I supposed I should start clearing out her toys and bed and water bowl, but I couldn't yet bear to.

Our hallway was lined with photos: my parents, Steven's father, a progression of the kids, from infants to toddlers to teenagers to adult. Another series followed Maddie's growth, with space for more in the years to come. Elsa as a gangly, scrawny puppy looked into the camera lens, then as a young adult, and finally the beautiful, mature dog she'd become. Jeff draped an arm around her as he held up his first *Defender Dog* book, and one-year-old Maddie sat astride her in another. Toward the end of the hall came one of my favorites, taken by Steven after an arduous climb to the top of Griffith Park: Elsa and I smiled at the camera with half of Los Angeles sprawled behind us. The last photo, completely out of chronological order, was our wedding picture: my twenty-seven-year-old self, all innocent happiness in my lacy white gown, clinging to my new husband's arm as we faced our future together.

So much time had passed, so much had happened during the years those photos were taken. Yet it seemed like only the blink of an eye. Where had the time gone, so quickly?

Steven hugged me. "We did the right thing."

"I know," I replied, "but..."

He blinked red-rimmed eyes as he released me and blew his nose. "I think we could both do with a drink, don't you?"

I'd never wanted one so badly in my life, and even though whiskey wasn't my first choice, I let Steven pour Crown Royal into two tumblers and add a couple of ice cubes. The liquor burned on the way down, but then the sensation mellowed to a soft glow.

I sank down next to him on the sofa and put my head on his shoulder. "This was a horrible day."

"It was," he agreed. "But we've gotten this far; we'll manage the rest."

Then, to my astonishment, he teared up again. I rubbed his back and let him cry.

"Oh Steven, I knew you were fond of her, but I didn't realize how much you cared."

He wrapped his arms around me and held me tight. "Don't leave me, Diane. Don't you leave me too."

I patted his back and tried to soothe him. "I'm not going anywhere, Steven. I promise you that."

I don't know if he believed me, but eventually he let go and took a shuddery breath. I grabbed a tissue, and as I wiped his face, I remembered how I'd tried to comfort Maddie not that long ago, in much the same way. *It all comes down to frightened children at some point, doesn't it?*

* * *

Sleep didn't come easy for either of us that night, and I dreamed of Elsa, dreamed she was young and frisky again. I woke with tears on my face, too.

* * *

"You should do something special today," Steven said over breakfast. "Something to distract you. Maybe call Maura and see if she's up for lunch?"

I shrugged. "We've... we've had a falling out. A big one."

"Let me guess—it has to do with that fellow she's dating. You don't trust him, and neither do I."

Oh, you dear sweet man—you have no idea, do you?

This, I knew, was one secret I had to keep. I'd already lost Maura because of Robert. Although Steven wouldn't give up on me that easily, it would still hurt him, even though nothing had really happened.

"No," I said, "I don't trust him. He's not good for her, but she doesn't want to accept that."

Steven rose, rinsed his coffee mug, and kissed my forehead. "She'll come around. You've been friends for so long. Although," he said, and shook his head, "I've never understood why."

"I know," I said. "I've been wondering about that myself." I stood and embraced him. "I love you, Steven. So much."

There was another unspoken thing between us, though, and it had to be confronted—*what are you going to do, Diane?*

I had only to say the words to make it real.

"I've decided," I said, and the confidence in my voice surprised both of us, I think. "I'm going ahead with the procedure, if Dr. Willis gets the okay."

He sat down again. "You're sure?"

I nodded. "Sure as I am about anything. I know the risks if I do, and I can guess at the ones if I don't."

He pulled me onto his lap. "I'll be with you, Diane, no matter what. We'll take a leap into the dark together."

An image from the movie *Thelma and Louise* flashed through my mind, when they drove their car off the cliff, but I didn't tell Steven that.

"Let's hope we get a soft landing," I said instead. "I don't know what to expect, but I have no intention of leaving you, darling. I want us to grow old together, if we can."

"You'll be giving up a lot," he said.

"We don't know that for sure," I replied. "But it's worth the risk. Totally."

Steven's forehead wrinkled. "Shall we call Dr. Willis then? I'll phone the office and tell them I'm not coming in."

"You've missed so much time from work on my account."

He smiled then. "What are they going to do? Fire me?"

* * *

He held my free hand as I called Dr. Willis's cell phone, and I didn't expect an answer, but Willis was on the other end of the line.

"It's Diane Devlin," I said. "And my husband is here, too. I'm putting you on speakerphone now."

Willis's voice was slightly distorted as it came out of the phone.

"Mrs. Devlin—I was going to call you today. I've gotten clearance from the university to use the procedure, if you decide to go ahead with it."

"That quickly," I said quietly.

"Yes. I emphasized your situation's urgent nature, and two of Dr. Banks's colleagues added their support. It wasn't quite a slam-dunk, but they did grant permission."

And I'm sure it helped that they've gotten all they need from "Mrs. Devlin's body." I didn't voice my suspicion, and in truth I didn't really care. That part of the situation was beyond my control and always had been.

"How soon can we begin?" Steven asked.

"The sooner the better. I'll send you the protocol—there are some things you'll need to do in preparation, but that won't take long."

I glanced at Steven. "Will it hurt?" I asked.

That got a worried look from Steven and a soft laugh from Dr. Willis.

"Not nearly so much as the bone marrow extraction," Willis assured me. "Now, I know we've discussed this already, but I need to reiterate—you understand this is experimental, the outcome is not guaranteed, and we don't know with any certainty how your body will respond after the mutation is removed. We would have some releases for you to sign to that effect."

I grinned at Steven, who bit his lip but held his hands up in surrender.

"Of course you will," I said.

"You're sure about this then? You're ready?"

"Ready as I'll ever be," I said.

And as I gazed into my husband's kind green eyes, I was telling the truth. I was—as ready as I'd ever be.

Chapter Twenty-Five
Six Months Later

Thanks to the wonder of Twilight Sleep, "The Procedure"—which is how we chose to describe it—turned out to be a relatively painless event. I awoke in the recovery room with Steven at my bedside, and as soon as I could sit up and take some water, Dr. Willis let me go home.

There would be no test results to await afterward, unless you count the fact that my whole body would yield the results. That part was anti-climactic.

Each morning after I woke up, I'd wiggle my fingers and toes, then stretch cautiously, seeking out any physical signs that my tired old self had returned to taunt me. One day I realized I was holding my breath, and when no aches or pains showed up, I exhaled an explosion of air that lifted the bedsheet. After that morning, I inhaled and exhaled gently before I began exploring my body for changes.

I thought I'd been doing it discreetly, until the morning I rolled over toward Steven, who presumably was still dozing. He wasn't. Green eyes wide, he watched my twitches and exhales with a mixture of worry and amusement.

"I'm okay," I assured him. "Just checking."

"And?"

"And I feel fine. Same as always—same as the new always."

It was true; I felt strong and energetic, ready to take on whatever the day dished out for me. I felt no younger, no older than I had the day before. No insidious little twinges in my knees or spine to remind me of time's passing.

Steven kissed the back of my hand. "Good girl."

So I'd progressed—or regressed—from "old girl" to "good girl." At least it wasn't "young lady."

I rose and stretched some more, then put on jeans and a t-shirt. This was Saturday, and we still hiked in Griffith Park on Saturdays. It wasn't any old Saturday, however; it was our wedding anniversary. Did Steven remember? Of course he did—he'd made reservations at The Smoke House for dinner that night. We'd celebrated almost every wedding anniversary at that well-known Toluca Lake restaurant.

Steven rose, grumbling and rubbing his back, as usual. He shambled toward the bathroom but stopped to kiss the back of my neck. "Happy anniversary, darling."

Another morning ritual: peeking at my reflection in the mirror, always with a little twinge of dread, followed by a surge of relief. Again, same as yesterday. No sudden onset of new wrinkles and sags, merely the ones I'd gone to bed with the night before.

Such a nice, normal beginning to a nice, normal day for the Devlins. A low-level hum of anxiety stirred at the sheer ordinariness of it all, and I began my daily bout of "what-ifs."

What if this is the day I start aging more quickly? What if I'm stuck at this one age, while my family gets old around me, like Elsa? What if…

I could "what-if" myself into a frenzy if I let it continue, so I tried to halt the ruminating and went downstairs to start breakfast.

* * *

The hike was pleasant, and we kept pace with one another. I might have been able to surpass Steven, but I didn't try. I'd learned to restrain those urges and simply enjoy being able to accomplish the climb without being winded. The day was clear and bright, the view from Mt. Hollywood as breathtaking as it ever got, with downtown Los

Angeles poking its few spires into the sky, and traffic moving smoothly on the main streets and freeways.

I hugged Steven, grateful for this moment of peace.

"I love you," I whispered.

* * *

I still felt a twinge of grief whenever we got home and Elsa didn't come to greet us. I'd finally worked up enough nerve to put away her leash, her water and food bowls and grooming tools. I put them in a box in the garage and would probably always keep them as a reminder of my beautiful girl. We'd scattered her ashes on the way to Mt. Hollywood a few weeks after she died; it had been her favorite place, and I always said a mental hello to her as we climbed and again when we descended.

We'd talked about getting another dog, but I wasn't ready, and Steven didn't seem to be either. I needed to honor Elsa's memory a while longer, and I believed (because I had to) that the universe would send us another dog when the time was right.

Steven went upstairs to shower before he tackled the pile of papers he'd brought home from the office—that part of our lives hadn't changed, either—except that as the new Senior Partner, replacing Victor DeWitt, Steven had leapfrogged over Teddy Royce.

I didn't begrudge him the time he devoted to his work—in truth I never had, at least not much—because I had work of my own to accomplish. It wasn't as high-profile as my old job at Gardner, but it was more rewarding.

I'd fallen into it by accident. One of Nancy's fellow teachers had been diagnosed with a rare form of cancer and was struggling to get a place in a clinical trial of an experimental drug that might well save her life. Because of my own medical misadventures, Nancy asked me to talk to Isabella, the teacher—not so much to offer advice but simply to lend an understanding ear. As it turned out, I was able to do far more than that. Isabella was a bright woman, but the mountain of application forms required to join the trial was enough to smother an elephant. Since I was no stranger to the bureaucratic hurdles she faced,

I hand-held her as she filled out the forms, and when she came to a release form similar to the one Dr. Banks had required from me, I cautioned her about signing it. We both knew her refusal would probably keep her out of the trial, so she did agree to it, but at least she went into it with her eyes open.

She got into the trial, and the experimental drug appeared to be working, but only time would tell for sure. At least I helped her get a fighting chance, and my new part-time career as a patient advocate was born. Mostly it involved acting as a liaison between patients and their doctors, or the hospital, and I hadn't saved any lives yet, but I'd made some of them easier, and I took pleasure in knowing my own ordeal had another upside.

That Saturday morning Steven and I both got texts from our son Jeff: "Happy Anniversary, Mom and Dad. Hope you're living it up today. Love you." A series of kissy-faces and red hearts followed. I smiled at the message. Jeff was midway through a draft of his novel and had been emailing me chapters to review. He'd also joined a critique group, and the members did most of the heavy lifting of notes and suggestions, so no pressure on me. I did enjoy being included, however, and his work was a genuine pleasure to read—a bit rough around some of the edges, but a damn sight better than many of the books sitting on the shelves at Barnes & Noble.

A bit later, Nancy phoned with her "Happy Anniversary" wishes. She and Nick had recently celebrated their own eleven-year anniversary, and judging by the loving glances they exchanged at the celebratory dinner I prepared for them, their marriage had survived that huge bump in the road. Both Nick's TV series and his supporting role in it had earned good critical reviews, so his employment picture seemed bright. The less-demanding workload gave him more time to spend with Maddie, and she'd entered several riding competitions, doing so well that Nick was seriously considering buying her a horse of her own. Nancy wasn't completely on board with that decision, but he was making good money, so she couldn't protest too much—especially since he'd convinced her to put some of that salary toward a housekeeper to lighten her burden. At their anniversary party, my daughter had looked lovelier and more radiant than I'd seen her in a long time, and I gave Nick part of the credit for that. Steven, too, had grudgingly acknowledged that Nick might not be the horrid husband material he'd once thought.

* * *

I answered a few emails from my new "clients," pruned my roses and did a little house cleaning, and by then it was late afternoon. Steven had finished reviewing his files and was taking a nap in the den while pretending to read the latest issue of *Time*, so I went upstairs to shower and get ready for our evening out. After all, a dinner at The Smoke House required dressing up. I didn't need the ball gown and tiara, but I wanted to look special, so I did all the usual preening and primping, shaving my legs and polishing my nails.

Steven was moving around downstairs, and I called out to him that it was time to start getting dressed as I took out the rose-print wrap dress I'd bought during that long-ago shopping spree with Maura. My eyes filled with tears at the memory.

* * *

Even though Maura and I never patched up our friendship, it had been real, and a source of enjoyment for so long. I'd thought about reaching out to her, but then I heard she and Robert had gotten married, and I figured it would be foolish to reconnect. I worried about her, but I had to keep my distance. I hoped Robert would turn out to be a good guy after all, although I had my doubts—doubts I swore to keep to myself. It was the least I could do.

* * *

The dress still fit perfectly as I tied the sash and twirled before the mirror and gave in to a burst of vanity. I did not look my age, but anxiety gnawed away. How long would this last?

Dr. Willis checked me out every month, ordering blood work and scrutinizing almost every inch of my body, seeking signs "The Procedure" had worked, as it apparently had. No more reverse aging; I seemed to be frozen in time, and he couldn't promise me that would or wouldn't change. He didn't know, nor did any of the best scientific minds at Wallace Taylor University know, what might happen. He couldn't promise that I would resume normal aging. He couldn't promise that I'd continue enjoying this younger body that was still me, only better. And he couldn't promise that I wouldn't wake up one morning and discover a shriveled old crone in place of the vibrant woman I'd been the night before. He promised nothing, but it seemed he had stopped the rejuvenation. I was still his human guinea pig, however, and I probably always would be.

Meanwhile, I scanned the newspaper often, searching for news of a miracle cure for some horrid disease, a cure that might have come about thanks to my mutation, which the university's scientists had succeeded in patenting. Dr. Willis couldn't share all the details with me, but he hinted that a local biotech company had purchased the right to market the mutation, although they were still testing its safety and effectiveness. I joked with him they should call it "Diane" when they packaged it, but he didn't laugh.

* * *

Steven had finished dressing—no cuff links tonight, but he looked pretty sharp, and I did my best imitation of a wolf whistle and helped him button his blue pinstriped shirt.

He wiggled his eyebrows. "You ready, gorgeous?"

"Except for my shoes," I said as I slipped my toes into the red patent stilettos I'd bought on that same shopping spree. Those I had worn a few times since then. There: picture complete. I pirouetted one more time in front of the mirror, and as I stepped off the bedroom carpet onto the wood floor in the hall, I felt an old familiar twinge that I thought was long-gone. My feet hurt! I took another tentative step. Ouch!

I looked down at the shoes, those shoes that had felt almost as comfortable as bedroom slippers the last time I'd worn them.

Steven frowned. "You okay, honey?"

I was probably grinning like a fool by then. "I'm fine. But I can't wear these shoes tonight. Let me switch real quick."

"Oh good," said Steven. "Those things always frightened me."

"What? Why didn't you say so?"

He kissed my forehead. "Because you enjoyed them so."

"No more," I said as I kicked the stilettos to the back of my closet, with only a tiny pang of regret. They were merely shoes—I didn't need them. I put on a pair of silver-gray pumps, with lower heels, and they felt fine as I walked out into the fragrant spring evening with the love of my life.

Acknowledgments

Turn Back the Clocks had an army of helpers to bring it into existence, including some generous members of the scientific community who sparked my imagination and kept me somewhere within the bounds of credibility. Dr. Felipe Sierra of the National Institute of Aging and Dr. Stuart Kim at Stanford University both gave me crash courses in genetics, aging, and cell biology. Any scientific errors in the book are completely my fault, however.

Other aspects of the novel also required expert advice, and in no particular order I thank Chuck Strathman for explaining the intricacies of patent law, Steven Cavallero for co-authoring the other Steven's tribute speech, Ann Hill for showing me the finer brands of whisky, and the friends and family members I queried about the behavior of eight-year-olds: Jayne, Marilyn, Morgan, and Tere.

If this book is an engaging read, you can thank my long-time critique partners, Heather Ames and Miriam "Miko" Johnston of the Pacific Online Writers Group. Also Kitty Kladstrup for her encouragement and developmental edits, and Dorothy Read for proofreading the final manuscript and fixing those pesky errors that slipped past the rest of us. And last but not least, Paula Johnson, whose title of "book designer" doesn't begin to describe the magic she works in bringing a book into existence.

Folks, I am ever-indebted to you all for helping me make this book a reality.

Book Group Questions
Discussing Turn Back the Clocks

1. Did the book's theme—be careful what you wish for— resonate for you? Have you ever gotten something you thought you *really* wanted, but then it turned out not to be as wonderful as you expected? What was that like? Did it color your outlook on life?

2. In Diane's place, would you have been excited or scared? Or something else?

3. Do you think our society often tends to devalue older people? When Diane begins to grow younger, the people around her have varying reactions. Whose reaction felt the most realistic?

4. Diane advises her daughter Nancy to try and move past her anger and pain at her husband Nick's affair. Do you agree with this advice, or would you help her find a good divorce attorney?

5. Do you believe it's possible to forgive someone for a betrayal like Steven's or Nick's?

6. What did you think of Nick's character? Do you think it's possible for him to resist temptation in the future, given his career?

7. Should Diane have told her friend Maura about Robert's seduction attempt? What did you think of Maura's reaction? Have you ever lost a friend over something so painful?

8. Diane has been feeling very critical of her husband Steven, but on the night of Victor DeWitt's retirement party, hearing Steven deliver a moving tribute to his friend and mentor, she remembers what a good, kind man he is. Have you ever experienced a similar reversal of your feelings about someone? How did that turn out?

9. Did you agree with Diane's final choice? Why or why not? What would you have done in that situation?

10. The medical community is mostly described in a negative light in this book, with one exception. Do you think this is a fair portrayal? Do you suspect that Dr. Banks attempted to use the mutation for himself?

About the Author

Bonnie Schroeder was bitten by the writing bug in the fifth grade and never recovered. In addition to *Turn Back the Clocks,* her other published novels are *Mending Dreams* and *Write My Name on the Sky.* Her published short stories include "The Go-Between," "A Losing Game," the award-winning "Vigilantes," and "Fault Lines." In the nonfiction arena, she wrote a weekly column in *Drama-Logue* on the subject of "survival skills" for actors and other theater professionals and has written e-newsletters for a chapter of the American Red Cross. She has also completed two feature-length screenplays, one of which, *Smoke and Mirrors,* was a semi-finalist in the Monterey County Film Commission's competition. Long-form fiction, however, remains her first love.

If you enjoyed *Turn Back the Clocks,* please post a review online. Visit BonnieSchroederBooks.com for more on Bonnie.

Made in the USA
Monee, IL
23 June 2023

36740025R00154